*Praise f*
all the walls o

"Compassionate, honest, and hopeful, *All The Walls of Belfast* celebrates the power of first love to build bridges and scale walls."

—**Marie Marquardt**, author of *Dream Things True, The Radius of Us* and *Flight Season*

"*All the Walls of Belfast* is the gripping story of courage and redemption in turbulent post-conflict Northern Ireland. Brilliantly written, this vivid fiction meets reality novel reveals how two teens navigate life with the fallout of their parents' actions."

—**Angie Stanton**, award winning author of *Waking in Time*

"*All the Walls of Belfast* is a powerful story about how the stones our parents throw in the past make ripples in our futures. Fiona and Danny's distinct voices weave a colorful tapestry of modern-day Belfast that will stick with readers for a long, long time."

—**Christina June**, author of *Everywhere You Want to Be*

"*All the Walls of Belfast* is fast-paced, compelling, and unputdownable… This is a story that transcends the scope of the plot and characters and speaks deeply to the needs of our broken world. I can't recommend it enough!" —**Jodi Herlick**, Author and WriteMentor Mentor

"I loved it! The story kept building and building as I was falling deeper and deeper for these characters, Danny and Fiona, the Romeo and Juliet of Belfast…a stellar debut!"

—**Jessie Ann Foley**, award-winning author of *The Carnival at Bray*

As cool, damp air wrapped around me on the Jetway, I caught a whiff of nostril-burning jet fuel. Apparently Ireland did not smell like Irish Spring. I'd have to tell Nevaeh her prediction was wrong. I hugged my green canvas jacket tighter around me.

Inside, signs in English and Irish directed people with European Union passports to the left, non–European Union passports to the right. The Americans from our flight stood stranded in a long line, but I walked right up to an immigration officer. I peeled my clammy fingers from my Irish passport as I handed it to the officer.

The immigration officer flipped through the empty pages, then raised an eyebrow at me.

"Um, I'm visiting my dad," I said.

His brow inched higher. My cheeks warmed.

"Welcome home, then," the officer said.

Right past immigration were a bunch of signs with Irish flags that said "In Ireland. Drive on the left." But one word echoed through my ears—home.

I'd always felt cool when I casually let it slip out that I was Irish, and not my-great-great-grandmother-rode-a-boat-over Irish. But now that I was here with actual Irish people, I wasn't so sure.

I was on another continent thousands of miles from home and everything I knew... and Mom. About to spend two weeks with a man who wasn't allowed to enter the United States because of his sketchy political past. My father.

Grainy images about the Troubles flashed before my eyes—men with guns, ski masks, and aviator glasses; bodies littering the streets; shattered buildings. A fresh wave of adrenaline pumped through my veins, firing my brain into a chaotic mess.

A week ago, the decision to come ASAP had seemed logical. I'd figured it would be like cannonballing into cold water rather than sticking a toe in.

But now Dad was waiting just a few yards away, and before this I'd only spoken to him for ten minutes on Skype. My heart pounded like I was waiting for the starter pistol at semifinals, times a hundred. My feet fused to the floor. Nevaeh was right—this was totally insane. And I hadn't even told her the whole surprise-Dad-was-in-the-Irish Republican Army thing. I hugged my messenger bag to my stomach. Maybe I could just hop on a plane back to Madison.

But it wasn't like he was one of the real bad guys. Mom had assured me, it wasn't like he'd killed anyone. He was just a small-time guy who knew some scary people. And things used to be different in Northern Ireland. His cause, Mom had said, hadn't been without justification.

We'd already lost fifteen years together.

Time to Polar Plunge.

I uprooted my feet and walked on through customs.

# chapter two

## *Danny*

Remember, Danny Boy, you've got the brains to be an officer." Mr. Sinclair pulled to a stop in the Palace Barracks car park. "Sit up tall. *Yes, sir, no, sir.* And for Christ's sake, don't say 'like' every other word."

"Aye, sure." I slouched in my seat.

Sinclair shot me one of his irritated looks over his glasses.

"I mean, yes, sir." Sinclair was still the only teacher at Ballysillan Boys' Model who wasn't a complete tosspot.

He turned off his car. "Right, then. Let's see if the candidate support manager thinks you're ready."

The Officer Selection Board was three days of mental and physical tests. And I'd be competing against a bunch of posh twats. I tightened my school uniform tie and checked my reflection in the mirror. My blond hair was getting a bit too long on top. I smoothed it down.

"I told you to get a haircut," Sinclair said as we got out.

"But all the wee girls think it's class."

"Sure they do, big man." He gave me a sour look as we walked up the footpath. I tried not to think about the fact that my trousers and blazer sleeves were almost an inch too short.

I walked into the army recruitment center clutching my letter. The whole place was filled with posters advertising the benefits of joining the army. Pictures of people in uniform "securing Britain in an uncertain world," looking brave as they stood on tanks, passing out food to kids from different countries, and pointing massive guns at things in the desert. The one from the Careers Suite at Ballysillan Boys' was up too—a soldier with a medic armband helping a Middle Eastern woman with a wee baby.

Sinclair nudged me toward the desk guarded by a secretary.

"Em, hi, I'm here for my appointment with Candidate Support Manager Flowers."

"Can I see that letter?"

I handed it to her. It was wrinkled and damp from my palm sweat.

She scanned it. "Just a moment."

My mobile vibrated against my thigh. The secretary was on the phone and Mr. Sinclair was inspecting posters, so I checked it.

Da: WHERE THE HELL ARE YOU???? GET UR ARSE TO PRACTICE NOW

I felt a bit bad about missing band practice since we'd the mini-Twelfth at the weekend, but I couldn't worry about that now. I shut off my mobile.

A glass door popped open, and a man in full uniform, complete with maroon beret and shined boots, emerged.

"Daniel Stewart?"

I almost laughed. Nobody ever called me Daniel.

"Support Manager Flowers. Pleased to meet you." He crushed my hand and shook it. I gripped his back. Firm handshake, like Sinclair said. He led us into his office, and I slid into a chair next to Mr. Sinclair. Flowers took a seat facing us. Behind him was a Union Jack and the flag of the Royal Irish Regiment—red, green, and blue stripes with the lyre and crown at the center. Flowers flipped through a file. I tried to peek inside, which earned me a disapproving look from Sinclair.

"Relax," he mouthed.

Easy for him to say. I slumped back and then remembered to sit up tall.

I'd been embarrassed two days ago when I'd had to ask Sinclair for a lift all the way to Holywood, but now I was a bit glad he was here. I'd already had to ask him if I could get my post from the army application sent to his house. I'd told him we were moving and that was why.

Flowers looked up from the file. "From the Shankill," he said. "We don't get many lads from there looking to become an officer candidate."

"Yes, sir," I said.

He flipped through more pages. I hoped my school discipline reports hadn't found their way in there. Principal Doyle had had it in for me since year eight. "Right, so you've done all the prerequisites. And you're interested in being a nursing officer?"

I caught my fingers drumming on my thigh. "Yes, sir. Em, specifically an adult health nurse."

He raised an eyebrow. "May I ask why?"

His tone almost made me lose my rag. *This is an interview, Danny. Don't muck it up.*

"Because I want to save lives, and the army seems like the best place to do it. I'm keen to go on humanitarian missions, see the world. And I think I've what it takes to be a leader. I want to be a career soldier, sir."

Out of the corner of my eye, I caught a rare nod of approval from Sinclair.

"So you know that involves forty-four weeks training at Royal Military Academy Sandhurst as well as specialized training in nursing." Flowers looked over something in my file. "You're sitting your A-2 Levels this week?"

"Aye. I mean, yes, sir."

"I'm confident Danny will earn the necessary points," Sinclair said.

Having a teacher at one of these things instead of a parent had its advantages.

Flowers closed my file. "I'll put you down for the Main Board on twelfth through the fourteenth July at Leighton House in Westbury."

Shite, the twelfth. And where the hell was Westbury? I glanced at Sinclair.

"It's near Bristol," he said.

In England. "Em, sir, excuse me. Isn't there an assessment center in Belfast?"

Flowers looked at me. "There is, but officer candidates undergo assessment at Leighton House. Here's all the information you need." He stood, thick packet in his hands.

I scrambled to my feet too, because you were supposed to do that when your superior officer got up.

"If you get accepted, be prepared to enlist immediately."

Which was exactly what I wanted. It looked like I'd be homeless come my birthday in a fortnight. "Yes, sir."

He handed me the packet. "Best of luck, lad."

Another hand-crushing shake.

"Thank you, sir."

As we left, the impossibility of it all smashed down on me. How was I supposed to buy a ticket to England when I couldn't even afford a frigging haircut?

And shite, it was on the twelfth. I'd miss the Twelfth of July parade for the first time ever. I didn't care for my own sake, but Da would kill me. I was supposed to be playing in the band.

I climbed into Sinclair's vanilla-scented car. It was half seven. By the time he dropped me off, band practice would be over. Now I had to worry about that text message from Da. He'd be raging I hadn't shown up.

"Distant Sighs"—my second favorite song by my secret favorite band, Fading Stars—played on the radio as we drove back to Belfast. As I focused on the slow twang of the banjo and the gentle plucking of the guitar, my nerves started to calm a bit. I dug out my mobile and looked up ways to get to Bristol.

Most of the plane tickets were around seventy pounds. I noticed the flight times. The earliest one didn't get to Bristol until ten in the morning, but the papers said I'd to be to Leighton House by 0800. So I'd have to fly over on the eleventh, which was more expensive. And I'd have to miss the Eleventh Night bonfire.

Bollocks.

I'd need to earn at least one hundred ninety-five quid to cover the ticket and rent.

I'd tried to get a weekend job, but Da was second-in-command of the West Belfast Ulster Volunteer Force and since businesses in the Shankill had to pay them protection money, most weren't too keen on hiring me. I did jobs for cash in hand, but it'd been an expensive spring—a hundred and forty quid for A-Levels, eighty-two for my passport, twenty-five pounds a week rent for Da, and buying minutes for my mobile. Thank Christ

I'd finally be done with school tomorrow, so I'd have plenty of time to work. But Sammy, the fella who usually had work for me, probably wouldn't need my help for the next few weeks. He was one of the collectors for the bonfire, which meant he'd probably already stopped working so he could spend his days gathering more pallets and tires.

Two months back, Sinclair and I came up with a list to get me ready for my Main Board. At the top were the things I could not do: get a criminal conviction or an offensive tattoo, like an Ulster Volunteer Force one. Then there were online reasoning and aptitude tests, interviews, training for the fitness standards, filling out loads of paperwork, finishing school, getting that passport and a physical. Sinclair had even taken me to some posh restaurant in the city centre so I could practice for the formal dinner. Put your napkin in your lap and eat slow enough to talk, but don't talk with food in your mouth.

When Sinclair had seen how high my GCSE scores were after year twelve, he'd convinced me to try for army officer, which meant going to sixth form instead of leaving at sixteen with the rest of my mates—and two more years of Da.

I shifted in my seat as I stared out the window at Belfast Lough. A patch of water glittered where the sun managed to break through the gray wall of clouds.

Now I could almost feel the army uniform on my skin, but the Main Board was all the way in Westbury. The farthest I'd ever been from home was Londonderry for parades. We passed the Clifton Street Orange Hall, where all the flute bands met on the Twelfth for the march out to the field. There was a white splatter of paint over the entrance. Some Catholic bastard had thrown a paint bomb, attacking our heritage again.

Da hadn't worked today, which probably meant he was blocked

already. Most of the time, we had a peaceful coexistence as long as I paid my rent. Da was always on about how his own da raised him with his fists and I was lucky he didn't, because I was a dirty wee poof who couldn't handle it. But missing band practice, me "abandoning my culture" again, would rile him.

Back in the nineties, Da had been the best boxer in the Shankill. If he knew what I'd been getting on to, he'd knock my bollocks in. I'd made the mistake of telling him my dream a year back. He said that no son of his would run off and be a wee nurse for the authorities. He hated the British government, because they negotiated and did deals with the IRA. They'd abandoned us, he said. They were supposed to be *our* government, and they were giving the Republicans more funding for their Irish language classes. No way was his son going to be in *their* army. After that, I let him think I stayed on in school to be a firefighter. Christ, I was dying for a pint.

The stack of army papers resting on my thighs burned through my trousers. It was dangerous for me to have them in the house where Da might see. But if I asked Sinclair to look after my papers, he'd ask a million frigging questions about everything in my life.

"Can you drop me off somewhere else?"

"Danny, you know school policy says I have to drop you at your address."

I clenched my hands in my lap to stop myself from drumming.

"Why?" Mr. Sinclair checked his mobile for directions as he drove up Shankill Road.

"For a wee swallow with the lads."

"I know you're counting on the fact you got all A grades while faffing about last year, but this is your future, Danny."

I didn't need him reminding me about my future.

"I'm not stupid." Sinclair glanced at me, evening sunlight framing his face. "You're not moving house, and your da's not working late. Those bruises last March, I'm fairly certain they weren't from getting into a ruck with the lads."

I glared through his insect-splattered windscreen. I wasn't a tout, and if those social workers had taken me away, they'd have put me in some boy's home and I wouldn't have been able to finish my A-Levels. Plus the UVF, Da's crowd, would end me if I told on him.

"As much as you try to hide it behind that generally piss-poor attitude, you're intelligent and you've a good heart, Danny Boy." Mr. Sinclair would not shut his gob. "But you need to get yourself out of the Shankill, away from that sectarian rubbish. And something tells me if you don't now, you never will."

"What do you think I'm trying to do?"

Sinclair sighed. "Right."

Christ, I wasn't some lost puppy.

Sinclair turned onto Lawnbrook. The lads were pouring out of the Supporters Club with their drums and flutes. Da's car wasn't in its usual spot, which meant he was probably home already.

I folded up my papers and shoved them in my blazer pocket.

Sinclair got to our dead-end street. Sure enough, Da's Astra was parked out front of our terraced house. Billy's Corsa wasn't. Maybe I could do a runner, just pop Sinclair's door open and roll out. Sinclair pulled into the spot next to Da's. Our curtains ripped back. Da's wide form filled the window, backlit by the flickering TV.

"Em, thanks for the lift." I pushed the car door open.

The front door near flew off its hinges. Da's eyes bulged over his puffy red cheeks as he glared at Sinclair, sun shining off his bald head. Grease stains dotted his Rangers top.

Sinclair knew who my da was. Everyone did. But he just stared right back at him like he didn't care. That wasn't going to make Da go any easier on me. Could he not go have tea with Mrs. Sinclair? I got out before he could say anything and shut the car door.

"Get your arse in here, you wee bollocks," Da growled, tattooed arms folded over his gut. "I messaged you hours ago."

"Sod off," I muttered. My heartbeat rattled my sternum like Da's Lambeg drum as I walked up the footpath.

Da slammed the door behind me. An empty bottle of Bushmills stood in the middle of the tin-littered coffee table like a guard tower.

"What were you doing with that hippy cunt?" he slurred. I almost got tipsy off his whiskey breath. "Letting him touch your wee ballbags?"

Tires crunched on the pavement outside. Thank Christ Sinclair was leaving.

On Da's spectrum of drunkenness, he appeared to be closer to "lie-down, black-out bollocksed" than "punching bag after a few pints." Which meant his motor coordination wasn't at peak capacity. Good for me.

"Revising for my A-Levels," I said.

"I just spent hundreds of pounds on your new band uniform because you grow like a frigging weed, and here you are mitching off practice." His fist pounded the side of my head. Pain plugged up my ears and spread to my brainstem. Da's tirade gradually came back into focus, but black spots danced in my field of vision.

"... disgrace. Too good for that job at Hardy's. Staying on in school like a posh twat instead of earning like a real man." Da ripped off my school blazer, nearly wrenching my arms from their sockets.

The front door flew open, and my brother Billy came in. I was taller than him now, but that square-jawed bruiser had two stone on me, all muscle. It was Billy that forced me to bathe and wrestled me into my school uniforms back when I was a wee skitter in primary school. He glanced in my direction. His brows knitted for a second. "Match is about to start."

The belligerent look left Da's eyes. "Why can't you be more like him?" He grabbed an upright tin from the coffee table.

My blazer tucked in his armpit, he pushed through the kitchen door. My enlistment papers were in there. That dirty beast.

"Aren't you supposed to be smart?" Billy folded his tattooed arms across his chest, muscles stretching the mechanic's uniform. "You provoke him. Wise the bap."

From the back garden, the rubbish bin lid snapped closed. It hadn't been put out in weeks. But since Da wasn't shouting, he must not have found my papers. My brain throbbed against the inside of my skull, but I could breathe again.

Billy ran a hand over his number one crop. "Have you applied to Queen's yet?"

Though part of me wanted to prove I could go to uni, I didn't want to deal with snobby professors and homework and even more posh wankers than in the army. "It's my life. What does he care what I do with it? Or you, for that matter."

Billy shook his head at me.

"I'll boot your hole to the moon!" Da lumbered back in. "Upstairs! Find some proper jobs to apply for."

Once upstairs, I dropped onto my bed. I checked myself with my camera app. There was a massive red lump on my forehead near my hairline. I brushed my hair down; it was mostly covered. I dug under my mattress and pulled out my baby book. I flipped past the picture of Ma snuggling me as a newborn, my baby footprints, a photo of me in a Christmas jumper, and loads of blank pages to my favorite page. There, written in pretty cursive, "*Danny, my sweet boy, I dream that you'll save lives instead of take them. Make the world a better place. Mummy loves you.*"

I traced over the last three words with my finger, felt the pen indentation on the page. Then after I tucked it back in its hiding place, I dug out the *Biology Revision and Practice* book Mr. Sinclair had shoved in my rucksack a fortnight ago.

# chapter three

*Fiona*

As I stepped through the sliding glass doors, I spotted him instantly. He stood at the front of a crowd, actively scanning the people exiting. His gray-streaked brown curls busted free of the product fighting to hold it in place. Beside him was the brother I recognized as Patrick: chin-length curls, the same brown as mine, and the same snub nose as me too. Patrick had maybe an inch on me, but my father—our father—was leaner and taller.

My dad's eyes locked onto me. His mouth crinkled as a huge grin revealed stained teeth. His eyes twinkled.

There was my father. My mouth, sticky with the sour taste of being trapped on a plane, went dry.

Dad ducked under the rail and walked up to me. On the laptop screen, it had been hard to make out facial features. But now I could tell I looked almost exactly like him—same high-arched eyebrows, peaked Cupid's bow on our upper lips, and narrow faces.

"There's my wee girl." He pulled me into a hug.

He smelled like the inside of a baseball glove mixed with a tiny hint of cigarettes. My dad. He drew in an uneven breath, crushing the air out of my lungs as he tightened his hold on me. "I can't believe it's you."

Dad cleared his throat and released me. His hazel eyes were speckled with green and gold, just like mine. He adjusted his pink-and-red-striped tie. He looked more like a teacher than a terrorist. Beside him, Patrick's hand brushed his earlobe, fitted with a nickel-sized green gauge, as he reached to scratch the back of his neck. His face split into a crooked-tooth grin as he smoothed his curls into a little man bun. "Welcome back, Fiona." They had the same singsong accent that Mom still had traces of.

"My car's in the shop, so I'm afraid we have to take the bus," Dad said. "Are you hungry? Do you need to use the loo?"

Loo meant bathroom.

I shook my head.

Dad gave me his umbrella as we walked through a cold drizzle past busses bound for other parts of the country, south of the border. I clenched the handle as I drew in slow breaths of air thick with the smell of wet cement, focusing on steadying my weak knees. Rain drummed on the umbrella fabric. Dad wore a raincoat, but Patrick's black Che Guevara T-shirt was quickly darkened by rain.

"Um, want to share?" I tilted the umbrella toward him. Cold drops of rain tickled my cheek.

Patrick shot me a smile as he rolled my suitcase up a curb. "It's barely spitting. Thanks, though. Bit cooler here than Madison, eh?"

"Yeah. Mom said I wouldn't need shorts." We walked by another row of tour busses. A long line of people waited to get on.

"How hot is it in Madison?" Dad adjusted his hood.

"It's been in the upper nineties for like a week. Heat wave." It sucked taking finals, because Memorial didn't have air conditioning. That memory already seemed so long ago.

"Nineties? That's boiling," Dad said. "You get snow as well?"

"We got like two feet in a day last year. We had to shovel the sidewalk four times." I kicked a rock at a gutter.

"Well, you won't be needing to worry about that here. Or tornados." Dad winked at me.

Our first real conversation in fifteen years was about the weather. Wow.

"Here's our bus, then," Dad said.

We loaded on, and Dad sat next to me. Belfast accents surrounded me. The bus pulled onto a busy interstate. Riding on the wrong side of the road hurt my brain. Houses and stores quickly gave way to rolling emerald fields. I tried to focus on the excitement of seeing where I was from. Food was the only thing Mom had ever really talked about—Jaffa Cakes, proper tea, bacon that comes in a slab, lemon Fanta, fish-and-chips with vinegar, and better chocolate. I wanted to try all of it.

Dad's arm sat inches from mine on the armrest. The aura of his body heat warmed my skin through my jacket. I stole a glance. He was watching me with a boundless grin. It was too intense. My cheeks burned. I picked at the rubber rainbow bracelets Nevaeh and I'd been collecting since sophomore year as adrenaline faded away and my brain clouded with exhaustion. I hadn't slept at all on the red-eye. A tiny piece of me wished Mom was there to break the ice.

"Have you got any pictures on your mobile?" Dad's voice came out like he thought I was porcelain.

I dug out my phone and showed him a selfie of Nevaeh and me sharing an ice cream cone at the Union. "My best friend, Nevaeh."

Dad leaned in. "What flavor is that?"

"Blue Moon. My favorite."

Patrick peeked through the seats at us. "Isn't that a beer?"

"I guess you guys don't have that flavor. It tastes like Froot Loops. Wait, do you have Froot Loops?"

They exchanged a look and chuckled.

"Wee Finny's favorite," Patrick said.

I flicked to the next photo, Nevaeh and me on Zion's arms at prom. Zion in a full-on black tuxedo with a red bow tie, dreadlocks pulled back. Nevaeh had worn a coral pink ball gown that perfectly complemented her skin. Mine had been sleek and midnight blue, covered with silver sequins like stars.

"You look lovely," Dad said.

I scrolled to the next, one Mom took of me crossing the finish line red-faced and gasping for breath.

"Is that a race, then?"

"Thirty-two hundred at the McFarland Invitational. I took first place for girls."

"I enjoyed running myself when I was your age," Dad said. "I wish I could've seen it."

"Me too." My fingers clamped the phone.

Shaking his head, Patrick turned around.

Mom had never missed a single track or cross-country meet, but a microscopic piece of me had always longed for a dad cheering me on too.

"What matters is we're together now." Dad's eyes wandered to Patrick.

"I spent the last fifteen years thinking you didn't want me." My throat tightened.

Dad's eyes, mirrors of my own, filled with tears. He tucked his arms around me. "I've *always* wanted you."

My teeth cut into my lip as I fought back the tidal wave rising in my chest.

❦

"That's the Royal, where you were born." Dad pointed out the cab window at a bunch of brick buildings.

Chills crawled up my arms as I pressed my fingertips to the cool glass.

"First time I held you, I was afraid I'd break you. You were smaller than Seamy and Paddy, like a butterfly in my arms. I could fit your whole wee body in my hand." He held out his cupped hand as if baby me was still nestled in his palm. "I swear you smiled at me. Your mam, she said newborns can't smile, but I know what I saw."

It sounded like something from one of the sappy Lifetime movies Mom always watched. But it was real life—my life.

The cab pulled to a stop at an intersection. Ahead were brick row houses and low green mountains. Dad said, "Welcome back to the Falls."

A sign attached to the side of something called a fancy dress party shop said Falls Road and *Bóthar na bhFál*. The yellow and red traffic lights flashed at the same time, then the light turned green. We drove past a bunch of stores—O'Neill's Family Butcher, Adams' Carpets, Oven Door Bakery. Lines of chimneys broken up by blocks of shops.

"A bit different to Madison, yeah?" Patrick asked through the plastic wall separating the front and back seats. "We haven't got all those massive houses with huge front gardens to play football in." His voice carried a hint of bitterness.

"What's your house like?" Dad asked.

I shrugged. "It's a three bedroom ranch. Not that big."

"There's Finny's school." Patrick pointed to another brick building surrounded by a rusting metal fence.

Row houses with no front yards pressed in around us, not a tree in sight. The street was so narrow that cars parked on the sidewalks. Our cab rolled to a stop in front of a wooden door with a clear stained-glass window. Next to it was a little plaque that said "*Teach Ó Ceallaigh Céad Míle Fáilte*."

"What's that mean?" I pointed.

Dad craned his neck as he looked out the window. "A hundred thousand welcomes to the Kelly house. I suppose you didn't learn Irish in America."

"We learn it in school," Patrick said.

"Did—does—Mom know it?"

"A bit, aye," Dad said.

Another thing I didn't know about her. I wished she'd shared *anything* Irish with me.

As we headed in, I noticed a massive wall loomed right behind Dad's house.

"What?" Patrick asked when I stopped.

"It's the peace wall she's looking at." Dad waved off the taxi.

The wall was about fourteen feet of concrete topped with at least ten feet of sheet metal topped with maybe twenty feet of mesh. "Is *Jurassic Park* back there?"

Dad chuckled.

"It's the Shankill. Protestant Loyalist area," Patrick said.

Before everything with Dad, the only thing Mom had said about the Troubles was that it was long over, but bits of what I'd read flashed into my brain. Protestant Loyalists, Catholic Republicans, both sides in a battle against their neighbors and the British government for like thirty years.

week ago, just minutes after I'd finished my last final of junior year, the truth had all come out. Mom had lied to me for a decade and a half; my "deadbeat dad" had always wanted to be in my life. Every time Mom had taken me to Olbrich Gardens, when I'd dropped my penny into the koi pond, I'd wished for a dad who would show me Jupiter through the telescope he bought me for my birthday. I'd never had that, and it was all thanks to Mom. I still couldn't believe she'd kept me from him. In a way, I understood her reasons, but...

The plane shuddered as we touched down. I was officially back on the island Mom had taken me and fled from. Tingles swelled from my stomach through my arms and legs.

"Welcome to Dublin Airport," a flight attendant with an Irish accent said over the intercom. She repeated it in Irish as the plane taxied past a row of other shamrock-marked Aer Lingus planes. Tall green letters spelled out "*Baile Átha Cliath, Dublin*" on the terminal we approached. Belfast apparently had an airport, two actually, but there were no direct flights from O'Hare, and Mom didn't want me navigating two layovers alone my second time ever flying. So Dad was picking me up in Dublin. The cabin filled with the clicks of unfastening seat belts and low voices. I pulled my messenger bag from under the seat in front of me and tucked my phone into it.

Following the slow flow of passengers off the plane, I wondered if the others would be waiting for me too. "The others" were Patrick and Seamus, my half brothers. I'd known they existed, but just as fabled, faceless beings. Patrick was seven years older than me, and Seamus three. Their mother, Dad's first wife, had died giving birth to Seamus. Mom was still their stepmom, legally speaking, since she and my father had never divorced. I even had a six-year-old nephew, Finn; he was Patrick's son. I couldn't believe all I'd missed out on. I was an *aunt*.

# chapter one

## *Fiona*

The plane broke free from a sea of boiling blue-gray clouds as we made our final descent into Dublin. Brilliant green pastures boxed in by hedges zipped under us. Just like I'd always imagined. The lady in front of me snapped a million pictures out her window. I wanted to too, but I didn't want to look like a total tourist. My favorite song by Fading Stars played on through my earbuds.

"Flight attendants, cross-check and prepare for landing," the captain's voice cut over Martin Benjamin's smooth voice.

My heart stuttered.

July 3, 2012. The day I'd meet my dad—my father, Peter, a man I'd never known—in the flesh. Yes, Mom and I had lived with him until I was two and a half, but I didn't remember a single thing about those years. And since then, there'd been nothing. Not a word from him in fifteen years.

And now he was down there. Waiting for me. Not the unshaven brute in a stained wifebeater I'd always imagined. A

For Norah and Ewan

Turner Publishing Company
Nashville, Tennessee
www.turnerpublishing.com

*All the Walls of Belfast*



**Cover design:** Olga Grlic
**Book design:** Meg Reid

Library of Congress Cataloging-in-Publication Data

Names: Carlson, Sarah J., author.
Title: All the walls of Belfast / Sarah J. Carlson.
Description: [Nashville] : Turner Publishing Company, [2019]
Summary: Wisconsin seventeen-year-old Fiona Kelly visits the father she never knew—and her half-brothers—in Belfast, Ireland, where she also connects with Danny, but their families' pasts may shatter what they have.
Identifiers: LCCN 2018040703| ISBN 9781684422524 (pbk.)
ISBN 9781684422531 (hardcover)
Subjects: | CYAC: Fathers and daughters—Fiction.
Family life—Ireland—Fiction. | Belfast (Northern Ireland)—Fiction.
Northern Ireland—Fiction. | Ireland—History—20th century—Fiction.
Classification: LCC PZ7.7.C4115 All 2019 | DDC [Fic]—dc23
LC record available at https://lccn.loc.gov/2018040703

9781684422524 Paperback
9781684422531 Hardcover
9781684422548 eBook

Printed in the United States of America
17 18 19 20 10 9 8 7 6 5 4 3 2 1

# all the walls of belfast

a novel

sarah j. carlson

TURNER PUBLISHING COMPANY

"The Troubles are over, though, right?"

"They are, but bored kids sometimes like to throw rocks and ball bearings at us," Patrick said.

Over *that* wall? You'd need a catapult.

"Belfast is one of the safest cities in Europe now." Dad opened the front door and waved me inside. "You don't need to worry about that rubbish."

A stairway met us at the entrance. To the left was a small living room. The smell of Pine-Sol overpowered me, just like after Mom's Saturday afternoon clean fests.

Someone stared at me from a ragged beige-and-cream plaid couch. I recognized him: Seamus, my other half brother. He had linebacker shoulders and freckles even darker than mine covering his pasty face.

"Where's Finny?" Dad hefted my suitcase onto the landing behind me.

The living room was crammed with the couch, a threadbare orange arm chair, and a coffee table.

"He's just watching Captain America." Seamus was studying me. "You dress like a boy."

I glanced down at my skinny jeans and flannel, then looked back at Seamus's tapered Adidas track pants. "Rev Run called. He wants his pants back."

Seamus snorted. "You said pants."

Right. Pants here means underwear.

Heavy feet plodded down the stairs. "Guess what I found hiding under the bed." Patrick emerged from the stairwell carrying his little boy, my nephew. He set him down and ruffled his curly hair. "Meet your auntie."

I crouched down to Finn's eye level. He was a mini-Patrick with brown eyes, which meant he looked like a mini-me too.

"Hey, nice to meet you."

Finn's eyes grew huge, then he ducked behind his dad. What had I done wrong?

I slipped a hand into my messenger bag and took out Bucky Badger, my stuffed toy bestie since I was five. I offered it to Finn.

"I brought you Bucky Badger. He's, like, the mascot of Wisconsin. Where I'm from."

Patrick took it from me. "Your aunt Fiona brought you your very own Wisconsin superhero. What's his superpower?"

Finn peeked one huge eye past Patrick.

"Uh... push-ups after touchdowns?" I said.

Finn's arms tightened around Patrick's waist. Maybe I should have just stuck with hello.

Patrick plopped down on the couch next to Seamus, wallet chain clinking. Finn scrambled into his lap. Seamus looked me over again like he was dissecting my face with his eyes. A painting of the Sacred Heart of Mary serenely watched us from above the TV. She held Easter lilies in one hand, like the ones Mom had painted on our mailbox last summer. These people I'd spent years imagining, there they all were. My head felt like a helium balloon attached to my body with a string.

"Sure you must be knackered, Fiona," Dad said. "I'll show you to your room."

"You mean *my* room," Seamus said.

"Shut your gob, you brain-dead bastard." Patrick smacked Seamus on the back of the head.

"Can yous not be civil for five seconds?" Dad rubbed his forehead.

I hugged my arms to my chest.

Dad let out a low, rumbling throat clearing. "Fiona, let's get you settled in, then." He lumbered upstairs, leaning heavily on one leg.

My wobbly legs managed to carry me up the stairs to a room swathed in floral wallpaper that smelled a little like a boy's locker room. A bedside table and two beds were packed in the tiny space; one had a *Cars* comforter adorned with a pile of action figures, the other was pink. On the walls hung two posters of nearly naked *Sports Illustrated* swimsuit models and a gold crucifix.

Now that I was here, I felt like a space invader. A thump vibrated the floor. Seamus had come in the door and stood over my suitcase at the foot of the pink bed. He shoved his hands in his pockets. "You used to hit me with pots."

I raised an eyebrow at him. "You probably deserved it."

Seamus guffawed. Apparently I'd landed on the right response. On his way out, he said, "Hope you like my bed, then."

Okay, maybe he didn't despise the fact that I'd come.

"Can I get you anything?" Dad inspected the room, hands on his hips.

"I'm fine."

"Right, well, I'll let you be." Dad loosened his tie. "If you're in need of anything, let me know. I've some time off tomorrow. Thought I'd show you about."

Chewing the inside of my lip, I nodded.

Dad squeezed my shoulder with a broad grin that obliterated the exhaustion from his eyes. "We're glad you're finally here." He closed the door behind him.

A damp chill in the air made me shiver. The big bottom window didn't appear to open, but the two smaller ones above it were cracked a few inches. I climbed on the *Cars* bed and pulled them closed. There were no screens. I guess they didn't have hordes of mosquitoes over here.

Across the world, Mom was perched on the edge of our couch that exact second waiting for me to call. I dug out my phone and opened Skype. She was online. My thumb hovered over the call button.

Mom had been my constant, my gravity. But my universe was expanding so fast not even Mom's gravity could slow it. I hated the growing distance between us, but she was the one who triggered it. If Dad hadn't found me, I might never have learned the truth.

I Skyped Nevaeh instead.

The blue call screen bleeped, then filled with Nevaeh's grinning face. Today, she wore bright-orange lipstick and her Marcus Point uniform, a black dress shirt and red tie.

"You working?" I asked.

"Zion and I are grabbing some Taco Bell fuel before our shift."

The image jumped, and then I could see Zion mowing down on a Crunchwrap Supreme. He waved a pinky finger at me.

"Hey, T Bell hiring?" I asked.

"Why? Didn't you apply to Marcus Point?" Nevaeh shoved the last of her usual Cheesy Gordita Crunch into her mouth.

I'd been selected from thousands for a spot in the field study program at Puerto Rico's Arecibo Observatory, but my golden ticket into MIT cost two grand by October 1. I hadn't shared that little fact with Mom just yet, because telling me it was impossible would shatter her heart. So I'd be scrambling for a summer job after this foray into discovering my long-lost family was over.

"Gotta cover my bases, cuz everybody wants the free popcorn perk Zion's always bragging about."

Zion laughed, covering his mouthful of taco. He grabbed their wrapper-littered tray and got up.

"How's Ireland?" Nevaeh asked. "Wait, Northern Ireland."

I'd corrected her a thousand times. "I've been here for like five seconds. But fine, I guess."

Another Skype call popped up on my screen. Mom. I hit ignore.

Zion plopped back down by Nevaeh. "They ain't hiring, but I'll see if you can help mow lawns with me. It'll get you a few hundred bucks."

God, if *only* Nevaeh hadn't been crushing on him since seventh grade. If only her outgoing personality wasn't already the perfect match for Zion's introversion. "You're the best, Zion. I still can't believe Mr. Fallon nominated me for Arecibo over you."

"I'm more of a quantum physics kinda guy." Zion draped his arm over the bench.

"You two and your crazy space talk." Nevaeh wrinkled her nose.

"Dude, quantum physics is subatomic," I said.

"Yeah, but all the atoms were made by stars, so..." Nevaeh shined a victorious grin.

"Dang, Fi, she treated you." Zion laughed.

The sound of explosive urination was audible through the door. A belch echoed from the bathroom, followed by a flush and a sharp, plastic slap. Seamus had just put the toilet seat down, for me.

"You all right?" Nevaeh eyebrows puckered. "Those people weird? Tell the truth, Fi."

I tugged a thread free from the rip in my jeans. I didn't know what to tell her. I loved Nevaeh, but her dad was a lawyer and her mom was an accountant. If she knew Dad's past, she'd hop on a plane and drag me back to Madison.

Zion might be able to understand, because his dad had done a brief stint with the Gangster Disciples in Chicago when he was a teenager. Oh, the irony. When Mom and I found out about his dad's past, she never let me go to Zion's again, even though his dad was now a part of an anti-gang task force. But she begrudgingly let me fly across the world without her to stay with an IRA "ex-volunteer."

"Fi, you're going all space cadet on me." Neveah waved a hand at the camera.

My cheeks warmed. "I'm just really tired. Couldn't sleep on the plane. I better go."

Nevaeh raised a cool eyebrow at me. "Fi. You're the worst liar."

"Veah, let her get some sleep." Zion gave her a gentle shoulder bump. "Interrogate her tomorrow."

"Fine. Byeeeee." Nevaeh stretched it out for her usual fifteen seconds.

I hung up and buried myself under that pink comforter, shoes and all. How could I expect to walk in the front door and fit into my long-lost family? I'd feel better tomorrow.

# chapter four

## *Danny*

The next morning while Da was having a shower, I rescued my school blazer. Thank Christ my enlistment papers were still in the pocket. I smoothed them out and stuck them in my rucksack for safekeeping.

My blazer smelt worse than that plugged toilet I'd helped Sammy unblock the other day. I sprinted for my bus stop, rucksack bouncing against my back. I was running dangerously late for my A-Levels, which could mean disqualification. But if I didn't wear the blazer, Principal Doyle might not let me sit it either.

Just as I closed in on the bus stop, the 81 pulled away. Sometimes I hated Da so frigging much.

According to my bus app, I could catch the 10F not a few hundred meters away, and it'd get me there by 8:45. But the 10F stop was on the Springfield Road, and that was in the Falls. If I went there in my Ballysillan Boys' uniform, those Taigs might murder me.

The 11A had a stop up the Shankill Road. It'd get me there at 9:00 . . . when the exam started.

I legged it through a wasteland, near lost a shoe in the mud. My lungs screamed, but I kept pushing myself.

*No surrender, Danny Boy.* I tore up the Shankill Road past shuttered shops. Sweat ran down my back, soaked into the band of my boxers. At least I could tell Sinclair I'd done my fitness training today—if I got the chance to speak before he ended me for being late.

"Oi, Danny! Have fun at school, wee lamb," I heard my friend Anto call after me, unleashing his usual hyena cackle.

"Sod off," I yelled over my shoulder without breaking stride. A gust of wind blew my tie in my face. I shoved it under my disgusting blazer.

The 11A pulled to a stop in front of Rosie Cole Beauty Salon as I reached the crossroads.

This old granny with a cane hobbled toward the open door.

"Hold him! A-Levels." I flailed my arms.

She scowled at me and climbed on.

Christ sake. I wasn't even dressed like a wee hood.

I threw myself on and tapped my card as the bus lurched forward. I half expected applause as I collapsed into the first empty seat. The stench of my damp, manky blazer cleared out everyone in the seats around me. At 9:02, the bus pulled to a stop outside Ballysillan Boys'. I slipped through the door as it opened and rushed across the car park. As I burst through the main doors, Principal Doyle snarled, "Mr. Stewart, get back here!"

He was too fat to catch me. The clicks from my heels echoed down the empty hall. The door to the gym was closed. I grabbed the door handle—locked. Through the window, I could see the other lads already writing. I tapped on the glass.

Mr. Sinclair had murder in his eyes as he got up from his desk. I ran a hand through my sweat-drenched hair. My fingers grazed the tender bruise on my forehead. I combed my hair down.

This old doll with blue hair, dressed in an official-looking pantsuit, intercepted Sinclair on his way over—an exam invigilator. They got into a whispering match for the ages; Sinclair threw his hands about as she shook her head.

That dirty wee arse-licker Foster smirked at me from inside the room. The gold buttons on his maroon prefect jacket gleamed in the strip lighting. The only reason he was prefect was because his mummy was always decorating wee bulletin boards.

Sinclair's eyes were nailed on me as he snatched the phone by the door. Angry whispering leaked under. Shite, he was calling up Doyle; he'd been told he needed to get permission to let me enter. My wet shirt turned cold against my back.

All the lads were scrawling in their exam books. My fingers tapped the rudiment we used for "Billy Boys" against my thigh. I needed only three Ds to earn the 180 points, but would that happen if I couldn't sit this one?

Sinclair hung up, veins popping out of his forehead. As he turned to me, the look in his eyes hurt worse than Da's left hook last night.

My enlistment papers weighed down my rucksack. I pressed my back against the wall, slid into a crouching position, and buried my throbbing head in my hands. This was it, then.

"On your feet, Stewart." Doyle's voice dripped with triumph. I pulled myself up and stood tall so I could look down on his shiny, bald head and he had to look up to me. The door to my future opened and Sinclair emerged.

"He was only five minutes late when he got here," Sinclair said. "Now we've wasted another five minutes of his time."

Principal Doyle's piggy eyes raked over me from my scuffed-up black shoes to the crusty mess of my hair. "After all your years here, Mr. Stewart, surely you've learnt that punctuality is a life skill. The army would never tolerate such tardiness, especially on such an important day."

"Please, sir," I forced myself to beg, "if I don't sit this, it'll ruin everything. I've my Main Board in a few weeks."

Doyle sneered at me, hands on his hips.

Sinclair glanced at his watch. "Glen, if Danny doesn't sit this, he'll be the first student who hasn't in five years."

Doyle's sneer deflated. "I don't want this yob mucking up our fine record." He turned on his heel and marched off like he'd something shoved up his hole.

"Jaysus, Sinclair, I owe you."

Sinclair's face relaxed as he looked me over. He unlocked the door. "Do your best, Danny Boy."

All the lads gawked as I walked in.

"Christ, did you bathe in rubbish this morning, Stewart?" Foster pinched his nose as I passed. A few sniggers spread through the gym.

"Aye, your ma," I muttered under my breath.

His face went red with rage.

"Mr. Foster, the exam has started. Silence," Sinclair said, "or it could lead to a penalty."

Someday I hoped to run into that twat in the city centre. I'd been fourteen when I won the Ulster Novice Boxing Championship for the seventy-five kilogram weight class, but I could still knock the shite clean out of him. I dropped my rucksack on the floor and sank into a desk chair. My forehead was grainy with dried sweat, and I couldn't even make saliva to wet my tongue.

Sinclair dropped the exam on my desk. The clock behind the

basketball hoop said it was 9:17. Seventy-three minutes left. I scribbled my name and signed it, then turned to the first page—a question about upwelling in the sea. Frigging biological molecules in the ocean; I should've paged through that revision book a few more times.

My mud-caked shoe touched my rucksack. Don't let Da muck this for you.

I flipped to a question about converting farmland to woodland and the impact on bird population.

All that I'd learnt over the past two years swam through my head. I grabbed the bits that I needed. Chicken genetics, ways to control malaria, humanity's role in global warming. I liked learning about the interaction of humans and the world, how we were all part of the same fragile ecosystem, tied to the same fate.

That old invigilator kept looking over my shoulder like she hoped to catch me with my phone out. Foster and his pack of fruits finished before me, but I took my time, gave loads of answers, and checked my work. I dragged myself up to Sinclair's desk with one minute to spare.

"How did you get on?"

"Brilliantly." I handed him my exam.

Sinclair scrawled something on a piece of paper and gave it to me. "Ring me if you're in need of anything."

I unfolded it. He'd given me his number.

"Well, I need to make sure you're off to Bristol," he said. "Otherwise it'd be like leaving a film before the end."

I slid the number in my trouser pocket. It choked me up a bit. "Em, thanks."

"I can't believe you've actually finished school." Mr. Sinclair's face cracked into one of his rare half smiles.

I grinned. "Me neither."

My throat still felt strangely thick as I walked into the empty halls. Rain lashed against the windows, rivulets distorting the courtyard outside. I'd gone to Ballysillan Boys' since I was eleven and hated almost every second of it, but a tiny part of me felt a bit sad that I'd never be back.

Foster and his shower of gobshites were having a wee chat in the foyer. They parted for me like I had Ebola. Nobody said anything to me, not even Williams, who'd been my partner in biology.

As I got to the door, they busted out laughing.

"Goodbye forever, you wee scrotes!" I threw open the door.

My fingers traced the cold railing as I jogged down the front steps of Ballysillan Boys' for the last time. I caught the 12A; it didn't go to the Shankill, but I couldn't wait one more second. I dug out my mobile, plugged in my earbuds, and put on "Hero's Heart," my favorite song. Guitars strummed in the background as Martin Benjamin sang, "*listen to your heart...*"

While everyone else was celebrating finishing school, I'd have to go round begging for work.

Most parents would be happy that their son hadn't turned out to be a wee hood. Not my da. He wanted me to fix cars for the rest of my life with him and Billy. Sign on with the UVF, extort protection money. Deal drugs. Run guns. But in two weeks, I'd board that plane to Bristol, pass my Main Board, and get accepted into officer training. Da wouldn't even know where I'd gone. Then in a few years, I'd come back in my army uniform and drive round in a nice car and show Da and everyone.

I just needed the cash.

The bus rolled to a stop by Castle Court Shopping Centre. Two lads about my age got on, both in O'Neills tops—Taigs. They leered at me. The crest on my school blazer had given me away as a Protestant. I hugged my rucksack to my chest and glared right back.

"*This is your life. Your only life...*" My song played on. "*Make choices that mean something...*"

Those bead-rattling scumbags went upstairs.

As the bus ground forward, water droplets streaked in jagged horizontal lines across the window. I got off at the Europa Bus Centre, then grabbed a job application at the Boots in the Great Northern Mall, a miserable hallway of shops connecting the bus station to Great Victoria Street. I'd leave it on the coffee table so there would be no doubt that I was collecting proper job applications.

As I walked home, my stomach was wailing. I'd had no dinner last night and no time for breakfast this morning. I messaged Jon, who'd been my best mate since before we could kick a football. He might give me a free feed again if he was working at the KFC. I crossed the bridge over the Westlink and passed the statue of a woman holding a banner: "Welcome to the Shankill." Brick terraced houses stretched toward Black Mountain and Divis Mountain to the west. Union Jack bunting—put up last week—zigzagged down the entire stretch of the Shankill Road. New Union Jack flags snapped against every lamppost. Everyone was getting ready for the Twelfth.

"Oi, Danny!" Jon jogged out of the KFC carrying a bag of chicken. "What's the craic?"

I grabbed the bag as we crossed the street, going from Ulster Defence Association territory to Ulster Volunteer Force territory.

"Thanks a million." I pulled out a steaming drumstick and tore off a chunk. The salty greasiness slid down my throat.

Jon shielded a cigarette with his freckle-covered hand and lit up. Raindrops spotted his maroon KFC polo. "You finally finish school, then?"

"Aye."

We walked up the Shankill in step out of habit from marching.

I finished off the first piece and grabbed a thigh.

Jon took a long drag. "Soon you're away off to your wee test."

He was the only one I'd told besides Mr. Sinclair.

"Eleventh." I took a huge bite from a thigh.

"But what about the boney? The parade?"

I shrugged as I chewed. The bonfire and the parade would just have to happen without me.

We turned down Lawnbrook, passing the boarded-up building that used to be a coffee shop. Someone had spray-painted "Policing supports Republicans" on the side next to "Police Service of Northern Ireland Scum."

"Where's your thing at?" Jon asked.

I kicked at rubbish collecting in front of a bricked-up door. "Near Bristol."

"In England?" Jon squinted. "How're you going to get there?"

"A plane."

Jon stared at me for an uncomfortable length of time. He took a long drag. "Well, you'll show all them poncy English tossers how it's done."

I grinned. I'd miss Jon.

The peace wall blocked the wind as we walked toward the wasteland where the Upper Shankill built our bonfire. Mrs. Donnelly said those walls protected us from the Catholics. She was our neighbor, and she'd lived through the Troubles. She knew how bad it could be. Security checkpoints, the steel ring round the city centre, soldiers on the streets, bars getting shot up, IRA bombs blowing people up and throwing shoes and hats and blood into the street. Not like our wee riots now.

Before we got to the boney, I nipped up to my room and hid my enlistment papers under my mattress with my passport and baby book.

Da's mate Gusty guarded the gate in the fence round the wasteland, wearing his usual Union flag hat backwards. "Mind yous don't get to drinking over by Top again, or I'll put my foot so far up your hole it'll come out your gob."

"All right, big man." I slipped past him. The paramilitaries thought they were local peelers, always chasing us off when all we were doing was having a drink, like they did all the time.

But Gusty was some kind of handyman. Anto sometimes worked for him.

I turned back. "Em, Gusty, I'm looking for a bit of work. You need a hand?"

Gusty threw back his Buckfast, and some trickled down his chin. "Come round at half eight the morrow."

Jon and I cut across the wasteland. Shards of wood and rubbish littered the paths from the rows of pallets and piles of tires that were being got ready for the bonfire. I knew from Physiology and Ecosystems that burning tires wasn't great for the environment, but it was only once a year and nothing compared to the carbon dioxide America pumped into the atmosphere every day with all their big cars. The council offered us money if we didn't put tires in it, but we wanted to celebrate our culture our way. A wee bouncy castle and a burger van wouldn't cut it.

Loads of lads were helping build the bonfire higher. We'd been at it a month, and I reckoned it was already over thirty feet tall—almost tall enough for the Catholics to see over the wall when we set it alight. This year we'd have the biggest boney, bigger than the Lower Shankill and Sandy Row and Newtownards.

I loved Eleventh Night when we lit it. Getting pissed up, watching the fire eat away at the tower. Hearing the roar as the heat boiled your eyeballs. I never left until it collapsed. But this year, I'd miss it.

I'd be back, though, after I was an officer.

I spotted Mrs. Donnelly cooking on her kerosene stove by the guard hut. Even with all the chicken, I was still famished. Skrillex blared out of the hut so loud it was a bit surprising the pallet walls and roof, made of old doors, didn't collapse. It was disrespectful, playing that rubbish round nice Mrs. Donnelly.

"Danny, hiya." Mrs. Donnelly pushed up her huge glasses. Frowning, she got on her tiptoes and brushed my hair back. Her cold fingertips grazed my bruise. I flinched and pulled away.

"Again?" Mrs. Donnelly asked, hands on her hips.

I combed my hair back in place. "I'm grand." I started to leave without any beans but then remembered Mrs. Donnelly had a cleaning business. "If you're ever looking for an extra hand with that cleaning..." I studied a footprint in the coagulated mud, the Nike swoosh imprint preserved like a fossil.

"Sorry, love. Not at the moment." Her soft voice had an apology in it.

"Right." I shoved my hands in my pockets and headed over to the band lads, drinking round a fire.

"Danny!" Clare rushed up to me. Her massive boobs almost jiggled out of her pink top. She'd a fake orange tan and bleached blond hair.

"What about you, Clare."

At a parade a few weeks back, I'd told Clare she was pretty. She'd pressed her boobs into me, which I took as an invitation to kiss her. Then she slapped me. Jon said it was because all the girls in the Shankill thought I was a wee fruit for staying on in school. In sixth form, we'd sometimes done stuff with Ballysillan Girls', but they were all posh tarts and thought they were too good for someone like me.

We joined Anto, Davey, and wee Jamie standing round their little fire. As the heat pricked my face, the smell of petrol and burning wood and garbage filled my lungs—I loved that smell. I grabbed two tins from a twenty-four pack of Carling and handed one to Clare.

"Thanks, love." She batted her crusty black eyelashes at me. I cracked my tin open and took a gulp. Anto leered at me as he supped his seven hundred milliliter bottle of WKD Blue, probably jealous. The fire cast dancing shadows over his acne-scarred face.

"How was school, Professor?" he asked.

"Piss off, you dirty wee bollocks," I said.

Jon joined us. He looked me and Clare over, then winked at me.

Davcy pulled off his Burberry cap and ran a hand through his number one crop. "Staying on in school with all the frigging retards. What's that all about? You used to be good craic, Danny."

"It'd do my head in, exams and homework and teachers telling me what to do," Clare said.

"Aren't you a bit old for school?" Jamie asked. "Is your da not raging?"

Jamie had the pleasure of hearing all manner of our family rows through the thin walls between our houses.

I looked at him. "We can talk about that after you grow real facial hair, not that wee bum-fluff tash."

Clare cocked her head to the side. "So you want to kill them ragheads in Iraq?"

Anto cackled. "No, he wants to be a wee nurse."

Now everyone was laughing except Jon.

I shoved Anto. "Fuck up, wankstain."

He pushed back. "Aye, your ma!"

He tried to scramble away but I dropped my beer, grabbed him by his Ranger's top, and swung my right hook into his pimply jaw. He was on the ground, fizzy blue WKD spilling in his lap.

"Alright, Professor. I'm only having a laugh with you," Anto whined.

As I walked away, Jon hissed, "You wee prick, you know Danny's ma got killed."

I snatched a near-full bottle of whiskey from the mud and set off. I twisted off the cap and let the drink rip down my throat until my eyes stung. I hated whiskey. Numbness spread out from my chest.

Screw Foster. Screw Anto. Screw Da. I'd get that money and get out of the Shankill.

# chapter five

## *Fiona*

A knock rattled the door. "Fiona, breakfast is ready."

I peeled my eyes open. My pupils protested. No plastic stars on the ceiling. Where was I? I sat up. My sour-smelling clothes from yesterday stuck to me like the fabric had tried to become one with my skin. The *Cars* comforter on the other bed appeared undisturbed.

"Fiona?" Dad's feet blocked the light oozing under the door.

It felt like I'd slept about ten minutes and my head was filled with packing peanuts.

"Are you coming down for breakfast?"

"Be right there," I said.

I changed, then stumbled to the bathroom, which was about the size of my closet. The sink ledge was lined with shaving cream and razors and man deodorant, but the toilet seat was still down. A cup with four toothbrushes, including a tiny Captain America one, teetered on the edge. The sink had two gleaming faucets. One was freezing cold, the other scalding. I splashed cold water on my face, then studied myself in the mirror. Dad's and Patrick's eyes looked back at me.

I checked the shower. Not even a hint of soap scum. In addition to the men's products, bottles of Sainsbury's Apple Shampoo and Conditioner sat on the ledge. The same scent as the generic stuff Mom and I used.

Talking and the clatter of dishes leaked through the floorboards.

*The more you're around them, the more comfortable you'll feel.*

Downstairs, Bucky Badger lay abandoned by a sofa leg. I followed the smell of frying meat. With yellow walls and a colorful backsplash, that cramped kitchen did not belong in a house with four dudes.

Dad froze mid-sausage flip. He grinned. "Good morning, Fiona."

"Hey," I said.

The sizzling pan began to smoke. "Ah, bollocks." Dad frantically scraped.

Shirtless Seamus snickered as he fidgeted on his phone. One of his biceps was covered with a Celtic cross. I took a seat between him and Patrick.

"Jet lag do your head in?" Patrick's face was buried in a copy of *Animal Farm*. He wore a green uniform shirt with a name tag.

I gripped my seat to stay grounded. "Yeah, it sucks."

Finn, next to Patrick, watched me with huge doe eyes. He wore a purple sweater with a crest on the breast, his school uniform. Thank God I never had to wear one of those.

"Do you have school today, Finn?" I asked.

He nodded once, gaze on the table.

"I saw your school yesterday. It looks . . . " Like a prison behind that iron fence. "Nice."

Finn's eyebrows pinched together.

"It's his last day before summer holiday." Patrick elbowed Finn.

"Seamy, put the kettle on," Dad said.

Seamus groaned but squeezed past Patrick and filled the electric kettle.

Awkward silence hung in the air with the burnt meat haze. Then I noticed the small window over the sink had an amazing view of the massive peace wall not twenty feet away. Between us and the wall was some kind of mesh cage. "What's with the zombie apocalypse sunroom over the backyard?"

Seamus squinted at me.

"Most of the year, everything's fine." Dad flopped eggs onto a plate and dropped some bread in the pan. "We've nothing to worry about." He cleared his throat. "We usually just do a full fry at the weekends, so this is a special Wednesday. Catherine, does she ever make her fry-ups?"

Catherine was my mom. It was so strange to hear him call her that. I wondered what he thought about her now. Even though she'd lied to me about him for years, he didn't seem that angry about it, more like resigned. Did he blame himself for the relationship ending? For her feeling so unsafe around what Dad was getting up to, that she wanted to move all the way to the States?

"Sometimes she makes pancakes and egg whites."

"Fiona, how do you take your tea?" Seamus poured water into the five mismatched mugs on the counter.

Mom didn't let me drink it until I was sixteen because she claimed caffeine stunted your growth, and then I discovered it was nasty. But I didn't want to offend anyone. "Um, regular?"

Seamus set a steaming cup in front of me. I took a sip and almost choked on the bitterness. They all stared at me like I was a Martian.

"Is it too hot?" Dad asked as even little Finn chugged his like it was soda. "Would you like a bit of milk?"

"It's fine." I set the cup down.

Dad reached over and put a chipped plate in front of me. Two runny eggs, fried tomatoes, two slabs of crispy Canadian-looking bacon, two sausages that were more like mini-brats than Jimmy Deans, and two pieces of toast, probably the legendary soda bread and potato bread Mom complained that she couldn't get in the US. I could not believe Mom used to make that artery clogger. What else was hidden in her past?

Dad dragged over a chair that didn't match the other four and squeezed between Seamus and Finn. "After breakfast, I thought I'd take you to Belfast Castle."

"Cool, I've never seen a castle before." I cut off some bacon and stabbed some egg, then dipped it in brown sauce. It was salty and delicious, but way more than I could eat. Seamus and Patrick fought over my leftovers until Dad intervened.

"Are you done, then, Finny?" Patrick dog-eared his page.

Finn nodded. He'd barely touched his food. I wondered if I made him too nervous to eat. Finn gave Dad a hug before he and Patrick headed out.

"Right, let's go, Fiona." Dad stacked the plates.

Seamus got up. "I'm coming with yous."

Dad raised an eyebrow. "I thought you were helping Mr. O'Neill with painting today."

Seamus shrugged as he checked his phone. Did he actually want to spend time with me? After he threw on a black McKenzie hoodie, we headed out.

"Sun's shining for you today, welcoming you back." Dad beamed as he held the front door open for me.

Four old-fashioned black taxis sat parked in front of the house. A rain-jacket-clad lady gaped at us as we emerged. People snapped pictures of the wall.

"Political tours, here for the Clonard Martyrs Memorial

Garden." Dad gestured at the fenced-in memorial in the lot between his house and another. A huge stone Celtic cross stood in the middle. On the peace wall was a billboard with faces and a black-and-red phoenix.

"That must get super annoying," I said.

"You get used to it." Dad rested a hand on my back and guided me down the street to a waiting black taxi.

After we were dropped off, I discovered Belfast Castle was more of a modestly sized graystone mansion. It didn't even have a moat and drawbridge. In the garden outside was a bush trimmed to look like a cat, complete with whiskers. I snapped a picture for Nevaeh and her cat obsession.

As we followed the paths through the castle garden, Seamus played on his phone, dragging a few steps behind, apparently not interested in castles or me after all.

"So your mam says you want to study physics at uni," Dad said. "That you'd like to go to MIT."

A gust of damp, cool wind whipped my curls into my eyes. I tucked my hair behind my ears. "Yeah."

"That's brilliant," Dad said. "But you know, if you don't get accepted there, Trinity College in Dublin offers free fees to EU citizens. Which you are."

Whoa. Slow your roll, Han Solo. I haven't even been here twenty-four hours.

Dad led us up into the hill paths above the castle. The wind cut through my canvas jacket. Dad leaned heavily on his left leg as we walked, but his smile never faltered as he interrogated me about every detail of my life. It made me feel like I was the only person in the world. Seamus's face was mostly still buried in his phone, but I caught him watching a few times.

Before we headed back to Dad's, he took us to a bench

overlooking Belfast—the spot of Mom and Dad's first proper date, he told me. Just like Madison, there weren't any tall buildings. Lines of brick row houses and chimney stacks stretched to the city centre. Sunlight glittered off Belfast Harbour, at the tip of a sea inlet called Belfast Lough, Dad said. I snapped a photo of the empty bench, Belfast spread below.

I tried to picture Mom and Dad prewrinkles, sitting on that bench. Dad playing with her long, straight hair before it started turning gray. I couldn't see it, even though they were still married. When I harped on her to get a life, she always insisted that marriage vows meant till death do us part. Dad still wore his wedding ring too.

When we got back to Dad's, a pack of boys swathed in Adidas hung outside the house across the street. If the Yung Guns, the gang plaguing Memorial, saw those poser white boys, they'd beat their asses.

"What are you at the day, wee Seamy?" brayed one wearing a baseball cap with dollar signs.

Seamus jogged up to him and they engaged in a pushing match. I was pretty good with Northern Irish accents, but I still couldn't decipher what they were saying. Seamus snickered.

"Yeoooo!" one of them yelled.

And then I realized Pimple Boy was leering at me.

"Mate, that's my wee sister," Seamus spat.

Pimple Boy hollered, "Do you wanna climb my pole?"

Dad gritted his teeth so tight the veins bulged out of his neck.

"I'll knock the feck clean outta you, Janty, you dirty wee prick!" Seamus shoved that punk into the wall. The rest of the pack started hooting and laughing.

I bit in a smile.

The boys scattered before Dad got halfway across the street.

"Why do you hang round with that shower of eejits?" Dad asked Seamus as they walked back. "Fiona, you needn't worry about those wee hoods."

"I've dealt with that before. I am in high school."

But still, Seamus could probably grow on me.

❧

Later in the day, Dad had to go to work. He was a community organizer now, trying to make sure the street youth had "positive outlets" and didn't grow up to carry on the violence. Seamus was going out too. Dad had asked a neighbor to come by—not to babysit me, he protested, but just to "keep me company" and to be here when Finn got home. Mrs. McMahon, it turned out, had grown up in the area and had been friends with my mom.

Mrs. McMahon told me stories about animals she and Mom had saved and things they'd baked. Mom winning the art show four years running at St. Dominic's Grammar School for Girls. Volunteering at the Falls Road Library to get free books. Singing in the choir. I imagined younger versions of them running around these grim streets in school uniforms. Telling secrets about boys. Sharing ice cream cones. In Madison, Mom had work acquaintances and some people at St. Maria Goretti, but her only close friend was Nevaeh's mom. She said she was too busy for friends, but now I wondered if she isolated herself on purpose. Because she was hiding her past from everyone, including herself.

The front door popped open, bringing a burst of cool, damp air. Finn hopped in, water splattering from his dinosaur rain boots. In place of his gray uniform pants were a pair of jeans with holes in the knees—and not the stylish kind like mine. He spotted me and froze like a deer in headlights.

"Hi, Finn. Did you have a good day at school?" I asked.

His freckled cheeks turned pink as his eyes fell. Seamus folded up the umbrella, then mussed up Finn's curls. "Take off your wellies."

Finn wobbled as he tugged at his rain boots. Seamus steadied him but exchanged a meaningful look with Mrs. McMahon. "Finny, go make sure we've flour, yeah?"

Head down, Finn darted between the couch and Dad's chair. The kitchen door clapped closed behind him.

"Again?" Mrs. McMahon's eyes lingered on the door.

Seamus sat in Dad's chair. "Second day. That's why he didn't have spare trousers."

*Oh*. He'd had an accident at school.

"What was Paddy getting on to that he didn't have time to do the washing for wee Finny?" Mrs. McMahon tutted.

After Seamus took Finn upstairs, Mrs. McMahon said her goodbyes. Thank God. Reaching to grab my cell phone from the scratched coffee table, I spotted a Batman coloring book. I flipped it open. The black and yellow never crossed the lines.

"Wow," I said when Finn reappeared in a Spider-Man shirt. "Whoever did this is really good."

Finn's huge brown eyes peeked at me through his curls.

I flipped to the next page. "This one too. Stayed in the lines and everything. Seamus, was this you?"

Seamus wrapped his massive arms around Finn. "Not me."

"Yeah, you probably couldn't color that well."

Seamus snorted.

A smile twitched on Finn's lips.

"Wait, was it you, Finn? Dang, you're like the best kindergartener at coloring."

Finn's eyebrows arched high. He looked up to Seamus.

"We haven't got kindergarten here. He's in primary two."

"Oh, well, you're probably the best in that grade too."

Finn peeled away from Seamus and sat on the other end of the couch. Seamus disappeared into the kitchen. I expected Finn to scurry after him, but instead he pulled an X-Men coloring book out of his backpack. Behind it was Bucky. I smiled. Round eyes fixed on me, he reached for a pack of crayons across the couch. His long-sleeved t-shirt sleeve rolled up, revealing two pearly circular scars smaller than a dime on his wrist. The hair on the back of my neck stood up. I flipped to Batman drop-kicking Joker.

"Batman's pretty much my favorite superhero," I said. "Besides Bucky."

Finn buried his face in Professor X, but at least he didn't run.

For the next hour, we colored together. Seamus was in and out of the kitchen, half watching some car show. The smell of chocolate filled the tiny living room.

Finally, Seamus set a plate of brownies on the coffee table. "Get that into ya. From scratch, no boxes here." So getting Finn to check on the flour had been for real.

I raised an eyebrow. "You bake?"

"That's a fine way to say thanks." Seamus got that upper-lip-curled look. "Even put frigging peanut butter in there."

"Okay… ?" I guessed he thought all Americans liked peanut butter.

His ears went pink as he stared at me.

I snatched one and took a bite. It was warm and gooey with the perfect balance of PB and chocolate. Mouth full, I said, "It's actually better than Mom's brownies."

His smile broke. "Well, I wouldn't know, would I?" He grabbed three brownies and left. The front door slammed. Finn's brownie hovered an inch from his chocolate-smeared lips.

Whoa. I played back the conversation. She'd been their stepmother. I guessed there were still some unresolved issues there. The front door popped open, and Patrick walked in still wearing his gas station shirt and a pair of black skinny jeans.

Finn bolted into his arms.

"Hiya, wee Finny. I'm sorry I forgot about your trousers." Patrick carried him over to the couch and shoved an entire brownie in his mouth. "Peanut butter? That's a first."

"So Seamus bakes?"

Patrick got a half smile as he swallowed and grabbed another. "The old biddies at Clonard are always on about his banoffee pie."

I raised an eyebrow. "He doesn't really seem like a baker."

Patrick jammed the second one in his mouth as he flipped through the TV channels. "He loved helping your ma in the kitchen." He stopped on that *Arthur* cartoon I used to watch when I was Finn's age. Licking his fingers, Patrick added, "Then he helped Granny while we lived in Fivemiletown."

So my innocent comment had triggered a land mine. And I was sleeping in Seamus's bed, which meant he was probably sleeping on the floor or the couch.

"What was Mom like back in the day?"

Patrick grabbed a pack of cigarettes from the end table and pulled one out with his teeth. Chewing on the butt, he said, "Catherine and our ma were friends. After our ma died, Catherine helped care for wee Seamy and me. She married Da two years later, and it was like we had a ma again. She was the best. Kept Seamy, that wee skitter, in line. Nice supper every night. Made the tea with proper tea leaves. Hot water bottles for our beds on cold nights. Read to us before bed. She'd sing 'Carrickfergus.'"

And then when she left, she took me, but not them.

Mom was the strongest person I knew. I'd never seen her yell or swear or cry, even though I knew her money dripped down to the last penny every month. She wore this mental armor that could stop even cosmic radiation. Did she hurt inside at leaving her stepsons, but just refuse to show it?

"She did what she thought she had to do." Patrick rested his chin on Finn's head. "But you don't need to be worrying about that."

But I *did* need to worry about it.

Mom had worked as a classroom aide at Orchard Ridge Elementary since I'd started kindergarten there. She was always baking her trademark brownies for kids whose parents couldn't afford birthday treats, but she'd abandoned her two stepsons like it was nothing.

I was still mad at her for not telling me about Dad. I hadn't spoken to her since I got here, even though I kept seeing missed Skype calls from her. Last night there'd been a message on my phone:

`Mom: I love you to the moon and back, sweetheart.`

And the day I boarded the plane, I'd felt it when I glanced back at her from the escalator to security—her whole being had wobbled like one of those spinning plates about to fall and shatter.

A sliver of me had reflexively wanted to type "love you to Neptune and beyond," but the words had refused to come.

❧

The next day at breakfast, Dad sat across from me reading the *Belfast Telegraph* while Finn nibbled on his toast. Today Bucky sat on Finn's lap. While I ate peanut butter toast, I sent Nevaeh the cat shrub picture.

> NevaehAngel: OMGGGGG I want that in my YARD! And you got to go to a castle! How's it going with your soap opera family?

I glanced at Dad, but it was the headline that caught my attention, "Dissident Republicans Blamed for Attack on Police." There was a picture of a blue-and-yellow-checkered police car with a scorch mark on the side.

I leaned forward and skimmed the article.

*At 1:03 a.m. Wednesday morning, a grenade was launched at a police patrol car on the Falls Road in West Belfast. There were no injuries, but police report both officers and residents could have been seriously hurt. Dissident Republicans from the IRA splinter group* Óglaigh na hÉireann *claimed responsibility.*

"I thought all this was over," I said.

Dad glanced at the front page. "Oh, that's just a few dinosaurs stuck in the past. They've no support from the community."

"Did it happen near your house?"

Mid-sip, Dad coughed, then wiped his mouth with the back of his hand. "It was miles from here." He folded the newspaper and drained his tea. "Sun's out again today. I'd like to take you and Finn to the Botanic Gardens before my bus driving shift at Translink. Your mam used to take yous for wee danders round the rose gardens there."

Finn smiled, hugging Bucky tighter.

"Cool." I shoved the last bite of toast into my mouth.

Dad summoned another taxi. It was funny how there always seemed to be plenty just waiting there, hovering outside the house.

As we got through downtown, I spotted a cylindrical tower built out of wooden pallets at least fifteen feet tall in a parking lot behind a Days Hotel. Around it were British flags and white flags with red crosses and a red hand in the middle, and a huge pile of pallets and tires. A few kids sat by it banging on snare drums.

"What's the deal with that?"

"One of the Loyalist bonfires. For the Twelfth of July," Dad said.

My eyes widened. "Wait, they're setting that on fire? That'll melt the hotel."

The taxi driver smirked at me in the rearview mirror.

Dad's hands clenched in his lap. "It's how they celebrate their culture."

I raised an eyebrow.

Dad cleared his throat. "Their bonfires happen in their areas one night a year. Everybody else's lives go on."

Finn unzipped his backpack. His Lego Batman shirt covered his arms, but I was reminded of those scars I'd seen. He pulled out a coloring book and flipped to a page with Batman in front of a moon, bats framing him.

"Wow, Finn, you even stayed in the lines for all his little bat friends," I said.

A smile flashed on his lips. He brushed the curls back from his face.

We drove past Queen's University, which looked more like a Harry Potter castle than Belfast Castle, then through a quaint neighborhood with pastel duplexes and cute little front yards.

Off the cab, Finn held the hem of Dad's Translink fleece,

cradling Bucky with his free arm. I fell into step with Dad, hands rammed into my jeans pockets. We headed down a path flanked on one side by red, yellow, and purple flowers and a huge green space on the other.

"What's that one, Daddy?" A little blond girl pointed to a purple globular flower.

Her sweater-vested dad tucked an arm around her. "Allium."

Mom had taught me the names of all the constellations visible in the Madison night sky. What would Dad have taught me? Maybe how to start a campfire. Last summer, Mom and I borrowed a tent from Nevaeh's family to experiment with camping at Devil's Lake. We tried for hours to light the fire, but we ended up eating cold Pop-Tarts for dinner instead of hotdogs.

The soft, rapid clicking of a bike coasting past brought me back to the moment. A light breeze trailed in its wake.

Dad frowned as he watched the father and daughter too. "So Fiona, is the room all right? Is there anything else you're in need of?"

I shook my head.

Finn ran into the lawn, curls bouncing. He grabbed a stick and started swinging it around, Bucky still tucked under his arm.

"He's pretending to be Obi-Wan Kenobi." A grin creased wrinkles around Dad's eyes. "Patrick had Finn watching *Empire Strikes Back* the day he came home to us."

That was one of Mom's favorites as well.

Finn's curls flew as he spun and sliced his stick lightsaber into an invisible Darth Vader.

"Finn has marks," I said, "on his arm."

Dad squinted against the sun splitting apart the low blue-gray clouds. A long, slow sigh flared his nostrils as his green-and-gold-specked eyes turned and studied me. He cleared some rattling phlegm from his throat. “His ma put another boy on the birth certificate, so we dropped it. Three years later, Child Protection showed up at our door. They did a paternity test and, there it is, Finn is Patrick’s son.” His face tightened. “Aoife burnt him with cigarettes when he cried. Now he’s always waiting for the other shoe to drop.”

I gasped.

Finn twirled and jumped as he swung his lightsaber.

“He’s already starting to come round.” Dad squeezed my shoulder.

Part of me wanted his hand to stay there, but then pink-faced Finn crashed into him. Dad pulled him into a hug.

“So you like *Star Wars* too?” I asked as we kept walking.

Finn looked up at me and nodded.

“That’s so cool. I love *Star Wars*. And Obi-Wan is totally the best Jedi Master.”

For the first time, Finn grinned wide enough to reveal his missing two front teeth. I risked it; I mussed up his hair. He didn’t flinch.

Dad’s arm tightened around Finn. “Fiona, here’s your mam’s favorite part.”

Birds warbled as the sun dripped onto grass paths between concentric circles of roses— red-tipped yellow, pink, red, white, and peach. I wanted to bottle the smell. Ten-foot-tall hedges walled off redbrick Belfast like it was the *Secret Garden*. Finn raced ahead, arms spread wide like he could fly. I could picture Mom sitting on a bench among the flowers watching Seamus and Patrick chase each other while she bounced me on her knee.

A rose caught my eye—creamy white in the center, spiraling out to a deep pink. Dew glittered on the petals. I pulled out my phone and snapped a close-up.

Dad's eyes were on me as I stood. "You took a huge chance, coming here like you did."

Finn did a lap around the inner circle, giggling as he held Bucky high over his head like Superman. His laughter was music.

"Yeah, I Polar Plunged it."

Dad raised a gray-peppered eyebrow. "Polar Plunge?"

"You know, where you jump into a frozen lake in just your swimsuit."

Dad let out a throaty, rumbling laugh.

"The cross-country team did it last February to raise money for the Special Olympics."

"Did you get hypothermia?"

"I was only in there for like five seconds." And Mom had five towels and a blanket waiting.

"And how's it going, then? This Polar Plunge?"

I nudged a small pile of rose petals back into the flower bed with the toe of my red Converse. "Good, I think."

Dad's entire face split into a grin so massive it filled parts of me I never realized were empty. He hugged an arm around me. My heart tingled. Each beat spread warmth farther through my veins. Squeezing my eyes closed, I relaxed against him, breathed in the leathery smell of his aftershave. My dad.

"I'm not a man of many words, because once they're out there, you can never fully take them back." His smile dampened. "The past is what it is, but what matters is the chance we have now."

If magic was a thing, I might say one of those pennies in the koi pond had granted my wish.

On the taxi ride home, Finn fell asleep against me, Bucky clutched to his stomach. Warmed by his body heat, I hugged his tiny, fragile form as I drank in that sweet little boy smell—like maple syrup. His stomach rumbled. Dad said he was making us cheese toasties for lunch, which was good because I was starving too.

Then at a stoplight, I spotted it—a mural of a bunch of dudes surrounding a casket covered with an Irish flag, a gun on top. A few guys wearing fatigues, ski masks, and berets pointed rifles at the sky. And then there was Dad—*Dad*—standing at the foot of the coffin. There was no mistaking the likeness. Across the top, it said, "IRA Final Salute."

"Hey, why are you on that mural?"

Dad peered out the window. He sighed as his head fell. "It's remembering one of our fallen comrades."

"Our deputy first minister's standing right next to him," the cab driver said. Wait...the cab driver was the same one who drove us down. Had he sat and waited for us? For two hours?

"Why are you on there with some bigwig?"

The driver laughed as he watched us in the rearview mirror.

Dad drew his gaze up to the rearview mirror. The tendons in his jaw bulged as the air boiled around us. Somehow Finn kept sleeping. The driver's eyes bolted forward. His knuckles turned bone white as he clenched the steering wheel.

A cold sweat tickled my forehead. The respect everyone threw at Dad, the personal taxi drivers, the freaking mural—it wasn't just because of his community work.

"What did you *really* do for the IRA?" I asked.

The color drained from Dad's face as the lines on his forehead deepened. "It was ages ago."

That sucked the air from my lungs like stepping into sub-zero winter. "Let me guess, it's complicated."

The taxi stopped in front of Dad's house.

I darted out and through the front door. Messages from Nevaeh popped up, but I opened Safari and typed in "Peter Kelly the Falls IRA."

A Wikipedia article was at the top of the results.

In the sidebar was a grainy picture of a man in a flannel shirt with his hair parted to the side—Dad.

The hair on my arms stood up.

*Peter Kelly (born 1964) was an Irish Republican activist brought up in the Falls area of West Belfast. He is believed to have been the quartermaster of the Provisional IRA Belfast Brigade from 1984 until 1997. It is suspected that Kelly orchestrated numerous bombings and mortar attacks in London, Belfast, County Armagh, and County Londonderry that lead to substantial damage to property, hundreds of injuries to both security forces and civilians, and at least twenty-three deaths.*

Dad had killed people. Ice water pumped through my veins.

*Kelly and his Active Service Unit were arrested on 25 September 1997 when an informant revealed a plot to bomb Belfast's city centre. Kelly was released on 28 July 2000 on account of the Good Friday Agreement.*

He'd served less than three years in prison.

The flower wallpaper and nearly naked swimsuit models and gold crucifix spun around me at dizzying speed.

Mom had assured me, told me he hadn't been that high up. That he hadn't killed anyone. Was it naïve of me to believe that? He was on a freaking no-fly list. But I'd wanted to believe he was innocent, a good guy. I tried the word out in my head... terrorist. Is that what he'd been?

I could never look in Dad's green-and-gold-freckled eyes again.

I couldn't breathe in that tiny room.

I forced my lungs to draw in air. I had Mom's credit card; I was flying home. Today. I'd get a job, mow as many lawns as possible, and spend the rest of my summer reading all the books off the AP English syllabus.

I remembered how to get to the bus station. I grabbed my messenger bag and walked out the front door.

# chapter six

## *Danny*

I spent ten hours ripping up moldy carpet in this disgusting terrace over in Glencairn. Gusty didn't lift a frigging finger. For all that work, I got forty pounds. Dirty, stinking bastard.

One hundred fifty-five quid to go.

I got home to find Da supping a Tennent's and watching *Top Gear*. His eyes were clear and focused, so he must have just got started.

"Did you have fun with Gusty, then?" Da stroked his double chin, thick with a three-day beard. "Too good for Hardy's, now look at you. Doing everyone else's dirty work."

I headed for the stairs.

He stuck out his oil-stained hand. "Thirty-five quid for rent."

"But it's twenty-five a week."

"Ten pound late fee. That's the way the world works, Danny Boy. Which you'll need to learn right quick, seeing as you're on your own soon."

I dug the thin roll of cash from my pocket and handed him three tenners and a fiver. My whole body ached and my fingers were raw, and now all I had to show for it was five quid.

Da scratched his gut, fingernails grating over his vest. "And stop wasting your time. Go collect some proper job applications. Go be a wee firefighter."

I dug the Boots application from my rucksack and dropped it on the coffee table, then headed for the door without a shower or a feed. As I grabbed the knob, Da let out a sigh that could melt tires. "Gusty's wee boy has a place over in East Belfast. Looking for a roommate. Asking two hundred twenty quid a month."

I glanced back. Da looked me over, face expressionless. His eyes jumped to the TV, and he took a long pull from his tin.

"Thanks." I opened the door. Every inch of Eddie's place was probably crammed full of fake Louis Vuitton satchels. I'd rather sleep under Jon's bed with his fat ma's seven cats.

After I got out of the Shankill, I knew where I was headed—to my thinking spot by the City Hall. But as I passed the bus station, a girl with long, curly brown hair leaned against the wall, looking unwell. Her head drooped, then she hunched into a ball, face buried behind her hair. Had she fainted?

I jogged over. "Hey, are you all right?"

She pushed herself to standing. I noticed she wore a Fading Stars top.

"Stop staring at my chest, pervert!" She was an American?

Heat flashed across my face. "Please yourself, then."

But as I made to turn, she caved against a lamppost. I was about to become an adult health nurse in the army; I couldn't abandon a sick person even if they were being a wee bitch. "Hey, careful there."

"Go away."

"I'm not going to leave you here to faint in the street." *Mind your tone.* I tried to sound like emergency responders on the TV. "Just sit down at least. Em, please."

The American bird planted herself on the curb and rested her forehead on her knees.

"I'm Danny Stewart, by the way."

"Fiona."

"Are you feeling light-headed, dizzy?"

"Yeah. Obviously." Her voice dripped with disgust.

"Have you eaten today?"

"Breakfast."

It was gone five. "Probably your blood sugar. There's a Burger King right over there." I pointed toward the city centre. "Let's get some food in you."

She pulled her head up and shot me a withering look. "I'm not going anywhere with you."

This was harder than my mechanics and biology exams combined. "I'll call an ambulance, then. Let them deal with you."

"Oh, my God." Fiona stood up. The color drained from her face again as she teetered against me.

"Steady on." I caught her—and caught a whiff from my pits. Fiona's head rested against my chest for a second before she pulled away.

"You stink."

My face blazed. "I was working before I came to your rescue. And for the record, I'm not a pervert. I was looking at your Fading Stars top, not your boobs."

She eyeballed me. "You like Fading Stars? You don't look the type."

My fingers drummed on my thigh. "Why not?"

"You're wearing track pants."

"Fine thanks I get for trying to help." I turned to go.

A sigh followed me. "Dude, wait. I'm sorry. I'm having a super crappy day."

"News flash, princess—you're not the only one. I worked ten hours of hard labor and have only five quid to show for it."

Fiona frowned and then made eye contact with me. "So the question is, is the universe conspiring to combine our separate crap into a Big-Bang-magnitude pile of crap that will destroy us all?"

"I'd have dressed a bit nicer had I known I might trigger the end of the universe."

A small smile cracked her face. She was pretty. "Might as well eat quick before the bus ride to Dublin."

As I led her to the Burger King, I asked, "So, what's in Dublin?"

"An airport. I'm flying home."

"Tonight?"

She rammed her hands into the pockets of her torn jeans. "Soonest I can get a flight."

"All the way back to America—with no bags?"

"I travel light."

When we got to the Burger King, I held the door open for her. The smell of fry and grease made my stomach grumble; I hoped Fiona hadn't heard. I hadn't eaten since that Tayto Crisp sandwich at breakfast.

Fiona ordered a cheeseburger, medium fries, and a Coke. The Taigy-looking cashier with his too-close-together eyes sneered at me like he could tell I was a Protestant. I almost started at him, but then I realized Fiona was waiting for me to order. I'd only the five quid, so I shook my head.

"Look, I've got my mom's credit card," she said. "Seriously. Order like the whole menu."

"Em, I'll have the Whopper."

The Taig looked between us. "Sit in or take away?" he finally asked.

"For here," Fiona said.

The lad set our tray on the counter. I grabbed it and followed Fiona to a corner booth. I sat in the swivel chair across from her and tore into my Whopper. Fiona stared at her food like it was Mount Everest. The lighting washed the color from her skin. She slid one chip out of the box and nibbled at it until it was gone. I dug the fiver out of my pocket and held it toward her.

"Seriously, keep it. Mom can pay the three bucks. My parents literally owe me more than they can ever repay."

I pocketed my cash, then took another massive bite. "So are you running away, then?"

Fiona picked up another chip. It drooped between her fingers. "How come there's no ketchup?"

She'd dodged the question, but I decided to go with it for now. "Oh, right, because you're American."

"Ketchup is totally not just an American thing."

"I was just teasing."

Not even a chuckle. I'd never talked to a real American before. Did they not understand sarcasm?

"Wait a wee second." I shoved the last of my burger in my mouth and went to deal with that potato-munching bead rattler at the checkout again.

"Red sauce," I said, "for the girl."

He sneered at me. What did he care if we needed a bit of sauce? He dug under the counter and produced a handful of packets, which I brought back to her. "So does it taste the same? As in America?"

Fiona squirted some ketchup on the paper covering the tray. "Burger King? I guess so."

"It's bonkers, yeah? That you can be on the other side of the world, but Burger King tastes the same."

"The power of preservatives." She dipped a couple chips in the ketchup and ate them.

"So whereabouts are you from in America?"

"Wisconsin." Fiona sipped her Coke. The color started returning to her cheeks.

"I only know California, Texas, Florida, and New York. Wisconsin by any of those?"

Her face scrunched up. "It's in the Midwest. By the Great Lakes? North of Chicago? Cheese and beer?" She took another bite of her burger.

"Right, got it." So in the middle somewhere. "What brings you round these parts?" I tried my best John Wayne impression.

Fiona frowned at the tray.

"You don't need to tell me."

She dropped her half-eaten burger on the tray with most of her chips.

"Are you done?" I was still peckish. "It's a sin to leave potatoes uneaten in Ireland. You know, the famine and all."

Fiona let out a choked laugh, then slid her tray toward me. I ripped off the bits she'd eaten from her burger and then devoured what remained and the rest of her chips.

She brushed her fingers under her eyes. "I'm here with my dad."

I looked up at her, mouth crammed with chips. I swallowed. "So you're on holiday?"

"But Mom's back in Madison."

"And you're going back there tonight without your da?"

Her eyebrows twitched. She grabbed a plastic saltshaker and spun it on the tabletop. She nodded once.

That tosspot behind the counter was eyeballing me again. The food was gone. No excuse to stay. But I could listen to her American accent all day.

"Hey, em, you want to get out of here? I could show you the City Hall if you'd like. Just until your bus is here, like. Unless you think it might trigger the end of everything."

Fiona's freckled nose wrinkled. She was cute when she did that. "I guess I could stay a few more minutes."

I almost fell off my chair. "Right. Okay then." I grabbed the tray and binned the rubbish. She followed, hands crammed in her jacket pockets. I held the door from the outside so she wouldn't have to walk through my BO. We walked along the shop-lined street flocked with people dressed for work, carrying shopping bags, pushing babies in prams.

"That's Belfast City Hall." I pointed across the street to the Victorian building topped off with a mint green dome and little turrets on each of the four corners. The Union flag stood tall over the entrance, reminding the Taigs that we're all British. "I come here sometimes to clear my head. Want to see my favorite spot?"

"Sure." She cocked her head to the side as she studied it. "It reminds me of Capitol Square back home. Madison's the state capital."

The green man appeared. I kept my eyes glued to Fiona as we crossed, just in case she fainted in the middle of the street, then led her through the gate to my tree. From my spot, I could watch the news on the massive TV across the lawn and see all the tourists pose in front of Queen Victoria's statue.

I sat with my back against the fence. Fiona plopped down a foot from me. My legs were so much longer than hers. She set her satchel between us. At least she didn't think I'd nick it. Her long hair slipped over her shoulders and past her chest. I could tell that under her jacket her boobs weren't massive like Clare's, but they were perky. *Call them breasts, Danny. It's more respectful.*

I sat there like an utter eejit drumming the rudiment we used for "The Minstrel Boy." It was a bit Taigy, but it was the same beat used in "Hero's Heart." The barely audible newscast from the TV filled the gap between us.

I thought back to the question she'd dodged. "So are you mad at your ma as well?"

Fiona picked at some colorful rubber bands she'd round her wrist. "Maybe I'll crash at a friend's house."

To stop myself from drumming, I plucked a dandelion. "I want to run away sometimes too."

Fiona looked up at me. The sunlight beaming through the leaves filled her hazel eyes with drops of honey. It was like she brought the sun. I wanted to ask her why she was running away, but then she might ask me. So instead, I held out the dandelion.

Fiona's pink lips curved into a small smile. "Just what I've always wanted." She rolled the dandelion stem between her fingers.

Just then the Albert Clock started chiming. I checked my mobile. It was half five. Ah, bollocks—band practice. I'd never talked to a girl this long in my life and she'd be leaving to America in a few minutes. But if I missed another practice, I might be joining Ma in the afterlife.

"Em, I've to go."

Fiona's brows knitted. She nodded. I felt bad, leaving her here alone when she was clearly upset.

"Are you going to get on the bus, then?"

Fiona shrugged.

"Here . . . if you don't leave Belfast and you're ever not busy and you don't think I'm a pure header, I mean . . . what I'm trying to say is, maybe I could get your number."

Fiona frowned at her dandelion.

My stupidity punched me in the face.

"Right, then. Hope you catch your flight." I got up before I cocked it up even more.

"Do you have WhatsApp?"

I glanced back at her. "Aye."

Fiona gripped her satchel by the strap. "My handle is FionaRuns. I can message when I have Wi-Fi."

A grin split my face as I added her to my contacts. "Em, right. So . . . hope you message me back, then."

"'Kay."

I left her there under my tree. As I walked down Howard Street toward the Shankill, I saw some posh restaurant called Flame had a *now hiring* sign in their window. I nipped in and grabbed an application, even though the hostess sneered at my trackie bottoms. Well she could shove those disco balls and candelabras up her arse. Who wanted to pay fifteen pounds for a burger anyway?

With each step closer to the Shankill, Fiona faded. She was away to America any second, and I was off to my Main Board and then hopefully Sandhurst.

But for a moment, I let myself imagine I'd see her again.

# chapter seven
## *Fiona*

I bought a ticket for the 7:00 p.m. bus to Dublin Airport. I felt bad about leaving Finn without saying goodbye, but at least he could sleep in his own bed again. As I sat on a bench waiting, rain drummed on the awning overhead.

I hopped on the bus terminal's Wi-Fi and checked my email. As scores of people unloaded from a bus from someplace called Derry-Londonderry, the sound of skateboard wheels rattling on pavement drew my attention. Patrick coasted toward me, wearing his soaked work shirt and usual low-riding skinny jeans and green-and-black plastic belt. Water sprayed from his wheels.

"Thank Christ, Fiona. We've been looking everywhere." Patrick pressed back on the tail and grinded to a stop a yard away. "Da's fit to be tied, so he is. Missed work."

"Yeah, really don't care." Seeing as he should be in *jail*. "How'd you find me?"

"Catherine checked her credit card account and saw the charge for the bus ticket."

My heel bounced in the puddle under the bench. Water seeped through the canvas tops of my Converse.

Patrick snatched up his board and whipped out his phone. "Aye, Da? I've found her. She's all right. We're at the bus station."

"The feck you doing out here?" Seamus jogged past the line of busses toward us, cigarette clenched between his teeth. He ran a hand through his wet hair, making a Mohawk that collapsed into a limp, curly mess.

I scoured some mummified gum with my toe. "Maybe you should talk to Dad about blowing people up."

Patrick squinted at me. "Is that why you ran away?"

"I thought it was just, you know, small-time stuff. Not, you know, *bombs* and things."

Patrick sighed and plopped down next to me on the bench.

"Well, at least now I know." I glanced through the window behind us. According to the digital timetable, my bus was leaving in fifteen minutes.

"I've better things to do." Seamus stiffly sauntered toward the street.

"Nice knowing you," I called at his back. Coldness radiated through my jacket, spreading goose bumps down my arms.

Patrick dug a crushed pack of cigarettes from his back pocket, pulled one out with his teeth, and lit it. "He was a volunteer, and it was fifteen years back."

"Bullshit. He helped kill like twenty people."

Patrick's eyes narrowed as he took a long drag. Blue smoke leaked from his nostrils. "It's the truth. Da was a part of a just fight to eradicate eight hundred years of cultural, social, political, and economic oppression."

"Not buying it."

Patrick pinched the bridge of his nose. A clump of ashes dropped from his cigarette. "You haven't got your suitcase, at any rate."

Yeah, my unexpected wannabe-runaway partner-in-crime Danny had already pointed out my rookie mistake. Of course, before today I'd never even snuck out of the house or broke curfew, so... "I have my passport."

A bus pulled into the spot in front of us, breaks hissing. Its scrolling marquee changed from "X1 to Belfast" to "X1 to Dublin Airport." People got off and started grabbing luggage from the bottom compartment.

As if on cue, Dad limped-ran through the gate, hair plastered to his forehead. "Thank Christ you're all right."

"Go away." My nails pierced the skin of my palms. I wanted to scream five million things all at once, but my brain couldn't zoom in on any one thing to say. At least we were in public.

People hiding under umbrellas started lining up by the bus. Clenching my ticket, I got in line too, fighting off shivers as the rain pounded on my hood. Dad peeled off his fleece and draped it around my shoulders. His body warmth leaked through my wet coat, but my skin crawled at the thought of a killer hugging me just hours ago. I shrugged it off. The bus door popped open.

Dad grabbed his fleece from the puddle. Raindrops left splotches on his blue dress shirt. "Please wait until tomorrow at least."

The line started moving.

"Not staying with a mass murderer."

Dad's head sank.

A sketchy-looking guy with short bangs plastered to his forehead gawked at us through the bus window.

Patrick trotted up to me, wallet chain jingling. "Wee Finny'd be gutted if you left without saying goodbye."

The only thing standing between me and the bus back to my real life was a little girl in a pink polka-dot raincoat.

"He'll probably be relieved," I said.

Patrick flicked his cigarette butt between the busses. "He talks about you nonstop."

The girl hopped on. The bus driver raised an eyebrow at me.

I stepped out of line. "What's he say?"

"That you're the best at coloring and have the same hair as him. That you're very nice and you love Obi-Wan too. He asks why you talk different, what kindergarten is, what your house is like in America. Things like that."

All I could think about were the cigarette burns.

"Fine," I said finally. "But only to say goodbye to Finn."

Dad's frown etched canyons between his eyebrows. I followed them to the perpetually waiting taxi—probable IRA bomber perk—and climbed into the back with Patrick, ticket still in my fist.

I turned my entire body toward the window so I couldn't even see Dad in my peripheral vision. Since yesterday, someone had spray-painted in black "heroin dealers will be shot dead. ONH" on the side of Falls Pharmacy. The dissident "dinosaurs" apparently shot police and drug dealers.

I pointed. "You in on that too?"

Patrick tensed next to me. The taxi driver's eyes darted from Dad to Patrick.

Dad rubbed his forehead. "I've supported the peace process since I got out. I swear on me boys' lives."

"Unfortunately, some of the youth, that's the only way they'll listen," Patrick said.

I picked at threads hanging from the rip in my jeans. Patrick shook his head at the window.

The taxi pulled to a stop in front of Dad's place behind two other black taxis doing those stupid tours. I got out.

Dad jumped out. "Fiona, please, I—"

As I yanked the front door open, a man in a Chicago Bears jacket gawked at me like I was a museum exhibit. "The Bears still suck." I slammed the door.

The front door opened again.

"Where's Finn?" I asked.

"At Mrs. McMahon's while we looked for you," Patrick said. "I'm away to get him now. Can you not just hear Da out?"

I said nothing. Patrick let out a long, heavy sigh. The rain briefly roared as the front door opened and closed.

Dad set a tray on the coffee table. On it were two mugs filled with steaming brown liquid.

"By the way, tea's nasty," I shot.

"I thought you liked it." Dad held out a rolled-up hand towel, his own hair dripping.

I snatched it. "I pretended."

Dad sank into the arm chair. He stared at the cup in his weathered hands.

"My family—your mother's family too—we fought for Irish freedom for generations. During the Troubles . . . political violence helped get us concessions, like the border poll, civil rights, more resources for our communities, and power sharing in a government that was free of direct rule from London." Dad's eyes tightened, deepening his crow's feet. "Catholics in the North were treated as second-class citizens for decades. We tried to protest peacefully but were met with violence. When the IRA went from being a necessary evil to an unnecessary evil . . . it's complicated." Dad's eyes were lost in his tea.

I felt each heartbeat in my temples. "You murdered like twenty-five people!"

Dad set his tea down and buried his head in his hands, gray-peppered curls poking between his fingers. Fingers I now pictured wrapped in wires, building bombs.

"Your mother... her brother Michael, he got killed by the UVF. Tit-for-tat retaliation. That's when she made the call."

The call? Pressure strained against my skin, threatened to rip me apart from the inside.

"She informed on us. On me. She couldn't watch it continue. I understand now why she did it. After she called the police... well, the IRA killed informants."

Words shot around my brain like quarks. "Were you going to kill Mom?"

"No!" The force of Dad's voice sent vibrations through the couch. "I never would have hurt Catherine or you, but I couldn't stop *them*."

Wow. *This* was why Mom left. *This* is why she fled all the way to the States.

The front door popped open. Finn hopped in, clutching Bucky to his chest. Eyes wide, he froze like he was a Vulcan telepath who sensed that shit just got real.

Patrick nudged him in. "It's okay, Finny."

Finn didn't move.

Dad pushed himself up with a grunt and headed for the door, leaning heavily on his left leg. Gripping the doorknob, he glanced back at me. Sunlight leaked through the cracked door. His nose cast a shadow across the sunken purple scar on his cheek. He left.

# chapter eight

*Danny*

I cut through the bar of the Ulster Rangers Supporters Club and ran upstairs, my drum kit bouncing against my thighs. The roar of drums meant I was late again. The walls were covered with the Union flag, Scottish flag, English flag, and the Ulster Banner. Our heritage. Wee lads too young to play cymbals crowded the sofas watching us. Fluters sat on one side of the packed room; drummers stood on the other. The stench of sweat already thickened the air. Da laughed with Billy and Gusty, eyes on me. At least Marty—the West Belfast UVF commander and lead tip—wasn't there yet, so technically I wasn't late.

Jon nodded to me as I took my spot by him. He started playing the cadence for the "Famine Song." I joined in, drumsticks vibrating against my palms with each strike.

Marty finally came. He wore his *Shankill Options* jacket, which meant he'd been doing cross community with people from the Falls. He played the kick beat for "The Sash My Father Wore." Billy stood next to him, veins bulging out of his cross-tattooed neck as he followed with another crushed five roll.

Gripping my drumsticks tight, I drew them high above my chest before striking heavy beats for the crushed five roll, then played another, slurred with the first. My eardrums rattled at our thunderous volume; it reverberated in my chest. The flutes launched into their bit, shrill and piercing. "The Sash" always got my blood pumping.

The wee lads watching belted out the words, "It is old but it is beautiful, and its colors they are fine..."

Strokes and bounces. Pulsating drumsticks numbing my hands. Sweat dripping down my forehead. I grinned. Last Twelfth, when we marched up the Crumlin Road playing it, the whole crowd of supporters—hundreds, maybe thousands—sang along. All of us celebrating. It had made the hair on the back of my neck stand on end.

Wee Jamie started dancing about as he "played" his flute; he still hadn't learnt all the fingerings. Red-faced and sweating through his mechanic uniform, Da pounded away on his Lambeg drum hard enough to make his hands bleed, like at the parades—blood and thunder. His drumhead said "Shankill Young Conquerors" in fancy blue-and-silver letters.

"...and it's on the Twelfth I proudly wear the sash my father wore."

I'd miss the band, but the army had one I could join. And someday, I'd come back. Show them all I wasn't abandoning my culture.

When practice ended, I still hadn't got a response from Fiona. It was probably for the best. I acted like a wee fruit around her, spewing my *feelings*, and she was away to America anyway. The message I'd sent her was stupid. It just said:

```
What's your theme song for the day? Like if your
life had a soundtrack.
```

Still, I'd hoped she'd write back.

As I stepped out into the cool evening, I found Clare leaning against the gate. "Hiya, Danny." She bit her sparkly pink lip.

"What about ye?"

Clare pressed her boobs against my arm, smoldering cigarette dangling between her fingers.

Jon took my drum and sticks off me and handed me a bag with two three liters of Frosty Jack's. "Here, mate."

"Aw, you remembered my favorite." Clare batted her eyelashes at Jon, but her arm tightened around mine.

"Thanks, mucker," I said.

As Jon headed off carrying both drums, Anto sauntered out of the Supporters Club with a sneer on his pimply face. His cheek was still green from when I'd punched him.

"What're you at the day, Professor? Hear you're looking to make some cash." Anto dangled a bag of benzos in my face. "Here, carry these for me. I'll give you a fiver."

"Carry your own ten deals, you wee scrote." I shoved his hand away.

Clare squeezed my arm. "Let's go to the park, yeah?"

Anto's face soured as I shouldered past him. I gave Clare a bottle of cider as we walked to Woodvale Park. Thin ribbons of clouds glowed golden pink as the sun sank below Black Mountain, casting rays up across the sky to fight back the rain. Clare took a long drink and then handed me the warm bottle. I felt my teeth decaying as I sipped.

I planned on taking her to the shelter, but Clare led me toward the toilets, pushed me against the wall, and pressed her hot body against mine. She tasted a bit like an ashtray. Fiona's heart-shaped lips popped into my brain. She'd smelled nice; probably tasted nice too.

I stuffed the thought away and kissed Clare back.

Her fingers slipped deep into my pocket. Gripping her sides, I shivered and pressed harder against her. Her long nail dug through the lining of my pocket into me. I flinched and tried to pull away, but her lips stayed suctioned to mine. This wasn't exactly how I'd imagined my first time.

My mobile vibrated against my thigh. Fiona?

I freed a hand from her waist and tried to sneak a peek.

FionaRuns: Dying for Tomorrow by Mad Rovers.

Clare released my tongue and pulled back, eyes on the screen. "Is that a girl?"

"Em, sorry?"

"You arse!" Clare slapped my chest hard enough to leave a stinging handprint.

"Shut up, you wee slag!" I shouted at her back as she ran.

As if on cue, a rain cloud directly overhead pissed down on me. I snatched the other bottle of Frosty Jack's and cut across the grass for the gazebo. Walking was a bit awkward. I adjusted my trackie bottoms, then tried to scrub Clare's slimy lip stuff off my face. Shite, if Ma was watching up in heaven, she probably wouldn't have liked that I treated a girl like that.

My mobile vibrated again.

FionaRuns: What's yours?

DannyBoy: Hero's Heart

By the time I got to the shelter, raindrops coated my bare arms. The gate was padlocked, so I hopped the fence. Someone had covered a post with KAT, *kill all Taigs*, and "I love Leah" again, and the park keeper hadn't got round to taking paint thinner to it. Rain dripped from a city council sign that promised a maximum penalty of five hundred pounds for drinking in the park.

I tapped on Fiona's profile picture to make it bigger. It was her and a black girl hugging, holding ice cream cones. Fiona wore this big smile she hadn't shown me when we met. She wasn't pretty—she was beautiful.

I took a long drink. The sweetness was already making my stomach rot, but the alcohol was finally reaching my brain. I played her song off YouTube. It was loud and angry, not what I expected. And the bagpipes mixed in with guitars made it a bit Taigy. Maybe that sort of thing was popular over in America.

A pair of hands shoved me forward.

"The feck's wrong with you, mucker?" Jon peered at me through the fence rails. "Clare's texting everyone that you kiss like a wee fruit."

I forced down more cider. My head was already getting a bit numb. "Sure I'd have just got some disease that would've made my dick fall off."

Jon sniggered as he climbed into the shelter. I stared at the Union Jack flags drooping in front of the terrace across the street, trying to think of something more to say to Fiona. Jon and Anto laughed about joyriding round North Belfast. I used to be fastest at hot-wiring cars, since Billy taught me, but I never got to have any fun anymore because I couldn't risk getting lifted.

"Feck all, Danny, were you even listening?" Anto took a puff from his spliff and passed it to Jon. Christ, I hope he didn't slag me off for not taking a hit yet again. They'd probably make us take a drug test at the Main Board.

"What? To you? You frigging gobshites." I snorted and checked my mobile again.

```
FionaRuns: That's my favorite song by them too.
```

Score another one for Danny. Maybe I wasn't rubbish with girls from across the pond.

Anto snatched my mobile off me. "Fiona runs,'" he said in this high, whiny voice. "That's who you were texting instead of bucking Clare?"

I grabbed it back.

Jon stared at me, gobsmacked. "Did you actually manage to find yourself a wee girl?"

"And she's American." I drank more cider. Now my head was swimming.

Anto took a long pull from his Buckie and wiped his oily gob with his hoodie sleeve. "Fiona. That's a leprechaun name, so it is." A Catholic name, he meant. He unleashed that extra annoying laugh he got when he was stoned—short and choppy like a machine gun.

"Quit talking shite, you ballbags you." I shoved him against the post.

A torch blinded me.

"How many times have I told yous?"

I shielded my eyes. Robinson, the community involvement officer, cut through the bushes at rapid speed.

Jon hopped the fence and took off running.

I ran north for the Ballygomartin gate.

"Feck the PSN-IRA!" Anto yanked down his trackie bottoms and flashed his pasty arse, then fell over the fence as he tried to climb it.

"You wee yobs!" Robinson chased after us.

Rain pounded on my head, ran down my face. Good thing I'd been running twenty miles a week for the fitness standards.

I glanced back. Anto chucked his bottle of Buckie at the footpath, laughing like an eejit. Red-faced, Robinson breathed down Anto's neck. I closed in on the gate.

"Run like my granny, Danny Boy!" Anto puffed behind me.

Robinson tackled Anto to the ground. "Shut your teeth, you wee hooding bastard."

And Anto had those benzos on him; he'd get another criminal conviction.

I nipped through the gate. After getting to Lanark Way, I slowed to a walk. My hands were still shaking as the rain cooled my head.

Alcohol giving me courage, I messaged Fiona.

```
DannyBoy: So you're not on a plane to America yet.
FionaRuns: Not yet.
DannyBoy: Will your family not stop you going?
FionaRuns: It's their freaking fault.
```

"Oi!" Jon jogged out from under the awning of Top Petrol. "What happened to Anto?"

"Got what's coming to him."

Jon smirked. "Right. Frigging melter, that one."

The rain eased to a sprinkle as we walked past the bonfire. Loads of the lads were working on it. Dubstep rattled out of the guard hut, lit up for the night. The clouds were thinning as moonlight fought to break through over Black Mountain.

"Where did you find yourself an American girl?"

"Outside the bus station."

Jon's eyes widened. "You're unbelievable, like. Can you find me one?"

I messaged Fiona back.

DannyBoy: If you don't go back tomorrow, can I see you again? If you aren't busy being a tourist.

Even though I'd drank about a liter of cider, I knew I'd sounded like an utter eejit.

DannyBoy: Or if you don't want to that's cool

DannyBoy: Is that something Americans say?

FionaRuns: Cool? I guess. And we'll see if I stay.

The Lanark Way gate to the Falls was closed since it was gone ten. Floodlights lit the mural of peeling skies and fading hills.

Clare could tell everyone in the Shankill I was a fruit if it meant I got to see Fiona again.

# chapter nine
## *Fiona*

A low knock sounded on the bedroom door.

"Fiona..." Dad's strained voice leaked in. His feet cast shadows under the door.

"Go. Away."

"You have to eat at any rate. I've just finished making some sausages."

"Not. Hungry."

He left. An argument seeped through the floorboards. I popped in my earbuds and blasted Mad Rovers.

Yet another Skype call from Mom vibrated my phone. I hit decline.

Mom knew. She knew what this man—*my father*—had done. How high up the chain he'd been. What pain and suffering he'd caused. I'd been so furious at her for lying to me, so insistent about coming here to make up for the lost time and all she'd denied me. If she'd really wanted to keep me from coming *here*, she should have told me the whole truth.

I guessed she was ashamed too. After all, hadn't Dad said her family was the same as his? That they believed the same things? For all I knew, my uncle Michael had been in the IRA as well. And Mom, for a while at least, had put up with—even supported—Dad's involvement.

She hadn't just lied to protect me from the truth about Dad; she'd lied to protect me from the truth about herself.

My phone vibrated. The screen lit up.

Mom: Sweetheart, can we talk??? Please let me try to explain.

My clammy hands trembled, but I managed to type:

I don't even know who you are anymore!!!!!

Mom's doppelgänger, that's who was stalking me.

A rattling knock cut through the ripping guitar and bagpipes. I paused the music. Patrick stood in the doorway clutching a shoebox.

I hugged my legs to my chest. "I heard you guys arguing. I know this is a conspiracy."

A smile twitched on his lips. "It is a bit of one."

Patrick settled on Seamus's bed a foot from me. His green-and-white Celtic FC jersey reeked of cigarettes. He grabbed *The Grapes of Wrath* off the bedside table. It had been my grand plan to start reading for AP English, but my brain hadn't been able to string letters into words.

"This book good? I've not read it."

I cocked an eyebrow. "You want to have a book club? Sip tea and have a philosophical conversation about theme?"

"You don't like tea." He handed me the shoebox. "Da wanted me to give you these."

I took off the top. In it were a few photos. I grabbed one. Patrick, about Finn's age, sat in Dad's lap holding a baby swaddled in pink. Finn looked just like him. Dad wore a face-busting grin.

"That's the day you were born," Patrick said.

The day he'd held me like a butterfly in his arms. The room blurred, but the picture stayed in focus. That was *me*. I'd never seen a newborn picture of myself.

I grabbed another, the whole family on a beach with black-and-white stones. Mom wore some spectacular stone-washed jeans. She grinned widely, head tilted to the side like in every picture. Dad had his arm around her waist, a smile almost as big as when he met me at the airport. He didn't have the scar yet. Patrick, probably eight, held toddler me in his arms again. Tiny Seamus pressed against Mom's side, his red hair blazing in the sun. I never imagined that linebacker could have been so little and cute.

Indisputable evidence of our life as a whole family, probably taken not long before we were ripped apart.

"You were a geg that day, after you learnt that if you ran toward the ocean we'd all chase you."

I grabbed the next photo of Mom and Dad. Dark clouds hovered on the horizon, but a rainbow spread behind them to a distant promontory. Mom's arms were wrapped around his neck, and he'd leaned down to meet her. Her eyes were closed, smiling as their lips touched. They both looked so happy.

I flipped it over. "Portrush, April 1993," with a heart around it—smack in the middle of Dad's reign as IRA quartermaster. I'd been born like a year and a half later.

"That's their honeymoon," Patrick said.

I rolled rubber bracelets up and down my wrist. "What do you think about all this?"

His nostrils flared as a sigh leaked out. "People can do bad things for a good reason, Fiona. The Brits forced Dad and the rest to take up arms. I think he's a hero. I think he should hold his head high."

"What, are you like in the IRA too?"

Patrick shook his head. "I'm a revolutionary socialist."

Sunlight burst through the window, glinting off the gold crucifix that watched over us. "So that's why you have that Che Guevara shirt."

Patrick balanced his forearms on his thighs. Loose curls concealed his face. "I want a society whose job is to meet the needs of its people, not the need for profit. I want the liberation of the working class from economic, political, religious, and social subjugation. That's why I don't have a problem with Protestants, because they're being oppressed, same as us."

Patrick glared in the direction of the peace wall. "It's the Loyalists, who *happen* to be Protestant, and their pro-imperialist beliefs that are the problem."

"Like the rocks they throw over the wall?"

"Among other things. It's quite sad, really, because Great Britain would be done with us in a heartbeat if they could." Patrick leaned back on his elbows. "But you asked my opinion about Da."

"What if one of his bombs had killed Finn?" I shot.

"What if Da's choices helped end it?"

Goose bumps prickled up my arms under my flannel shirt.

"The past is what it is, and it doesn't change that we're family. Now we've a chance for a different future. I think you should hear Da out."

"Yeah, except he, like, doesn't talk. Probably knows none of his precious words could ever make anything right again."

Patrick chuckled. "Sure, you're getting to know him."

"Is he really done?"

"That I can assure you." Patrick checked his phone and then got up. "I'm away out, but keep the pictures."

A cool burst of damp air flowed through the cracked window. I climbed on Finn's bed to close it. For the first time since I'd arrived in Belfast, the night sky was clear and I could see Scorpius. Reddish Antares in its tail flickered—stellar scintillation due to the Earth's atmosphere. It was logical that the sky would look the same here—I was still in the Northern Hemisphere—but it felt like the Belfast night sky should be a mirror image of Madison's.

I pulled myself into a ball on Finn's bed, pushed my forehead to my knees. Now all I could see was the picture of us all together on the beach.

Danny and I had messaged until after midnight. His favorite animal: elephants because they mourned for their dead. Favorite food: fish-and-chips. Favorite show: *Band of Brothers* because it was about brave men standing up to evil and there was a heroic medic. At least Mom had finally gotten the hint and left me alone for a while.

Seamus and Patrick had come home at three in the morning belting out some song about the fields of Athenry. Apparently Celtic or whatever won. I'd prayed drunk Seamus didn't forget I was sleeping in his bed. When I drifted out of the haze of near-sleep, I could hear plates and dishes clattering and low voices talking. Finn's bed was undisturbed again.

DannyBoy: Good morning, miss America. What's your favourite sport to play? I like football. Or soccer as u Americans call it.
DannyBoy: Shite sorry just realised its early hope I didn't wake you
DannyBoy: And sorry for the curse word

All sent within thirty seconds of one another. He was adorably awkward.

FionaRuns: Lol I run cross-country and track. I figured you'd be a basketball player. You're sooooooo tall.
DannyBoy: Ha you're a right geg. How fast can you run?
FionaRuns: Best time 17:32 on a 5K
DannyBoy: I can do that in 20 minutes. Not as good as you.

The door inched open. Finn peeked in.

"Finn, it's okay, you can come in."

Looking dapper in a collared shirt and khakis, Finn tiptoed in carrying a tray with two pieces of peanut butter toast and a "Home, Sweet Home" mug filled with hot chocolate. Seriously?

I took the tray. "Thanks, Finn. Did you make it?"

Pink bloomed on his freckled cheeks. He shook his head.

I just wanted to hear him laugh again before I left. "Hey, wanna hang?"

Finn climbed onto my bed. Even though my stomach was too knotted to hold food, I ate some to make Finn feel like he'd accomplished his mission. He slid closer.

"You tried peanut butter toast before?"

Finn shook his head.

"Want a piece?" I held the plate toward him.

Finn took a small nibble and smiled. He took a bigger bite and chewed big, like it was stuck to the roof of his mouth.

"Like it?"

He nodded, then took a few more bites.

"Want to color?"

Finn shoved the rest of the toast in his mouth and grabbed his Spider-Man backpack. He pulled out two coloring books.

"What should I color?"

Finn flipped through an Avengers coloring book to Captain America, then poked my upper arm.

I chuckled. "Yeah, I guess I mostly am."

Finn handed me a box of crayons. I got to work on Captain America running with his shield up. Finn, his little tongue sticking out, leaned against me and colored Superman. How had I not known this adorable, tiny human existed two weeks ago?

My phone vibrated.

`DannyBoy: Are you away to America then?`

Finn held up his book. He'd colored Superman pink. He exploded into giggles as he drew a heart at the bottom and wrote his name in it. My heart almost literally melted. I wrote "+ *Aunt Fiona*" under it. He beamed up at me.

"Finn," Patrick called up the stairs, "it's almost time for Mass." His voice had a frog-like quality to it.

I hoped they didn't try and drag me along. Mom stopped making me go after confirmation, so I could make an informed decision when I was older. I hadn't even been to confession since.

Hugging Bucky to his chest, Finn grabbed my hand; his was so little and soft in mine.

If I left today, what would it do to Finn? And how could I leave without hearing his voice?

I let him pull me downstairs. The smell of laundry detergent previewed the explosion of wet clothes draped over the radiator and drying racks crammed between the TV and the coffee table. Boxers and tighty-whities just hanging out. I averted my eyes to the ceiling and headed for the kitchen. Another rack had been crammed between the stove and the open door to the backyard.

Dad froze mid-sip of tea. A smile creased the lines around his eyes. "Hiya, Fiona."

Right then, in his Translink fleece, he looked like just a dad, not a murderer. But now I knew the truth. I took my seat by Patrick. A cloud of alcohol and cigarettes surrounded him. Finn crawled into his lap.

Dad's smile evaporated as his eyes fell. Patrick scooped up Finn. "Let's go, Finny. We'll grab a sausage roll on our way to Mass."

"See you later, Finn," I said.

Grinning, Finn made Bucky wave goodbye to me.

But now it was just me and my father trapped in that tiny kitchen with men's underwear. Ugh. I got up, walked outside, and sat on the stoop to their tiny, pebble-filled backyard. The peace wall towered forty feet over me, the chain link on top scratching the blue-gray clouds. Dad stepped past me; pebbles crunched under his shoes. The awning shielded him from rain dripping through the zombie apocalypse sunroom. Dad pulled a pack of cigarettes from his front pocket. His hand shook as he lit one.

Dad let out a slow, tired sigh. Smoke curled from his nostrils as he stared past the mesh at the billboard of black-and-white faces over the memorial garden. Most of the pictures were of men, but some of the boys looked like they were high schoolers. One was a little kid about Finn's age. In the middle of the billboard was the red-and-black phoenix.

"Those are the faces of some of the volunteers and civilians murdered by Loyalists and Crown forces during the Troubles." Dad took another puff from his cigarette, then let out a guttural throat clearing. "I want to talk to you about why I signed on."

"So you're going to enlighten me with some of your priceless words?" I folded my arms across my chest.

The ghost of a smile twitched on his lips. Unexpected. "You know the sign on the side of our house that says 'Bombay Street, Never Again'?"

The one with burning houses and the boy hugging his mom. I shrugged.

"That's our street, August 1969. I was just five years old. A Loyalist mob from the Shankill invaded our area and burnt the whole street out of our homes. Your mother's too. She was just a baby then, she wouldn't remember."

"Why?" I caught my leg bouncing and forced it to be still.

Dad took another puff. A clump of ashes fell to the wet pebbles. "Loyalists were afraid we were planning to overthrow the government that day, which we weren't. The police, almost all Loyalist, took up position between the Falls and the Shankill, but they didn't stop them coming."

"They stood by as a lynch mob burned kids out of their homes?" I asked.

A burst of raindrops rattled the mesh around us. A few fist-sized rocks littered the top. Maybe they really did have catapults in the Shankill.

"The IRA did fire some shots at the police. And perhaps they couldn't stop them. That night was chaos. But we were just trying to defend ourselves." Dad rolled the slowly shrinking cigarette between his fingers. "My family took refuge at St. Paul's. All we had were the clothes we stood up in. Fifteen hundred people were left homeless. We put up barricades to stop Loyalists and the police from invading. The army eventually came, but the Loyalists kept burning our homes and shooting. The army built the peace wall. It was meant to be temporary, but they've kept building it higher. More and more peace walls went up round Belfast between Protestant and Catholic areas. They're all still there too."

He sucked his cigarette to the filter, then flicked the butt toward the wall. "The Provisional IRA arose from the ashes of Bombay Street—that's what the phoenix is about. We learnt we had to protect ourselves, and we'd never let that happen again."

The rocks on the cage were a literally concrete reminder that the descendants of those people lived twenty feet away. I snapped a green bracelet against my wrist over and over again.

"Before I was even a teenager, I remember being stopped by the British army, having my name taken. One of my mates was killed by their plastic bullets. Every day in the news, more bombs, more indiscriminate killing. My da, a teacher who wasn't in the IRA, was interned and beaten. I signed on when I was sixteen, right when Bobby Sands died on hunger strike. Our plan was defense, then retaliation to prevent more Loyalist attacks, then an offensive war to force Britain to come to the negotiating table and agree to withdraw its forces from Ireland.

"I didn't see myself as a petty criminal running guns and laundering fuel. I saw myself as a soldier in a war for independence. A freedom fighter, not a terrorist. You know, like your American Revolution."

I bit my lip hard as my heel bounced.

"But by the time I married Catherine, the armed struggle had been going on for so long without getting us what we wanted. We hoped the bomb planned for the city centre would be the end of it. It was to damage property and disrupt life, but minimize casualties. I'd..." Dad seemed to age ten years; the bags under his eyes darkened, his crow's feet deepened. "I'd learnt my lesson from the Shankill bomb. This time people would have been evacuated."

"The Shankill bomb?" I ripped at the frayed edges of the tear in my skinny jeans.

His gaze wandered to the wall. "Our intelligence said UVF leadership would be meeting above a butcher's shop on the Shankill Road. I made the time bomb with a short fuse. Two of our volunteers were to enter the shop and evacuate the customers. But the bomb"—Dad pressed his fingers to his forehead—"detonated prematurely. Killed eight innocent people, injured fifty-three. And, turns out, the UVF had changed their meeting. So it was all for nothing, and it was my fault."

A butcher shop? On a main road? Couldn't they have at least stuck to military bases? I felt sick just sitting within arm's reach of Dad.

"It wasn't supposed to go that way. There was supposed to be a warning given so no one died. We always tried to be careful." Sweat glistened on Dad's brow, even though it was only like sixty out. "When I was arrested, I knew Catherine had done it. The Army Council had me tortured, but I told them nothing."

The scar... maybe the limp too. I gasped.

"It took me a long time, but I know now your mam did the right thing. The city centre bomb likely would have derailed the peace process. I hated every bomb I made... what I had to do." Dad massaged his forehead.

Yet you still kept hanging with the dark side.

"But without the armed struggle, we'd still be second-class citizens fearing for our safety," Dad said.

"So I should just look the other way?" I yanked more strings from the rip in my jeans.

"I know you'd like black-and-white answers, but this isn't a law of physics. This isn't evil versus good. I've spent the past ten years trying to build bridges between the communities." Dad's breath caught. His eyes squeezed closed. "My hope is that a person's past doesn't have to define their future."

Fat raindrops pooled and dripped from the mesh protecting us from the Shankill rocks.

The pebbles crunched under Dad's feet as he went inside, but I didn't have the strength to lift my head.

Maybe I could tolerate staying under the same roof as Dad the "freedom fighter" for a few more days. I'd get to spend more time with Finn and Patrick. If I couldn't handle breathing the same air as the terrorist, I'd hide in Seamus's room. And there was Danny...

FionaRuns: I'm not leaving today.

DannyBoy: I'm free in the afternoon. If you are. Unless you're busy being a tourist.

Crap. I'd kind of lied by omission yesterday, but I technically was a tourist even though I'd been born here. I should probably tell him the truth, but that might open the whole "Dad's a terrorist murderer" Pandora's box, which I really didn't feel like doing with a stranger. Or anyone.

My phone vibrated in my clenched fingers.

DannyBoy: Or you don't want to.

```
FionaRuns: No, we can meet.
DannyBoy: 15:00? City Hall? Same tree?
```

Right, people sometimes used military time over here. That was three o'clock.

"If I stay, you have to let me go for runs," I called to the kitchen. "I've been seriously sucking at training for cross-country."

Dad filled the doorway to the living room, gripping the doorjamb. "Just to city centre and back."

"Fine."

Dad's eyes lingered on me as silence undulated between us. This was all too much, pressing against my skull.

The flash of pain in Danny's blue-gray eyes when he'd said he wanted to run away suggested he probably had some bad stuff going on too.

# chapter ten
## *Danny*

Things kicked off during the mini-Twelfth parade.

Gusty and Da as well as some of the Orange Order wearing orange-and-purple sashes, pushed against the peelers' riot shields. I felt the tension rising, the buzz, the anger, the craic. Heat and bodies and drum kits pressed against me. Flutes glinted in the sun. The stench of tangy sweat charged with adrenaline filled my nostrils.

Mr. Donnelly had told us not to play anything sectarian in the Short Strand, but Anto and wee Jamie played a few bars of "Billy Boys" while we marched past St. Matthew's Cathedral. Then some papist scumbags had thrown rocks over the police lining the street between them and us. One hit wee Willy—just ten—in the head.

It was the Queen's highway, and we'd been marching that route—approved by the Parades Commission—forever to celebrate the Battle of the Somme. If the Taigs didn't like our songs, they could stay in their houses for a few hours once a year while we walked a couple of feet through their area. Instead, the Catholics rioted and got what they wanted, just like the Provos during the Troubles.

I ached to let out everything I'd had to keep trapped inside for the past four years. To get pissed up, scream "Billy Boys" at the Taigs, throw rocks at the peelers, feel the heat of a petrol bomb through the glass as I lobbed it. To feel the release.

And Willy had cried his wee lamps out as blood ran down his swelling forehead.

But the beat of helicopter blades warned more police were coming.

Jon eyeballed me. "Mate, you should get out of here."

Jon was right. I couldn't risk being lifted for riotous behavior. I hated it, but I had to peel myself away.

"No surrender!" Jon yelled over drums and shattering glass and lads shouting "The Famine Song" as he pushed his way through the crowd toward the police.

Bandsmen from the Ardoyne Protestant Boys, the East Belfast Sons of Ulster, and Carrickfergus Volunteers fought to get to the flash point as I scarpered in the opposite direction, surrendering like a yellow bastard. One fat, red-faced lad wearing a Sandy Row Defenders uniform fell against my drum and almost bent the rim.

"Watch it, wee tosser." He'd the nerve to scowl at me.

Clenching my drumsticks, I forced myself to move on.

The crowds thinned as I crossed into the safety of Loyalist East Belfast. Two peelers dressed in full riot gear waited on either side of the street, eyeballs glued to me as they guarded the only bridge across the River Lagan for more than a mile.

Shite.

*Keep your calm. You haven't done anything wrong*, that's what Sinclair would say to me.

Steeling myself, I jogged across the street to face the taller one, drum bouncing against my thigh. I conjured my best phony smile. "Morning, Constable."

"What have you been getting on to, wee lad?" The sun reflected off his face shield so I couldn't see him, but his voice dripped with disdain.

The other peeler jogged across the street.

I hadn't even done anything other than walk round in my band uniform. They were discriminating against my Protestant culture. *Steady on, Danny.* I stood up to my full height, about a foot taller than the short one. "Just trying to get home. Sir." I forced that last word out.

"Sure you are, big lad. Hands up," said Prick Two as he knelt next to me.

Death clenching my drumsticks, I put my hands up. I shook with rage as they groped up my legs. "I'm not looking for any trouble," I spat through my teeth.

"Well, your mates are causing quite a lot of trouble at the minute."

The Taigs started it.

The first fellow rammed a hand into my pocket, his sausage fingers dangerously close to my knob. The second fellow's hand jammed into the other. *Don't give them a reason to lift you.* I bit my tongue to stop myself from accusing him of child sexual abuse. Tight fingers felt up my sides.

Finally the first one gave me a shove. "Get a move on, you wee yob." He sounded disappointed.

I shot a triumphant smirk over my shoulder. As I jogged across the River Lagan, drum bouncing against my thighs, the roar of the riot and the helicopter slowly faded. I checked my bus app for the quickest way back to the Shankill. Walking through the city centre in my band uniform was the same as wearing a target; I didn't have time to get into a ruck if I was to get cleaned up and meet Fiona at three o'clock. I managed to catch the 11B direct to the Shankill from Castle Arcade.

My uniform earned a nod of approval from the bus driver. I set my drum on the seat next to me and then ran my fingers over the shiny, new brass buttons. My band uniform made me feel proud, but I'd feel even more proud in an army one, because I'd be saving lives. I got off on the Shankill Road and legged it home to change and spray myself with some of Billy's Lynx. I caught another bus back to the city centre.

Through the wrought iron fence rails, I spotted Fiona lying under my tree. She'd come.

My heart thumped against my rib cage as I forced myself to walk casually through the gate. I wasn't quite sure what to say, but what came out of my gob was, "What about you, Miss America."

Fiona started and jumped to her feet. She was wearing leggings that left nothing to the imagination, especially that tight, round runner's bum.

"Seriously? Perving on me again?"

"No! I—" My face flamed as I threw my hands up.

"I'm just playing." Fiona tapped my arm with her fist. Heat pulsed from the spot she touched. "I told my dad I was going for a run"—her eyes fell—"because I didn't want to go to the *Titanic* museum. So I ran, hence the sweatiness. But I can probably stay for only like forty-five minutes."

All I could smell was apples. "I like your sweat."

Fiona raised her eyebrow.

Scundered, I scratched the back of my head. "That was a bit weird to say, yeah?" It was a lot easier to talk to her via WhatsApp.

Fiona's freckled nose wrinkled as she giggled. It drove me pure mental when she did that. "Kinda."

"Well, I'm a bit smelly as well." I sat in the grass. She plopped down next to me, a few inches closer than yesterday.

My fingers drummed on my thigh to the rudiment we used for "Billy Boys," adrenaline from the parade and the blood running down Willy's forehead still heating the insides of my veins. "So the *Titanic*."

"Yeah, Leonardo DiCaprio sinking into the frozen abyss even though there was totally room on that door."

I laughed. "She was fine when she left here."

Fiona squinted at me. "Oh, the *Titanic*, you mean."

"Well, I wasn't talking about the *Santa Maria*."

Fiona looked me over. "Wow, I just got here and you're already bringing Columbus into the conversation."

"Score one point for Danny in American history. So, em, how are you?"

Fiona's knee bounced off the ground, the hot pink laces of her trainers jerking with each beat. "I didn't run away yet."

"Lucky for me. Is your da not raging, that you keep mitching off all your family things?" I knotted my hands to stop myself from drumming.

"I'm running, remember?" She leaned back on her elbows. "And you didn't run away either."

I leaned back too. Our arms almost touched. "Nah. I've just finished my A-Levels. I'm away for my tests to be an army officer in five days. I can wait that long."

Fiona's nose scrunched up. "What are A-Levels? Are they as evil as the ACTs?"

"Yeah, those always sound horrible in American films, but I've no idea what they are either." A nervous laugh slipped out. "Here you take your GCSEs or leave without qualifications at sixteen, then you can be finished with school and go to work or continue on with A-Levels for two years and go to uni."

Fiona's eyes grew huge. "Wait, you can legit finish school at sixteen? That's crazy."

I loved it when she said American-sounding things like "legit." "Why, how old are you when you finish in America?"

"Technically you can drop out when you're sixteen with your parent's permission, but most people are eighteen when they graduate senior year."

I sat up. "Right, you've fancy names for years at your American high schools, like in *Glee*." Now that we were talking about schools, perhaps I could get her sorted. Not that it mattered, seeing as she was just a tourist. But I'd never properly talked to a Catholic before, and I didn't want to say the wrong thing. "So, em, do you go to some manner of Catholic school over in America?" My fingers pounded on my thigh.

Fiona's eyebrows twitched. "No, it's just a normal school, where everybody on the far west side goes."

I relaxed. I knew Anto was wrong; she wasn't a Catholic.

"So, the army. That's why you like *Band of Brothers*. Do you want to, like, blow stuff up?"

"Actually, I want to be a nurse." I braced myself for her to slag me off like everyone else apart from Sinclair and Jon.

A smile played on her lips. "That's so cool."

"You taking the piss?"

"What?" Her noise wrinkled. "You people say weird things."

"Are you joking, like."

She poked the back of my hand. "No, seriously. I don't know any guys who want to join the military. But I imagine the ones who do just want to shoot things."

"I want to save lives, do humanitarian aid in war-torn countries, and the army seems like the best place. And you get to travel to different places, maybe see proper mountains or hear people speaking different languages."

A smile stretched her soft-looking lips until it consumed her, and it made me feel like a million American bucks. "You're willing to risk your own life to help others. That's really heroic."

I sat up taller. "First I've to get to Bristol for my Main Board. If they accept me, then I'm off for training. Em, what about you, then? What do you want to be?"

"An astrophysicist. I love black holes and space and superstring theory."

"No clue what half of that means. Em, biology was one of my A-Levels." I threw in that last bit in a desperate attempt to sound halfway intelligent. "But it sounds brilliant. You're really smart, aye?"

She tapped her toe on my shin. "You tell me."

I laughed. She was class. "Smart enough not to answer a loaded question, anyway."

"I really want to go to MIT. And I even got picked for this field study that may be my golden ticket to acceptance." Her lips tugged down.

"That's grand." I could listen to her accent all day. "So, em, have you decided how long you're going to stay, then?"

"Fourteenth probably."

Days and days from now. "Brill." I tried to sound casual.

Fiona picked at a purple rubber bracelet round her wrist. "How long have you wanted to run away?"

"As long as I can remember. My ma, she got killed when I was a baby. And my da, he's an arse."

The color drained from Fiona's face, making her freckles pop even more.

My whole body cooled. I'd never told anyone me ma got killed. Everyone just knew. Here's me, puking my feelings all over the City Hall lawn like a wee fruit. Again. To some bird I'd been talking to for five frigging minutes.

My fingers hammered against my thigh. If she apologized, I was leaving.

Fiona's wee, clammy palm pressed against the back of my hand. My fingers stilled. Her eyes met mine, hazel dripped with honey. Our noses almost touched.

"What happened to your mom?" she asked.

"It...it was car related." Something burned in my eyes, perhaps a bit of dirt. I blinked hard at the leaves rattling overhead. "Actually, it was an IRA car bomb. Meant for some peeler—police officer."

Fiona's hand fell from mine. A nice girl like her couldn't handle my life.

"Was it the Shankill bomb?" Her lips had gone white as her knee bounced again.

"How do you know about that?"

Fiona picked at some grass, a frown twitching on her lips. "Oh, I had to go on one of those political tours."

"Oh. Em, no. Not that one. She happened to be walking by a pub in North Belfast when the bomb went off."

Fiona's eyes jumped to me. She chewed her lip.

"Anyway, my da's a bad person most of the time, to be honest."

"Not as bad as mine," she said, her voice barely a whisper.

"Why, what did your da do?" I grabbed a clump of dirt and pitched it at a patch of sunlight dripping through the leaves.

Now her cheeks went pink. She plucked some blades of grass and rolled them between her fingers. "Stuff. He wound up in jail for it."

That knocked me back a bit. She seemed posh.

"My da, he did a stretch too. More than one. I've always wanted to ask my ma why she was with him in the first place. Why she stayed. He's treated all his other women like pure rubbish. Maybe she was scared he'd kill her if she left. I'll never know."

Her eyes widened. This was why I never talked about it. "I know she loved me, and she'd her reasons. But things might've been quite different if me ma was still alive."

Her eyes met mine; her eyelashes had golden tips. It was too much, like she could see into my brain. I dropped my gaze to the broken, knotted shoelaces of my Adidas.

I tried to dig myself out. "But your ma, you're mad at her as well?"

"She lied to me my whole life. All to cover up the fact that she was totally down with my dad's . . . stuff. Which is insane. So she's like a criminal by default. Then she split us all apart and spent the past fifteen years pretending everything was cool." Her clenched fists shook in her lap.

"You can be angry for the choices she made in the past but still love your mum today."

Fiona's eyebrows knitted as she glared at her freckled hands.

I took her hand. Her fists opened. Crescent nail imprints marked her palms. I stroked them with my thumb. Her skin was so smooth compared to mine. "How much longer have you got today?"

She pulled free and checked her mobile. "About ten minutes."

I pressed our palms together. "Want to listen to Fading Stars?"

"Yeah."

I dug out my mobile and handed her an earbud. "Hero's Heart" filled our ears. I freed my fingers from hers and slipped my arm behind her back. Our eyes met. Fiona's lips pursed. Bollocks, I'd pushed it too far. I moved to sit up, but she leaned her head against my shoulder. My heart skipped. I tightened my arm around her waist and breathed in her apple smell mixed with a hint of sweat.

It pained me when she pulled her headphone out a few songs later. "Um, gotta get back."

I jumped up. "Here, I'll walk you to your hotel."

"If Dad saw me with a boy..."

"Sure, no, right, of course." I shoved my hands in my pockets.

"Um, so if you ever want to see me again over the next few days, just let me know." The toe of her trainer tapped the tree root.

I couldn't stop my grin. "Brill. I've to work tomorrow, but the day after? If you're not busy touring round Ireland."

"Cool. I'm sure I'll go for a run." She winked at me.

As I walked toward the Shankill, I felt naked after everything I'd shared but also a bit lighter. Fiona was a puzzle, and I'd like to find all the pieces. Christ, what she was doing to me after less than twenty-four hours.

I checked my mobile. Messages from Anto and Davey slagging me off for running away from the riot like a wee girl.

A small price to pay for my future.

# chapter eleven

*Fiona*

I couldn't stop shivering the whole run home, even though it was above seventy and sunny for once.

As I passed the Royal, where Dad had held me like a butterfly, my stomach wrenched; I almost puked into the gutter. I wiped my mouth with my shirt sleeve and caught a whiff of cedar wood and grapefruit mixed with a little bit of sweat.

It wasn't Dad's Shankill bomb that took Danny's mom from him, but it could have been one of his many others. He'd been at it for fourteen years, after all. God, when Danny talked about his mom, his adorable goofiness died as his voice flattened. Those pale-blue eyes rimmed with midnight blue avoided mine. I felt terrible about bald-faced lying, especially given how lies were tearing my life apart, but thank God Danny thought I was just a tourist.

The pain on Danny's face when he'd said his things might have been different.

Blasting Fading Stars, I picked up the pace past the stores lining Falls Road. Green posters with guys' faces that said "*vótáil*

*Sinn Féin*" and fliers advertising Irish language classes clung to lampposts. I ran along a long wall covered with murals: Martin Luther King Jr. and Patrick's revolutionary socialist mentor Che Guevara, appeals to join Sinn Féin and fight back against Tory cuts, and something about POWs in Long Kesh, maybe Dad's former prison home. Today, a black-and-white one caught my eye. I stopped as Fading Stars played on. It was of a bunch of women marching in the street toward an armed soldier. In the corner it said, "Falls Curfew, July 1970—dedicated to all those women who faced up to military aggression." Framing it in white: "oppression breeds resistance" and "resistance brings freedom."

Patrick had said the British army forced Dad and his IRA buddies to take up arms. Yes, fact, the British government and the Loyalist paramilitary people did terrible stuff. All those things, including the Bombay Street burning and internment, were true. But Martin Luther King Jr., right up on their wall, resisted oppression *without* blowing things up.

I thought of the pain and regret in Dad's eyes when he'd said he hated what he'd had to do. But he'd do it all again, wouldn't he? Would he?

By the time I got back to Dad's, gray clouds hung low enough to scrape the peace wall. I opened the door. Dad sat in his orange arm chair, staring blankly at a muted soccer game. His weary eyes brightened. "Hiya, Fiona. How was your run?"

I folded my arms across my chest.

Dad hefted himself up. As he pulled on his Restorative Justice Ireland fleece, he said, "I've a cross-community meeting tonight. Seamus will order yous a pizza." The deadbolt clicked behind him.

Seamus emerged from the kitchen with a glass of Guinness.

I picked at a green bracelet that had slipped below my sleeve cuff. "Was your cake okay?"

Seamus choked on his chug of beer. Coughing, he wiped his mouth with the back of his hand. "First cake layer was burnt to feck."

"I'm sorry it was ruined."

Seamus squinted at me, pint of Guinness hovering inches from his curled lip.

"I'm not being sarcastic."

He shook his head like he was startled. He took a drink then let out a loud, long belch. "You do my head in."

I sat on the couch. "And, um, thanks for the brownies. And letting me use your bed."

Seamus settled into Dad's chair. "It's bonkers you've an American accent."

I raised an eyebrow.

"Well, you did talk like us before. Sure it was baby talk, but still."

Yeah, I was pretty much completely American. "You're… bonkers."

He drained his beer and belched again. "So are you." He grinned.

Seamus was growing on me.

# chapter twelve

## *Danny*

The next day, while helping Jamie's da paint the Orange Hall, I messaged Fiona all the questions I could think of. Her favorite food: chicken burrito with fiery habanero sauce. Favorite pizza toppings: pepperoni and green olives, dipped in ranch. Favorite TV show: some science fiction one called *Battlestar Galactica*. I'd never watched those kinds of things, but now I wanted to.

My grand total was now sixty-five pounds. I'd no more job prospects, and there might not be many the week before the Twelfth. As I walked home down the Shankill Road, arms speckled with white paint, Marty eyeballed me from outside his tattoo shop.

"Billy says you're need of work. I've work needs doing."

He was talking about dealing drugs. "Thanks, Marty, but I'm grand now. See you at practice."

"If you change your mind, let me know." Marty grinned like a gorilla baring his teeth. He'd a fight story for each tooth he was missing.

I slipped home. Selling for Marty would be an easy solution, but peelers were always searching us and lifting us for a spliff. And once you started working for the UVF, they owned you and you could never leave.

At practice, I let the Shankill Young Conquerors drown out the Main Board and Da and Marty. Mrs. Donnelly caught me on the way out. She needed help with some cleaning tomorrow. That meant not meeting Fiona, which was a liver punch to the gut—but I needed the money.

"You bucked your Taigy American girl yet?" Anto squinted at me with his hamster eyes.

"Piss off, you dole-leecher."

Jon laughed, smoke coming out of his nostrils in sharp bursts.

"And she's not a Taig," I said. "I checked."

Through my clenched fingers, my mobile screen lit up.

FionaRuns: Your future is waaaaaaaaaaaaaaaaay more important ☺ Besides, I want to spend max time with my nephew.

She sent me a picture of a little boy with dark-brown curls and loads of freckles like her.

I grinned. Christ, what she was doing to me.

When I got home, I did hundreds of sit-ups and press-ups until my abs burned and my arms shook.

I headed to the Donnelly's at half seven the next morning. Before I was away, I'd grabbed some crisps, only to find a pile of Sten machine guns on the kitchen table again.

As Mrs. Donnelly drove us to the house we were cleaning, we passed Sandy Row's bonfire in the car park behind Days Hotel. Their base was massive, but it wasn't even fifteen feet tall yet and they barely had any tires or pallets left. They just dumped wood in the middle rather than building and stacking properly. Then we headed far south on the Stranmillis Road to this religiously mixed neighborhood with semidetached houses and no flags anywhere. The posh people out here didn't build bonfires, even if they were Protestant. We stopped in front of a house with sculpted bushes in the front garden.

Family pictures lined their hall; a ma and da and two wee boys posed in front of Disney Castle wearing Mickey Mouse ears. There weren't crucifixes hanging everywhere, so I decided they probably weren't Catholic.

"I'll be cleaning downstairs and bedrooms. You work on the bathroom." Mrs. Donnelly handed me a bucket of cleaning supplies.

And I needed the most powerful stuff known to man, because hidden behind that lovely front garden was an ugly secret—a bathroom even more disgusting than ours. Piss caked the base of the toilet. I spent three hours in their bathtub scrubbing black scum from between the tiles with a toothbrush. Then I'd to unblock the drains. I'm sure the mum was a nice lady, but she shed like a dog.

While the toxic cleaning supplies killed more of my brain cells, I tried to picture myself on a plane to Bristol. Once I got to Leighton House, I hoped they gave us uniforms straightaway. I didn't have nice clothes like the posh tossers I'd be up against. The practice tests showed I was good enough on the numerical, verbal, and reasoning, but I hoped I showed "the ability to problem-solve under pressure" and be a leader during the practice field exercises. And feck all, I'd to give a five-minute lecture.

After five hours of cleaning, the bathroom gleamed. I cut the grass in the front and back gardens. We left before the family came home. As Mrs. Donnelly drove us back, singing along to her Christian music, I tried to imagine a life where I'd a mum rich enough to hire someone to do the cleaning and a da who wore ties. I'd probably be a tosser like Foster, but families like that, they'd celebrate me passing my A-Levels and see me off to my Main Board with a wee party.

When Mrs. Donnelly dropped me off, she pulled out three twenty notes from her massive knockoff Coach purse. "Here you go, love."

"But I worked only eight hours."

She pressed her bright-pink lips, matching her pink tracksuit, into a smile. "You've earned it, the state of that bathroom."

"Thanks a million, Mrs. Donnelly."

She squeezed my knee. "You're welcome, love."

Da and Billy were both gone, so I had a shower and a shave, then nicked Billy's one polo to look respectable for this next thing I had to do. I put on my school uniform trousers and shoes and set off to open a proper bank account. The money would be safe from Da, and I could buy my ticket online with a bank card.

Before I nipped out, Ma's picture next to the flat-screen TV caught my eye. It had been taken up at Belfast Castle; I knew the exact bench. Smiling, she was brushing away a strand of hair from her forehead. I touched her face, then set the faded picture down and legged it over to the Ulster Bank in the city centre. If I went to the one on the Shankill Road, Da would hear about it and wonder what I'd been getting on to. I walked up to the first open counter. This posh-looking bank teller with a skinny tie eyeballed me like he thought I was going to burgle the place.

I dug out all my cash and piled it on the counter. "Em, hi. I'd like to open a current account. Please." I snatched back a twenty note for rent.

The bank teller sneered at the notes like I'd pulled them from a rubbish bin. "I'll need proof of identification, proof of address—"

From my back pocket, I pulled out my passport and an electric bill I found buried under a pile of magazines. Their website said it was okay if the bill had your parent's name on it if you were under twenty-one.

"And proof of affordability."

Shite, I'd missed that bit. "What's that?"

His eyebrow inched up. "A pay slip. Taxes. Something to prove you have a job."

"Doesn't this money prove I have one? Are you having a laugh?"

Now that dirty wee prick laughed at me. "Not about proof of affordability."

"Sod off." I snatched up my crumpled notes and change. On my way out, I grabbed an application from a pile by the door just to see the look on that knob's face. When I was earning my big army paychecks, I'd never use frigging Ulster Bank, not even their cash machines.

My mobile vibrated in my pocket.

FionaRuns: How's work going?

My heart picked itself up.

DannyBoy: I'm done, if you're free.

FionaRuns: I can come.

DannyBoy: Grand.

FionaRuns: K b there in 30.

I lay on the grass under my tree listening to Fading Stars, watching sunlight glow through the shifting leaves as it warmed my arms. Something nudged the sole of my scuffed-up black shoe. I looked up to find Fiona standing at my feet, brown hair spilling over her face. Christ, she was beautiful. Today, she wore a tight top that hugged the slight curve of her breasts.

"Hey, perv. Up here."

My face blazed. "No, I—"

Fiona's face broke into a sly grin. "I'm just taking the piss." She plopped down less than six inches from me.

I breathed a silent sigh of relief as my face cooled. Her hand lay between us, blades of grass sticking between her fingers. I wanted to take it, but I twisted my fingers in my lap to stop myself from drumming. "So would it be a bit creepy if I said I missed you?"

Pink spread across her cheeks along with a cute smile. "I missed you too."

My chest filled with this warmth like I'd had a few pints. I coiled my fingers through hers. Her soft palm pressed against mine. I hoped it wasn't sweaty.

"And what other tourist destinations have you conquered while I was slaving away?"

Fiona frowned at her lap. "Botanic Garden and Belfast Castle. So, um, are you all ready for your big test?"

I shrugged. "It's a bit weird to think I'll be on a plane soon. I've never even left Northern Ireland before. I could be in the army in a week."

Fiona leaned her arm against mine. Sparks shot through my skin as I breathed in her sweet apple smell.

My mobile vibrated against my thigh. I didn't want to check it, but I had to.

`Da: If ur not home in fifteen minutes ill end u`

My heart pounded faster than a triple-stroke roll. I mustered an utterly pathetic attempt at a cowboy accent. "Em, I've to hit the old dusty trail."

Fiona's eyes were on my phone, a look of pure horror on her face.

Ears hot, I freed my fingers from hers.

"Don't go home. That's crazy."

"It'll be worse if I don't like. Most of the time, we get on fine. It's just if I forget to pay rent or skip band practice or he's taken too much drink."

"Wait, you have to pay rent? You just finished school. And what if he's drunk right now? You shouldn't go back there. Ever." Her eyes searched mine.

Anger pricked my chest behind my sternum. I rubbed at the grass imprints itching my forearms. "You don't know the situation, and it's none of your business at any rate."

Fiona recoiled. "Well, excuse me for actually caring about you."

Shite. My anger cooled. I ran a hand through my hair. "My enlistment papers are back there," I mumbled, face burning. "And I haven't got anywhere to go."

As Fiona chewed her plump bottom lip, she took my hands. I'd never seen that much worry on someone's face, even Mrs. Donnelly.

"Can I see you tomorrow?" she asked.

My fingers tightened around hers. "Aye, sure."

"And I'm going to text you like sixteen thousand times asking if you're okay," she said.

The tourists snapping photos in front of the statue of Queen Victoria and teenagers hanging out faded away. Sunlight glowed around us. I leant down, tucked my fingers around the back of her head, and pressed my lips against hers. They were soft and warm and it was so right, I had to pull away. "I probably shouldn't have done that."

This massively beautiful grin even bigger than the one on her profile picture left me clean melted. "No, you totally should have."

"Are you taking the piss?"

She giggled, then caressed my cheek. "Keep me posted so I know you're okay."

"Aye, sure." Her silky curls slipped through my fingers as my hand dropped.

As I legged it home, I felt her ripping farther away with each step, but at least we had tomorrow. It was mental, but I was already counting down the minutes.

I turned down Lawnbrook and headed past the bricked-up terraces. The dark second-story windows stared down at me like dead eyes.

Da's car sat parked out front.

A bus of tourists unloaded across the street, cameras ready to take pictures of the peace wall.

The front door sprung open. "I oughta kick you the length of the Shankill!" Da loomed in the doorway with his UVF-tattoo-covered arms crossed over his gut. His watery eyes scanned slowly, but his eyelids weren't sagging yet. Fiona was right; I should run. That fat bastard would never catch me. But all my paperwork was in that house.

No surrender, Danny Boy.

A tourist with massive glasses gawked at me. He drew up his camera.

"What did I tell you?" Da grabbed my arm and near ripped it out of the socket as he dragged me up the stairs.

He threw me into my room. I tripped over my drum. My

clothes covered the floor. He'd shredded my army poster. The only things untouched were the Union Jack on my wall and my band uniform in the cupboard. My mattress was on the floor. My mattress, under which I'd hidden everything.

"I pay rent. What are you doing going into my room?" I slabbered. Not my smartest move.

"You're still living under my roof," Da roared. "Filling your massive gob with my food while I pay your school fees!"

"Well, you are legally responsible for keeping me alive for three more days."

Da rammed an oil-stained finger into my chest, almost knocking me back into my mattress. "I told you to get a proper job, earn like a real man."

"Where's my stuff?"

"You mean this?" Da rammed a fistful of my enlistment papers in my face. "Jonny big balls, is that it? Going to fuck off to England on Bonfire Night so you can be a wee nurse in the army. After I bought you that new uniform."

Seething, I clenched my fists at my side. "What do you care? I'll be out of your hair, and that's all that matters, isn't it?"

"You're gonna turn your back on us?" Da's voice shook the walls. He tore up my enlistment papers and let the pieces fall to the floor like snow.

I scrambled to grab them. Da rammed his fist into my cheek. I bit my tongue. Blood filled my mouth. My brain slammed against the back of my skull. Something wet and warm ran down my cheek. I fell back and couldn't get back up.

"Get up!" He screamed, whiskey-drenched spittle wetting my skin. A foot struck my side. I balled up to protect my organs. A hand jammed into my pocket. "What's this?"

My money.

"Get up!"

I coughed, tried to suck in air. My ribs screamed. Da grabbed me by the collar. Billy's polo ripped as he threw me against the wall.

"Was this for your wee plane ticket? Now it'll pay for the uniform you'll never frigging use."

My throbbing head was filled with molasses as my vision narrowed in on my mobile a meter away by shards of the army poster. Da reached for it.

"No!" I lunged.

"You haven't got what it takes to be in the army, even as a wee nurse." Da laughed. "I'll tell you this right now, no son of mine is going to turn his back on his culture. Absolute disgrace."

My door slammed.

All my money was gone.

# chapter thirteen

*Fiona*

As I showered, I relished the memory of Danny's lips brushing mine, that adorable, embarrassed smile as he pulled away. Then that text message; he'd tried to play it off like it was nothing, but I'd seen the panic flash across his face.

I checked my phone. We'd been apart for only like an hour, but I needed to know Danny was okay.

FionaRuns: Hey, John Wayne wannabe, how's it going?

Crickets. God, and Danny usually responded in like thirty seconds.

I Skyped Nevaeh instead.

"OMG, I was about to fly over there," Nevaeh said, lips coated with brilliant red. She lay on a lounge chair in her teal bikini, pop music barely audible over splashing and children's shouts. If I hadn't opened Dad's letter, that's where I would be right now, coated in gallons of sunscreen.

I fought back the burning sensation creeping up my throat. "I'm fine."

"Zion, I got Fi here." She tilted her phone to Zion next to her. Beads of water glistened on his ebony skin.

"Hey, Fi." Zion leaned against Nevaeh's shoulder to get closer to the camera. Her nose scrunched in excitement. "I talked to my lawn guy. He'll hook you up."

"Cool, thanks." God, my return flight to Madison felt years away. But at least it delayed facing down doppelgänger Mom; I had no idea how I was going to do that.

"But seriously, Fi," Nevaeh said and rammed a pointer finger at the camera, "you haven't even posted a single picture on Facebook. What's really going on?"

I chewed the inside of my lip. Hiding the truth from Nevaeh and Zion didn't bother me half as much as hiding it from Danny, because Danny kept baring his soul to me as I told bigger and bigger lies. But still, the three of us shared everything. I could at least tell them about Danny. I wanted to share his amazingness with someone.

I told them everything except the whole Dad-might-have-killed-his-mom thing. Nevaeh and Zion both stared at me. I'd just gushed about practically falling head over heels for some guy I'd known for a few days. Back home, Nevaeh and I wrote out pros and cons lists for guys I was crushing on before strategizing if and how to pursue. I'd had a few boyfriends before, like "go out on a few group dates, eat lunch together, text all night" boyfriends. There had been some awkward kisses after homecoming and the winter formal—all flat soda compared to the fizz with Danny. But, even though Fiona from two weeks ago would never have believed it, I was glad I'd gone to Burger King with that sketchy-looking dude. Because *Danny*.

"But you're going to be there only a few more days," Zion said.

Fact, obviously, but Zion had just made it real.

Nevaeh poked Zion in his ticklish side, unleashing a chain of his contagious laughs. "She's gotta have something to do in all that rain."

"You tell Belfast Boy, if he does *anything* to you, I'm gonna have to hop on a plane."

"But don't mention Zion won't even step on an ant." Nevaeh giggled. "You should've seen him hopscotching the anthills on the walk to Ridgewood."

His nose wrinkled. "Nobody said I was gonna get violent. I'd just sit him down and talk about his life choices."

"Speaking of life choices, Zion, it's too hot out here. Let's go get some frozen custard."

God, what I wouldn't give for heat. "Someone better get chocolate peanut butter in my honor and send me a selfie."

"I got you, Fi." Zion shined his full-on dashing Prince Charming grin.

"Byeeeeee," Nevaeh said.

As soon as we disconnected…

NevaehAngel: You got a pic??????

I took a quick screenshot of Danny's WhatsApp profile picture and sent it.

NevaehAngel: Dang he's like Axel Lurgen, New York Supermodel Male Edition, hot. And I know he's got that accent.

FionaRuns: Exactly!!!!

Part of me was glad I told them, because I wanted our brief whatever to feel real.

Since Dad was at a cross-community planning thing with the Shankill, I headed downstairs without fear of his awkward desperation.

I settled on the couch between the usual Patrick/Finn combo and Seamus. Shining a gap-tooth smile, Finn crawled into my lap. I curled my arms around him and savored his sweet maple syrup smell, mixed with Patrick's secondhand smoke. On TV was some baking show with snobby-sounding English people in a pavilion tent.

I raised an eyebrow at Seamus. "Are you seventy?"

Patrick snorted from behind *Animal Farm*.

Seamus belched so loud I felt the vibration through the couch. "If you listen to these posh tarts and imagine them talking about sex, it's frigging class."

"Totally not why you watch it."

"See if I give you any of my lemon fudge cake." Seamus slouched back and splayed his legs wide enough to knock knees with me.

I shoved Seamus's thigh.

He stared blankly at me.

"That means scooch over. You're taking up like half the couch."

"Oh." Seamus closed his legs a few inches. "I don't speak American."

Finn's high giggles resonated in my chest.

"That's not American, that's like normal body language."

The old, pastel-swathed English lady took a bite of some chocolate thing, pinky up as she licked her thin pink lips. "Mmm. It's delightful. Moist and warm."

Seamus guffawed as he slapped his knee.

"Oh, my God, seriously. I cannot sit on the same couch as you with this show on." I kicked Seamus's gigantic Nike.

Snickering, Seamus flicked through the channels until he got to a news program.

"Loyalists have been hard at work building their bonfires, all in preparation for the Twelfth," a news anchor with an English accent said. "Jim Donnelly from the Shankill claims theirs will be the biggest ever."

So there was more than one of those monstrosities.

The newscast cut to a balding man in a red-white-and-blue plaid shirt. "This is a family-friendly celebration of our British culture. We residents didn't take money from city council to pay for our fire. We've no bought culture here."

Seamus pointed the remote at the TV.

"Wait." I touched his thick, freckle-spattered wrist. "So what's the deal with that?"

"There's loads of them all across the North." Patrick's wallet chain jingled on his thigh as his heel twitched. "They build it high enough for us to see over the wall. Always put tricolors on it, sometimes statues of the Virgin Mary."

I was pretty much an awful Catholic, but even I knew that was immoral. "There's tires in it—that's terrible for the environment. Why are they allowed to do that?"

"Same reason they're allowed to have their wee parades," Patrick said. "And not just on the Twelfth."

"What's the deal with the Twelfth?"

"Loyalists celebrate the 1690 victory of Protestant King William of Orange, who was actually Dutch, over Catholic King James." Patrick sounded like my World History teacher. "They light them on the Eleventh. On the Twelfth, they have a massive parade right through our areas with all their flute bands, carrying banners celebrating the murder of Catholics."

"Going to the toilet in people's gardens," Seamus jumped in, "spitting, giving us the finger. Them inbred Huns can march round every day and cover their lampposts with flags, as long as it stays on their side of that wall."

I hugged my flannel tighter around my chest. "That's crazy! Why don't the police stop them?"

Patrick glowered at the newscaster. "The Loyalist political party still has a slight majority in the government."

"Protestants'll wreck the place if the Parades Commission reroutes it," Seamus said.

"Like you should talk, Seamy." Patrick's voice cut like razors. "Brendan says yous were at the riot the other day."

"Wait, riot?" I asked.

Seamus scowled, but his ears turned pink. "It was just a bit of craic."

"It's nothing to worry about," Patrick said, voice cool and collected again. "Just a few bored kids looking to get into a ruck. And it was on the other side of the river."

I should just keep a running tally of things not to worry about at this point. Seamus would have been a little kid when the Troubles ended, but clearly there were still issues—because peace wall and bonfires burning the Virgin Mary and riots. It struck me then. When Danny asked about my school, he'd been trying to figure out my religion. He'd mentioned being in a band.

Finn's body heat made a sweat break out over my upper lip.

But Danny wanted to be a nurse and see the world. Save people. He wouldn't want to stir up violence in his own backyard. I checked my phone again. Still no response. My heart sank.

Seamus flipped past a car chase and some singing show. And then I saw Beau Braxton. "Go back."

"What?"

I grabbed the remote from his beefy hand and changed it back to *New York Supermodel.* Girls dressed in steampunk getups posed in front of a train engine. I hated hair and makeup, but Nevaeh had gotten me addicted to it last year.

"Are you frigging joking?" Seamus asked.

I set the remote on the coffee table. Finn clapped his tiny hands.

"I need to understand what they're wearing," Patrick said.

"Bloody hell," Seamus muttered.

The show cut to Simone, the mega-snob. "Imani looked like she was trying to ride that train like a cowboy with her boobs oozing out of that bustier. So trashy."

"She's well fit. I'd take a buck at her," Seamus said.

"Oh, my God, Seamus."

"Don't chat shite round your sister." Patrick reached behind me and smacked the back of Seamus's head.

"Besides, her boobs are totally fake," I said.

Seamus's big ears turned red.

"You're embarrassed I said boobs, after you presumably just talked about screwing her?"

"You're mad," Seamus said.

"You're weird." I elbowed his arm.

He grinned and pushed back. "Will you give my head peace, will you?" I was glad I decided to stay.

Seamus rated all the girls according to fitness while we watched a few more episodes. But with each passing commercial break, my worry over Danny swelled until it started compressing my lungs. Maybe his cell phone was dead. Or he had an actual life. Eventually, Patrick took Finn up to bed and Seamus headed out "for a few tinnies."

The front door opened halfway thought the "Zombie Edition" episode. Pounding rain drowned out Beau as the former IRA quartermaster for the West Belfast IRA walked in. Even though it was past ten, it was still light out.

"Hiya, sweetheart." Tiredness weighed down Dad's eyelids, but he dredged up his usual brilliant grin for me.

I should have gone to bed after the last episode. Every time Dad had seen me the past few days after long shifts or washing mountains of dishes, his whole being lit up. He must have searched the internet for lists of corny icebreaker questions, because he had hundreds at the ready, ranging from what planet I would visit to what I would do with a million pounds.

"Hey," I muttered.

He shrugged out of his Restorative Justice Ireland fleece and sank into his arm chair. "I've the morning off tomorrow and my car's out of the shop. I'm taking us all up the Antrim Coast to Giant's Causeway. I think you'll quite like it. It's like a *Star Wars* planet."

"Cool." I picked at a thread hanging from the rip in my jeans.

"How was your day? Did you have a good run?"

Patrick's feet drummed down the stairs. He stuck his head into the living room. "Any troubles at the interface tonight?"

Dad kneaded his knee. "Just that blighter Jonty and some of his mates looking to nip over to the Shankill to give their bonfire an early start."

"That cheeky wee knob." Veins popped out of Patrick's forehead. "We'll have a chat."

Dad's eyes flashed up to him. "That won't be necessary. We've got him sorted, Paddy."

"Joyriding twice last week. The riot. Now this?" Patrick folded his arms over his Mad Rovers shirt, wallet chain jingling against his black skinny jeans.

"Patrick, let him alone." There was a sharpness to Dad's voice I'd never heard from him.

"This is the last time. Finn's sleeping. I'm away out." Patrick locked the door as he left.

I raised an eyebrow. "If Patrick takes his mentoring job so seriously, maybe he should work a little harder on Seamus."

A corner of Dad's lip almost twitched into a smile. "He's tried with that wee hellion, rest assured." His glassy eyes squinted at the TV. "What's this you're watching?"

"A model show."

Dad pulled off a shoe; the outer sole had started to split from the upper part of the shoe. With how much it rained here, his sock must be constantly soaked. A heavy sigh leaked across the living room. I glanced up at him through my hair. Dad stared blankly at the TV. He hadn't gotten himself tea or even taken off his other shoe.

Had he finally run out of questions?

Whatever. Danny's mom was dead, along with a lot of other people, and Dad was watching *New York Supermodel* "Zombie Edition" with me.

# chapter fourteen

*Danny*

When I peeled my eyes open, Billy was standing over me with a bag of frozen peas and a Tennent's.

"Jaysus, what did you do this time?" he asked.

My head pounded like Da was taking his Lambeg mallets to it, and my insides felt like a squished tomato. I squinted at Billy, but my eyes refused to focus. Something crusty crinkled the skin around my eyes.

My passport and baby book were by the cupboard. My shredded enlistment papers lay scattered across the floor. I scrambled to gather the pieces of my future. Bolts shot through my throbbing brain with each movement.

"Back off, you wee skitter. I'll see to that. Go clean yourself up," Billy said.

I limp-crawled across my blood-speckled floor to the bathroom. In the mirror, half of my face was lumpy and bright red. Not even Gusty would take me on a job looking like that. Billy's ripped polo hung off my shoulder. I started my systems check.

My face and ribs pulsed heat and my eye was swollen shut, but my nose looked okay and my teeth were all intact; two small things to be grateful for, because I wasn't keen on having a smile like Marty's or a crooked nose like Billy's.

My brain squeezed against the inside of my skull.

Billy's voice slowly came back into focus over the ringing in my ears. "Danny. Danny! I'm talking to you."

Da took all my money. My stomach rolled and lurched. I leant over and puked bile in the toilet.

"What?" I gripped the sink to stay up.

Billy studied my reflection from the door, jaw clenched so tight the tendons popped out of his thick neck, distorting his cross tattoo. "Christ." He handed me the Tennent's.

I took a long drink. The cool bitterness slowed my heart. I wet a flannel and dabbed at the dried blood around the split in my eyebrow. The pain made me flinch.

The mirror caught sunlight leaking from my bedroom window. "What time is it?"

"Half eight. In the morning." Billy shoved his hands in the pockets of his trackie bottoms. "What did you do now, you wee hellion?"

"Da found out about my officer test on the Twelfth. He stole all my money."

"Oh, for Christ sake, is your head cut?" Billy ran a hand over his number one crop, still holding his cigarette. "You're still on about that? I thought you were supposed to have some brains, staying on in school with all those snobby wankers."

I glared at him with my good eye. "It's my life, and I want more than working at Hardy's and being owned by the UVF."

"The UVF has been fighting for us since before World War I. Show some respect."

"And I'm trying to join the British army, fighting for God and Ulster."

"Feck sake, would you just apply to uni already?" Billy's voice softened. "Go learn to be a wee nurse there."

He wasn't having me on; he actually wanted me to go to uni. "Why do you care if I join the army?"

"You've no respect for any kind of authority. I've no clue how you've managed to finish school, what with all the calls from that eejit Doyle. Your temper gets the best of you and you can't stop yourself slabbering. Can't even get a proper weekend job, and you somehow go weeks without doing the washing." Shaking his head, Billy took a long drag. "You're no officer."

"What would you know about it?" I fumed. "I've got my army test in a few days. In England. If they accept me, I'll be gone. You won't have to worry about me again."

Billy jabbed his smoldering cigarette butt at me. "And just how are you going to get there?"

He was right. My legs couldn't support me any longer. I sat on the piss-caked floor and buried my head in my hands.

Billy exhaled slowly through his nose. His feet pounded down and back up the stairs, then a crisp ripping sound came from my bedroom. I dropped my hands. Billy sat on my mattress, still on the floor, tearing a piece of tape.

"We have tape?"

Billy taped two more shards together. "Jaysus, you do my head in, you do."

My heart wobbled. "Em, thanks."

Billy shook his head as he ripped another piece.

After washing down a handful of paracetamols with beer, I slowly laid myself down on my overturned mattress and pressed the peas to my tender face—a sharp burst of needles then biting cold.

"Where is this test?"

Beads of cold water ran down my cheeks. "Westbury, near Bristol."

"How much do you need, then?"

"Hundred twenty quid."

Another crisp rip. "By when?"

"The Eleventh."

"Jaysus, Danny."

I lifted the peas from my face. Billy had two reconstructed pages sitting next to him. "I know a way."

"I'm not dealing."

"See, here you are thinking you're above us again. It's *your* dream, so it is."

"I can't risk getting lifted, or the army will never take me." I put the peas on my face again. A bead of water ran down my throat.

"All these years, I've been lifted only a few times, and you're talking about dealing for two frigging days." My door shut.

I screamed into the bag of peas. Each breath hurt. My head was an accordion, squeezing and expanding over and over again so hard my brain felt like it might pop. The peas slowly turned into a soggy, thawed mess.

Da and Billy left for the Whiterock parade without me, and it was my second favorite parade after the Twelfth. But at least Da would be gone until the wee hours of the morning getting blocked afterward.

I was supposed to see Fiona today. That fat bastard better not have taken my mobile. I shoved my repaired enlistment papers, passport, and baby book into my rucksack. It was never leaving my sight again. I limped downstairs.

By some small miracle, my mobile sat on the coffee table.

A tiny part of me liked to think he'd left it there on purpose. Sometimes I thought perhaps Da felt bad for what he'd done when the drink wore off. The word "sorry" did not exist in his vocabulary, but sometimes he'd make me breakfast the next day.

And sure enough, I'd at least twenty messages from Fiona. A smile tried to form on my lips. The last one had been sent two hours ago.

> FionaRuns: K seriously I wasn't joking about checking 16000 times. You're scaring me. Are you okay?

I hugged the mobile to the one part of my chest that didn't ache. She was sitting in her hotel room worrying about *me*.

My mobile vibrated.

> Sinclair: Have you got your ticket yet? Do you need a lift to the airport?

Crap. Crap.

Going on missions. Traveling the world. Saving lives on the battlefield. Being a leader. Even the class car I'd drive round the Shankill someday. It was slipping away.

I staggered to the kitchen and put the kettle on. I rinsed out a tea-stained cup and set it between towers of moldy plates. Reaching for the box of Barry's almost ended me.

Just as the kettle finished boiling, a knock rattled the front door. "Daniel Stewart, you open up this instant!" Mrs. Donnelly called.

Why wasn't she at the parade? Shocks shot through my side as I limped to the door. Mrs. Donnelly's eyes danced across my face, bright pink lips pressed into a tight line, hands on her wide hips.

"Just a fight with the lads."

"Don't lie to me, Daniel Robert Stewart. I've helped raise you since you were a wee baby." She shoved her finger in my face. Her nail varnish was blindingly pink too. "Jamie's mum rang and told me what she heard."

A wave of dizziness rushed through my head as my vision narrowed.

"Do you need to go to hospital?"

Her frown was like that look in Sinclair's eyes when he dropped me off before my last beating. And even if I did have a concussion, I was sure the doctor would just tell me to rest anyway. I closed the door on her.

"This isn't over!" she said.

I pressed my back against the door. My throat felt thick and clotted. I squeezed my good eye closed, which made the black one smart.

I didn't want Fiona to see me like this.

# chapter fifteen
## *Fiona*

I still hadn't heard anything from Danny at six thirty the next morning, when we left for Giant's Causeway. Something had happened to him; I could feel it.

On the drive, the sky was the most brilliant blue as the sun spilled over rolling green pastures dotted with sheep. The country roads were so narrow hedges scratched the car, but it was warm enough to roll down the windows. I let the wind sweep through my curls, carrying with it the smell of freshness, maybe a hint of Irish Spring. Then the hills opened to the glittering cerulean ocean lapping against craggy cliffs. Every once in a while, we passed through tiny towns with pastel downtowns that belonged on postcards. Some had a crap-ton of British flags and some purple-and-orange ones; some didn't. Belfast was a lot of brick, but otherwise just a city. But this landscape was so different from Wisconsin's forests and cornfields and red barns. And, even though I'd been here for days, it struck me hard: I was in another country. Minus Seamus and Patrick in the back seat farting to make Finn laugh, this was how I always imagined Ireland would be.

Dad's eyes were on me every second he could peel them from the road as his questions continued. When was the last time I climbed a tree? If I had unlimited funds to build a house, what would it be like? Since it was a three-hour drive, he asked for play-by-plays of every cross-country and track season, lists of every class I'd ever taken, and all the school clubs I'd been in.

A tiny sliver of me was relieved Dad still had questions to ask, but my worries for Danny ate away at it. My arm pressed into the car door as Dad turned off the road into a gravel parking lot. Ahead was a beach of black-and-white stones. Waves crashed into white cliffs, spraying whitewater high into the air. A clear sky framed the the sparkling aqua sea.

When I got home, I'd get two summer jobs and mow a million lawns if I had to. Two grand, then Arecibo in November. Puerto Rico's sandy beaches would probably be cram-packed with bikinis and towels and beach balls. But this beach was something out of a fairy tale—and the setting for the last photo of my whole family. Clearly, there was photographic evidence the beach existed, but now I was in the parking lot. Whoa.

"Let's take a wee picture," Dad said as his car door creaked open. Patrick, Seamus, and Finn climbed out too.

I pushed open the heavy door. A warm breeze kissed my cheeks, carrying with it the briny smell of salt and seaweed.

Grinning, Dad waved us over to a pile of huge rocks almost identical to our last stage fifteen years ago. He had a tourist with a Southern accent take a picture of us. Finn had one arm around my waist and the other around Bucky. Patrick hugged my shoulders. Next to him, Seamus stood with his arms folded. Dad was a foot away from us, eyes on me. In the original photo, Mom had stood in that space between with Seamus hugging her side.

This beach was real; so was the fact that we were physically the same people. Mostly.

"The only thing missing from this picture is Mom," I said.

Finn was pulling Dad toward the bathroom. Dad leaned on his left leg more than usual, shoulders caved. I wondered if he'd heard what I'd said about Mom.

I'd never been mad at Mom for more than a few hours. I didn't like this emptiness between us. I didn't like being unmoored.

*Fact*, she chose to marry a terrorist because she was down with the violence.

Fact, my rational brain argued back, Mom works her butt off to pay rent and your cell bill and buy you clothes from places other than Goodwill. She keeps nothing for herself.

And that was still true, so she hadn't become a total doppelgänger. But I wasn't ready to talk to her.

Car tires crunched on the gravel. I drew up my gaze. Three kids jumped out of the back seat of a car.

"Ready, steady, go!" shouted one boy about Finn's age.

The two older ones left him in the dust. Laughing, their mom gave chase.

I shook the thoughts from my head and made for Dad's rusted-out silver car. Patrick's phone sat in the back seat. Maybe I could use his data to check my WhatsApp.

A lighter flicked behind me.

"She could be in the frigging picture if she hadn't been a tout." Seamus took a long drag from his cigarette and then skulked off toward the bathrooms.

I sat on a boulder as warmth from the sun leaked through my jeans. In an alternate reality, maybe we could have been one of those TV-perfect families. I'd drink tea every morning, and Dad would help me with calculus, since Mom gave up after algebra. Patrick would wear argyle sweaters instead of plugs in his earlobes and would be studying for his PhD in twentieth-century literature. Seamus would be a pastry chef instead of a rioter.

Patrick's wallet chain clinked on the rock as he took a seat.

"I wish we all could've been together," I said.

"Me too."

I leaned my shoulder against his. "We can do a book club if you want, bro."

Patrick pressed back into my arm. It was weird to think the smell of his cigarettes made me feel safe now.

"So now I'm your bro, eh?"

"Yep."

Patrick grinned, the sun catching honey drops in his eyes.

When we finally got to Giant's Causeway, I discovered their visitors center had Wi-Fi. Thank God. While Dad waited in line to get us waters, I sat next to Finn and tried to connect, heel bouncing. I glanced up at the cartoon playing on the big screen in front of us. It was about the legend of Giant's Causeway. Finn's eyes lit up when he learned the hero of the myth's name was Fionn mac Cumhaill.

My phone finally connected.

DannyBoy: Sorry!!!!!!!! Da took my mobile off me.

Relief washed over me. A tremulous grin split my face.

FionaRuns: OMG thank God I've been so worried!!!! We're at Giant's Causeway. Using visitors center wifi. Are you okay?

DannyBoy: I'll be ok. Sorry I worried you.

FionaRuns: You'll BE ok? That means you're not ok. Are you safe?

Finn looked up at me wide-eyed.

I messed up his curls. "I'm fine."

DannyBoy: Da and my brother are away till the wee hours of the morning. I'm safe.
DannyBoy: ☺

I hugged my phone to my chest and wished it was him.

DannyBoy: It's ok if we can't see each other today.
FionaRuns: No I want to see you. I'll "go for a run" when we get back.
DannyBoy: What time are you back?
FionaRuns: 3.
DannyBoy: Grand. Send me some wee pictures of Giant's Causeway. I've never been.

It broke my heart even more that his ass of a father hadn't even taken him to the main tourist attraction in Northern Ireland.

Dad held out the water bottle, eyes lit up with their near-perpetual twinkle. God, how could he be so unfailingly cheery toward me when I was being a total brat? I took the cold, condensation-slick bottle and slipped it into my messenger bag. "Thanks."

Back in the sunshine, we cut through crowds of tourists with American and English accents.

"Want to be a giant, Finny?" Seamus asked.

Finn grinned huge as Seamus hoisted him on his shoulders. Patrick snapped a picture of Finn pretending his hands were binoculars. I managed to catch a photo with all three of them, the smooth sea and rocky cliffs as a backdrop.

As we walked on a path nestled between a steep hill and a

precipice into the ocean, Patrick started grilling me about my opinions on the symbolism in *The Grapes of Wrath*. Dad watched us with a quiet smile. The path rounded a bend and there it was, Giant's Causeway. Thousands of interlocking hexagonal basalt columns reached out into the waves like a broken bridge, some towering almost as high as the wall behind Dad's house. Dad was right; it did look like an Outer Rim planet, except for the tourists climbing all over. Finn hopped across the stepping stones toward where they disappeared into the sea, Patrick barely a step behind. I snapped more pictures.

After we explored, we headed back along the top of a high sea cliff with a cool view of the columns. Warm, salty wind swept across the grass on the other side of the path. Sheep and cows masticated their food as they watched us. Finn ran ahead, arms wide. Patrick chased him. Dad lumbered after with a rumbling laugh. How could a murderer be so freaking sweet?

That left me and Seamus. He squinted against the sun as he sucked on his cigarette. His copper hair blazed as he pitched his butt over the edge. I gritted my teeth to stop myself from scolding him. Mom would have made sure Seamus never started smoking. At the very least, she'd have raised him not to litter in a World Heritage Site.

But Seamus hadn't had a choice, just like I hadn't.

Up ahead, Finn squealed as Patrick gave him a piggyback ride. Chewing the inside of my lip, I snapped a few more pictures. Of Seamus walking away, head hung low. Of Patrick racing Finn while Dad laughed. It was all part of our family's story.

On our way back through the visitors center, I checked my messages. I sent Danny, Nevaeh, and Zion selfies with some of the basalt columns.

`DannyBoy: That's brill. Wish I was there.`

FionaRuns: Me too.

But then, of course, he'd meet my dad and brothers. My lie would be exposed. I shuddered.

I wondered if Mom pulled away from people these days not just to hide her past but also because of the burden of her pain and guilt. Danny had said I could hate her choices but still love her. And maybe I should feel more grateful that I had a mom who loved me—or a mom, period. That crushed my chest like I'd been thrown at ten g's.

I dug out my phone. Two bars of Wi-Fi left. I sent her the picture of us at the beach.

❧

As we drove into Belfast, I spotted a mural on the side of a building that said "Prepared for Peace" and "Ready for War." It featured two men dressed in black, wearing black ski masks, and holding big guns. At the top was a hand ringed with the words "UVF, For God and Ulster."

"What's the deal with that?" I asked.

Dad said, "Dinosaurs."

Patrick glared out the window. "Just touched up the paint."

So the Protestant side had dinosaurs too.

As soon as Dad parked on the sidewalk in front of our house, the rain unleashed. Crap.

I changed into my running gear and plopped down on the couch.

Mom: Thank you, sweetheart. This means the world to me. Please send more, when you're ready.

I could almost feel her happy tears across the Atlantic. The pressure still crushing my chest lifted a few centimeters. I sent her a selfie, then messaged Danny.

FionaRuns: Hey, back.
DannyBoy: ☺ but it's meant to rain all day. If you want you could come over maybe.

Seamus slurped tea from a dainty, rose-detailed cup. One of these times, he was going to stick out his pinky.

DannyBoy: If you don't think it'd be bonkers or too far. And if you still want to meet.
FionaRuns: Where do you live?

He sent his address. I tilted my body away from Seamus and opened my map app. A dot popped up literally across the street.

But there was a wall in the way.

Danny lived in the Shankill, where the torch-bearing lynch mob had come from. My hair stood on end under my hoodie.

DannyBoy: But if you don't want to, that's cool. It is probably a bit of a walk. Maybe tomorrow.

We'd driven through a bunch of Protestant towns today and there had even been British flags in the parking lot of Giant's Causeway, and it had been totally fine. Plus the burning of Bombay Street happened like forty years ago; even if the people involved were still alive, that didn't mean they were still dangerous. Dad was case in point. But it wasn't just a question of if I felt safe going to his house. It was about my lies—my lies of omission. I'd thought they didn't matter. I'd told myself it couldn't matter to Danny whether I was Catholic or Protestant, or who I was related to. But living where he lived, it would matter—a lot.

```
FionaRuns: I can come over whenev. Now even
DannyBoy: Give me 30 minutes.
FionaRuns: See you then.
```

I closed my map app and shoved my phone in my kangaroo pocket.

Dad came down wearing his Restorative Justice Ireland fleece.

"I'm going for a run."

Dad pulled back the heavy orange curtain. "It's lashing down."

"The only things that cancel races are lightning and tornados."

Patrick peeked over his book. "The Whiterock parade is today."

"The one where they pee in people's yards?" I asked.

"It's not the big one, but they still might," Seamus said.

Finn's eyes grew hugc as he sank back into his throne on Dad's chair.

"You guys are always saying how safe Belfast is. And I can't mess up my training routine any more, or there's no way I'll make State. This year is my last chance."

"She runs to the city centre and back," Dad said. "The parade is the opposite direction and crosses into the Shankill a half mile west of here. She'll be fine."

Seamus pulled on his Nikes. "I'll run with you."

I scoffed. "You can't keep up with me."

"How do you know?"

"You smoke like five packs a day."

Seamus shot me a sour look.

"Just go straight to the city centre and back," Dad said.

"Sure." I slipped out the front door before Seamus could tie his shoes.

I almost crashed into a beer-bellied man taking pictures of the billboard remembering the burning of Bombay Street. I got a few weird looks as I wove through the tourists clogging the road like this was not a place where real people lived. My Memorial Cross-Country sweatshirt wasn't something the locals wore. Distant shrill flutes and drums echoed off the row houses, the melody blurring into a cacophony. Danny was home, so at least he wasn't *that* kind of Protestant.

I flipped up my hood and jogged past Finn's school toward the gate in the peace wall. A thrill ran up my spine. I wanted to see the other side. Seamus and Patrick had to be exaggerating. Jonty and the Tracksuits hung out under the awning of Kashmir Bar, smoking. I waited for them to start catcalling, but they just stared.

Within the three minutes it took to reach the gate, my sweatshirt was drenched. What a crappy day for a parade. Two blue-and-yellow-checkered armored, tanklike cars sat parked on the road to the open gate. My Mizunos skidded to a stop on the wet sidewalk. One tank said "Crimestoppers" with a 028 phone number. The other had a camera surrounded by a cage. So the police needed *Mad Max* tanks for protection.

The rhythmic thump of a helicopter cut through the rain and the flutes. I looked up, cold drops spattering my cheeks. A police copter hovered almost directly overhead. All this for a parade.

The thrill evaporated.

The open gate loomed directly ahead. At some point in the distant past, someone had painted the ten-foot-tall, solid metal gate with a scene of rolling hills. Now it was chipped and faded, covered with "KAH," "KAT," "AYH," and random people's names. A new-looking sign read, "Do not enter hatched area whilst gates are in motion." A bunch of cameras watched down from tall poles.

I thought back to that creepy mural—*prepared for peace, ready for war*—and the new rocks that kept appearing on our zombie apocalypse sunroom.

But the people from the Shankill were just humans, and I needed to make sure Danny was okay.

I scurried through the gate. The police didn't do anything. On the other side, fences cut off an empty grassy lot. Beyond that were more brick row houses that looked older and crappier than on Dad's side. A red-and-yellow double-decker bus that said "City Sightseeing Belfast" roared by and took a right at the first intersection. Danny's street.

As I made for Danny's, I spotted the bonfire from the news in the middle of a muddy, garbage-littered lot. It had to be at least forty feet tall, a lot bigger than the one by the hotel. Today a massive Irish flag hung from the side with IRA on it, one letter in each color, along with some "*vótáil Sinn Féin*" posters like I'd seen in the Falls and Celtic jerseys like the ones that Seamus and Patrick always wore. All this not even a half a mile from Dad's house—and Danny's.

I hoped Danny wasn't helping to build that thing.

No, he wasn't like that.

Maybe... maybe I could even tell him the truth. Set *something* right. Danny would understand why I lied.

I ran to his street. It was lined on one side with row houses and the other by the wall. A little white sign that said Cupar Way sprouted from the sidewalk. Their street signs didn't have Irish and English like in the Falls. A tourist bus was parked along the peace wall where artist-caliber graffiti started. A bunch of them huddled under umbrellas as they wrote on the wall. Someone had painted in gold letters over the graffiti art: "It's time to kill all Republicans."

Goose bumps rippled up my arms. Maybe it was just some stupid kid. I slipped through a gate in the fence that separated Cupar Way from Danny's little side street and found his pebble-covered row house.

Before I had a chance to knock, the door popped open.

Danny had a swollen black eye and a busted lip. Half of his face was eggplant colored.

"You're not okay," I gasped.

Danny's eyebrows twitched. "You're soaked. Get in out of the rain."

I stepped into the stairwell; it was the same floor plan as Dad's house. Danny closed the door and locked it.

"You're worried about me?"

Danny scratched the back of his head. "Looks worse than it feels."

"Your dad did this."

The place was so thick with the stink of cigarettes and stale beer—and a faint trace of lemon—that I had to breathe through my mouth. A massive British flag hung above his torn couch. Yellow foam stuck out at the seams. Stains dotted the once-cream carpet. A red-white-and-blue flag that said Rangers hung on the other wall. Seamus and Patrick had been trash-talking that team a couple days ago. What would Danny think of the Celtic flag hanging on Seamus's wall?

"Em, sorry about the state of the place, like." Danny looked back. "Maybe I shouldn't have invited you. I'll grab you an umbrella so you can go back to your hotel."

The lie. I dug my nails into my palms. I couldn't fess up now, not after Danny had been beaten to a bloody pulp. What if he was seriously hurt? I hadn't even taken a babysitting class, let alone a first aid one. I didn't know how to fix him.

Danny continued, "I just wanted to see you and, and it's raining, and—"

"Should you, like, go to the doctor or something?"

His ears went red. "I've had some medical training. It's just bruises, perhaps a mild concussion."

Just like yesterday after I'd told him to run away, his voice hardened. It was like Finn; push too much, even with good intentions, and he'll shut you out.

A photo of a woman in a delicate silver frame by their unnecessarily massive TV caught my eye. "Is that your mom?"

"Oh, em, aye." His whole body relaxed.

Chewing the inside of my lip, I followed him deeper into the lair. Danny handed me the faded photo of a young blond girl with blue eyes and an oval face.

"She's beautiful. You look just like her."

"Em, thanks." Danny got that lopsided grin that filled my stomach with butterflies.

Then I realized the implications of what I'd just said. "I mean, not to say you're beautiful or anything."

Danny's grin widened. His swollen eye squeezed shut. Did it hurt to smile?

A shiver quaked through my body. My teeth chattered.

"Ah, here you are freezing, and here's me showing you pictures." He took the picture and set it on the TV stand, then adjusted it a centimeter. "Em, let's go to my room. And you needn't worry. There'll be no perving, I swear."

Upstairs, the stench of pee wafted out of the bathroom. Danny opened a door and ushered me in. He left it open a crack as if to signal that I could escape. His room smelled like him—fresh-cut grass with a bit of sweat, plus some overdone Axe. Just past his rain-streaked window was the peace wall. My house was just on the other side.

"Here, take your top off."

I raised an eyebrow.

"I mean, if you've another top on underneath and you don't want to wear that soaking one—"

"I'm just playing." I peeled it off. My Physics Club T-shirt was mostly dry. He draped the dripping hoodie over the radiator. I sat on his neatly made bed. Each mattress spring poked me. A British flag hung right next to me. At the foot of the bed was a shredded poster; one piece had a soldier with a medic armband.

"Will you take tea?" Danny asked.

"I don't drink tea." I just wanted some tape to fix his dream.

"Right, yous threw it all in the Boston Harbor." He opened his closet door. A drum sat on the floor and a navy-blue military-looking uniform hung from the rod. The brass buttons glistened. My leg twitched.

Danny held out a black McKenzie sweatshirt identical to the one Seamus wore pretty much daily.

"Thanks." I pulled it on and pushed my hands through the super long sleeves. I got dizzy off of the Danny smell.

Then I noticed his door had caved in the middle.

He followed my gaze and ran a hand through his hair. "If you want to leave—"

"Danny, relax." I studied his profile, his strong jaw, straight-edged nose, high cheekbones, and ears that were just a tiny bit too big. "I'm not going anywhere."

"Right." The bed creaked and sagged as he sat next to me. He winced.

I grabbed his huge hand, rough with callouses, and slipped my fingers between his. At least that wasn't bruised. Heat prickled up my arm. I tucked my fingers around the nape of his neck into his sandy-blond hair. His eyes closed. I gently brushed my lips between his swollen black eye and purple jaw. He trembled.

"Did I hurt you?"

Danny pressed his sweat-slick forehead against mine. Our noses touched. He shook his head. His warm breath tickled my upper lip. I wanted to kiss him, but then he straightened. My hand slipped from his neck, but his long fingers stayed laced with mine. "Da found out that I was planning to be a nursing officer. See, he doesn't want me joining the British army."

"But..." I pointed to the flag.

"The British government betrayed us when they signed the Good Friday Agreement and gave Republicans joint power. And now we've a former army council member as deputy first minister, even though he helped murder loads of people."

My gut wrenched.

"Da doesn't think I can do it, and he doesn't want me abandoning my culture." Danny sniffled, then wiped his nose with the back of his hand. "He took all the money for my plane ticket."

"That evil asshat! Call the cops. Do they have restraining orders here?"

"And what, be a tout on me own da?" The flash of fear in his eyes told me there were threats worse than his bruises. "They'd send social services. Put me in a boy's home."

"There must be somebody. Another relative? Friends?"

His palm grew sweaty against mine. He shook his head. "It's just a few more days."

"But how are you going to get the money?"

Danny's eyes fell to our knotted hands. "There might be a few people looking for help before the Twelfth."

I traced my fingers along his jaw, his stubbly cheek. Danny closed his eyes and pressed his hand over mine.

"How can I help?" I whispered. "There must be something."

Danny's eyes opened, and I fell into the pale-blue expanse. Heat swelled in my chest. I wanted to kiss him again.

"Can I show you something I never showed anyone before?" he asked.

"Sure."

Guilt lanced my heart. Yet again, Danny showing me everything while I hid behind lies.

With a grimace, he leaned over and grabbed a faded black backpack. He pulled out a blue book with a stork carrying a baby on the cover. Our arms touched. Electricity flowed between us. Danny flipped past a picture of his mom cuddling him in the hospital, pages about his favorite toys and stories, first tooth, a picture of him crawling. The page for first word was blank, and all the ones after it until the last one. A message from his mother.

"That's why I want to be an adult health nurse. To make her proud."

His life shattered my heart.

"Well, you rescued me from fainting in the street, so you're off to a good start."

"Aye, sure." A smile twitched on his lips. "But you were the one who bought me that burger."

I caressed the flesh between his thumb and pointer finger. "Don't let anything stop you from being who you want to be. Do whatever you have to do to get the money."

His eyes jumped up to me.

"Okay, I was a little dramatic. Don't rob a bank or anything."

Danny's eyebrows drew together. "Course not."

Silence swelled as his fingers tapped a beat on his thigh. I scrambled for something to say, but then…sometimes things were better left unsaid. Ugh, Dad and his precious words. I grabbed my phone from my hoodie pocket and held out an earbud. The corner of Danny's mouth pulled up as we popped in our earbuds. "Distant Sighs" filled the space between us. Danny tucked an arm around me. I rested my head against his chest, felt his slow heartbeat against my cheek. His breath came out shaky as his arm tightened around my waist. Martin Benjamin sang in his low, raspy voice as a banjo plucked in the background, "*You're miles away, but sitting right next to me. Silent, but I can hear your heart. Another sigh leaks through the line.*"

❦

When I opened Dad's front door, my whole family was waiting for me like a scene from *Intervention*.

"Hi." I shoved my hands into my hoodie pocket.

Dad let out one of his trademark sighs, eyes on his hands.

"You were in the Shankill," Patrick said, rolling an unlit cigarette between his fingers. Finn buried his face in Bucky's red-and-white-striped chest.

Crap.

Seamus sneered at me. "You went into that Hun's house. Jonty saw you."

I pressed my back against the wall. Icy fingers ran up my spinal cord. "Are you guys having people stalk me?"

"Those Orange wankers are beasts!" Red-faced, Seamus shouted close enough to fill my nose with the stench of cigarettes and beer.

"You don't even know him," I spat up at him, fists clenched.

Seamus brushed past me as he headed for the door. "Feck all, I don't care what happens to her, anyway."

That stung. "I don't care what happens to you either, little boy!"

He yanked the door open. "I'm not little!"

"It's an expression, dumbass!"

Seamus slammed the door behind him.

Bucky muffled Finn's high, tiny cries.

I darted upstairs. If they wanted to duke it out with me, fine, but it would be away from Finn. Dad's heavy footsteps pounded after me. He caught the door before I got it shut.

"Aren't you supposed to be at work?" I shot.

"I was, until I heard where you went." Dad's voice came out flat. I'd finally broken his perpetual cheer. "Even Paddy and Seamy have never gone there."

"Well, maybe they should. It's no different than here."

Dad's jaw tightened as he shook his head. "Does he know where you're from?"

"He knows I'm from the US."

"Does he know who I am?"

"He's a good guy."

Dad pressed his fist to his forehead. "I can't let you take that risk."

I folded my arms across my chest. "What are you trying to say?"

He let out a slow, heavy sigh. Probably trying to craft his treasured words into something that wouldn't piss me off. "You're only staying for a few more days at any rate. I don't want you seeing him again. For your own safety."

"I've done just fine without you the rest of my entire life. I don't need you telling me what to do now."

Dad pulled his silver-peppered curls. "You lied to me and went to the most dangerous place you could. What if something had happened to you?"

I hugged my arms tighter to my chest. "Nothing did."

"I'll take your mobile off you."

"Wait, are you trying to *ground* me?" I laughed in his face. "You lost your right to parent me because you're a murderer. And you don't pay my cell bill anyway."

Dad's face contorted like I'd slapped him, then went red. "I'm still your father, and you're under my roof."

The force of his words knocked me back a step. Shaking, I snapped, "One of your many bombs might have killed his mom!"

Dad's breath hitched. His face grayed.

"Now leave me alone."

To my complete shock, he withdrew and closed the door behind him. I hid the box of pictures under Seamus's bed, then buried myself under the covers, let them shield me from the world. How *dare* he think he got any say about my life.

Now I didn't feel bad at all about Seamus sleeping on the floor or Dad's crappy shoes.

I should go home tomorrow so I could get a job a few days sooner, because none of this even mattered.

Then come November, I'd be working with an astronomer at the world's largest radio telescope. Helping catalog radio waves from pulsars, track asteroids, record data from brown dwarfs. In a little over a year, I'd be moving to Cambridge and settling into a dorm specially selected for me based on my interests, surrounded by highly motivated, like-minded people. Strolling along the Charles River in between lectures. Standing below the oculus of the Great Dome in the rotunda of Barker Library reading room. I'd be able to get into any grad program I wanted.

None of this even mattered. Except Danny and Finn. Maybe I'd go home on the Eleventh after Danny left.

I'd find a way to see him again.

❧

When I opened my eyes, Bucky mean mugged me from the edge of my pillow. And, for the first time, wild curls poked out from under Finn's *Cars* comforter. My chest squeezed. Finn threw the comforter off. His freckled cheeks were pink. He smiled. I could fill my lungs again. That kid.

"Morning, Finn." I dropped to my knees beside his bed and held out Bucky. "Thanks for lending me Bucky. He kept the nightmares away."

Finn hugged him to his chest and beamed.

I stroked his chin. "I'm sorry I got so angry yesterday. I bet it was scary. You know it had nothing to do with you, right?"

Finn wrapped his arms around my neck, Bucky squished between us. His warm, baby-soft cheek pressed against mine. I hugged him back and breathed in his smell, secondhand smoke mixed with maple syrup. "I'd hang out with you for forever."

"Can you have breakfast with me?" he asked.

I let him go so I could see his face—make sure I hadn't just imagined that sweet, high voice.

Finn cocked his head to the side.

Tears filled my eyes. I loved that kid.

"Did I make you sad?" Finn tugged at the hem of his Captain America pajama shirt.

"No, you made me really happy. Yeah, let's get breakfast." I'd even face freaking Seamus for Finn.

But I was seeing Danny today. I threw on a pair of repurposed Levis and my favorite ever Goodwill find—a T-shirt featuring Ursa Minor—so I could slip out after breakfast. There were adults in the house, so I wasn't abandoning Finn. Through the kitchen window, the peace wall loomed. Danny was just a few feet away, but it might as well have been a hundred miles.

I made us some peanut butter toast while Finn colored. When I turned around with the plates, shirtless Patrick stood right behind me.

"Good morning, Fiona." Patrick dropped *To Kill a Mockingbird* on the table. My copy was still up on Seamus's bedside table. Patrick switched on the electric kettle. His entire back was covered with a tattoo featuring the words "*Tiocfaidh ár lá.*"

"Can we have a wee chat?"

"Dad struck out, so now you're up to bat." I rolled my eyes.

"For the record, I didn't tell Jonty to follow you. He saw where you were going and took it upon himself."

"Whatever."

"Look, you scared us."

"Why, because I am capable of looking beyond someone's religion?"

Patrick shot me an annoyed look as he pulled his curls into a man bun. "You know it's about history, not religious beliefs. And the vast majority of Protestants, just like most Catholics, want to move on. Working class folks from the Shankill, though . . . that lot are proud of their culture, and they don't care who it offends."

"You can't judge Danny based on what some people in his neighborhood do. That's discrimination."

"Right, get that." Patrick threw up his hands. "But you need to understand the context. The Troubles may seem like ancient history to you, and it is in the past, but that history still lives and breathes in some parts of Belfast."

"Yeah, I know."

He squinted at me. "I've grown up here. I've seen the truth. You haven't."

My knee bounced. "Danny's sweet and intelligent. He just graduated or whatever you call it over here. He's going to be a nurse. And he wasn't at the parade yesterday."

Patrick released a slow breath, shaking his head. "Finny, shall we have a wee *Star Wars* marathon?"

"Yay!" Finn bounced in his seat. "Can we watch the Ewok one first?"

Finn's voice melted my heart again.

Patrick eye's widened. He smiled as he mussed up Finn's hair. "Aye, sure. Start at the end."

Part of me already regretted what Fiona in five seconds was going to do, but I had to see Danny. I'd explain to Finn later.

The kettle switch clicked off. Patrick took out the box of tea bags from the cupboard. As he poured his precious tea, I darted for the front door.

I'd just tell Danny the truth. Prove them all wrong.

# chapter sixteen
## *Danny*

The next morning, my ribs still ached too much to do my sit-ups and press-ups. I stared at the light cast through the broken blinds onto my ceiling. All I had to do was sell a few ten deals, and then I'd be out of the UVF's reach in England.

Billy had been dealing for years, and he'd been lifted only four times. He was right about my odds. Ma would probably say it was wrong, but Fiona said do whatever it takes. It was me doing a bit of wrong so I could do a whole lot of good. I wasn't forcing them to be drug addicts. They'd buy it somewhere anyway.

Marty would probably be at the Supporter's Club. I could stop there before meeting Fiona.

I threw on my last clean clothes, sprayed myself with Billy's Lynx, and took some paracetamols. My stomach was too knotted up for food; a rare situation. Before I left, I dumped some of Da's whiskey into a water bottle. My nerves might need a bit of drink to get through my first day as a drug dealer. I put it in my rucksack with everything that mattered in my life—my baby book, passport, and my enlistment papers.

As I walked up Lawnbrook, the gray clouds looked ready to piss down.

"Oi!" wee Malcolm called from the gate to the Supporters' Club, a huge grin on his pudgy face. "Danny Boy, what about ye. Here, did you see Napalm Pimp beat Brock the Rock in *SmackDown* last night?"

"Class like." I nodded toward the Supporter's Club. "I better not leave Marty waiting."

"Sure, I'll finish telling you when you're done. I'm keeping lookout."

I pulled the door open. The burst of fresh air failed to fight back the stench of old, musty beer. Yellowed strip lights tried to eat away at the dim coolness, but the brick walls must've absorbed most of it because it was a cave in there. A spotlight reflected off the Battalion of the Dead mirror honoring the volunteers that got killed in the Troubles and the wars.

Smirking, Marty looked me over from his usual booth.

I shoved my hands into my pockets to stop myself drumming. "Okay."

"Okay what?"

I puked out the words, "I'll take you up on your offer."

Marty spread his arms on the back of the booth, revealing his sweaty pits.

Oh, feck sake. "Please, Marty."

Marty took a swig of Tennent's. "The Republicans get everything, and what do we get? Fuck all. They want us ruled by Rome. It's about time you joined the fight."

All selling drugs did was line Marty's pocket, but I didn't say so. *See, Billy? I can control my gob.*

He reached into a black holdall and tossed a bag of blues on the table. “Tenner a pill. You’re to hang round Europa Bus Centre.”

“That’s right by the police station.”

He shot me a toothless grin. “I take the busiest spot off that wee shit Anto for you, and that’s how you thank me?”

I shut my gob.

Marty dropped a blue baseball cap with a B on it. “That’s to show yourself to the customers. Your cut is three quid a pill.”

I snatched up the hat and bag of ten deals. As I left, I caught Ma’s picture staring at me from the wall commemorating all the people killed by the IRA. Ma was about sixteen in the picture. It had been taken just before she had Billy.

I’d walked by that picture a thousand times; she smiled like always, but today her eyes looked sad.

I’m sorry.

As I stepped into the soggy morning, Malcolm chased after me. “Hey, Danny! I’ve not told you about Napalm Pimp’s finishing move. Wait up, Marty’ll be cross if I leave the area.”

“Sorry, gotta get on with the day.” I legged it down the Shankill Road, each foot impact stabbing my side, but at least I was getting in some fitness training. Rain rattled the Union Jack bunting and ran down my face, but it couldn’t cool the burning in my chest. Forty frigging pills, that’s what I had to sell. The ten deals weighed down my pocket.

I should go to work straightaway, but Fiona said she was slipping out for a few minutes to see me. Replaying the sensation of Fiona’s lips brushing between my bruises fought back the pain. But everything I knew about Fiona told me she wouldn’t be too keen on kissing a drug dealer.

By the time I got to the city centre, the clouds had broken into shockingly clear blue skies and it was proper warm.

Fiona brought the sun.

I checked my reflection in a window of the Crown Bar. My eye opened a bit more. I ran a hand through my hair and tried to spike it up. When I got to the City Hall, Fiona was lying under my tree, hair fanned round her head. She jumped to her feet when she saw me, that heart-melting grin on her face. A rush of heat blazed through me so fast I got light-headed. More than anything, I wanted to kiss her. If she'd any idea how often I dreamt of touching her in places I'd only seen in Billy's dirty magazines, she'd know the dark truth that I really was a pervert. But with Fiona, it wasn't about that.

Fiona put a hand on my chest and got on her tiptoes to inspect my face. My heart drummed to the beat of a multiple bounce roll.

"No new bruises, I swear."

Fiona's eyes lingered with suspicion.

"So, em, want to see Big Fish?" I asked in case she was bored of sitting in the same spot. "It's a sculpture. It's not really that exciting, but I dunno, I thought maybe you'd like it. Unless you've already seen it while touristing."

"Haven't seen it." Fiona frowned at the grass.

"Are you all right?"

She put on a smile that felt too bright. "Peachy."

I wanted to take her hand, but she walked in my shadow as we cut across the lawn, head down. Today, she wore red Converse, ripped jeans, and a T-shirt, not her running clothes. She'd little legs, so I took smaller strides, but still she drifted away. Perhaps she'd x-ray vision and saw the drugs in my pocket. Instead of reaching for her hand, I gripped the straps of my rucksack.

A double-decker bus roared by as we passed the shops. Her loose curls danced around her face. She brushed the strands behind her ears. "So, did you find any more jobs?"

All I could muster was a shrug.

Fiona's brows furrowed as she chewed the inside of her lip. Her fingers pried mine from the strap and squeezed the back of my hand. Tingles spread from my hand through my entire body as we passed the Albert Clock.

"And there's the Big Fish." I nodded toward the ten-foot-long, blue tile fish sculpture across the street.

She swung our arms. "It's more of a medium fish."

I laughed.

When the green man appeared, we ran across hand in hand like a proper boyfriend and girlfriend. Pain sliced my ribs. I steadied my voice. "Each piece's got a different news article about the history of Belfast."

Her palm slipped from mine, and my whole body got cold. "That's cool." Fiona inspected the blue-and-white ceramic tiles, her nose an inch away. "Never knew you were a tour guide *and* a paramedic."

"My primary school helped make some of the tiles back in the nineties."

We walked round the fish and sat on the steps facing the River Lagan. Sunlight danced off the water as boats slowly drifted under the bridges. Couples, mums and their kids, and grannies walked by, but it was only me and Fiona in the whole world, and the smell of fish.

"See those yellow cranes over there that say H&W?" I pointed past the bridge. "That means hello and welcome."

Her freckled nose wrinkled.

"Right, so it actually stands for Harland and Wolff. The *Titanic* was built at that shipyard."

"Thanks, personal tour guide." Fiona caressed my bruised cheek.

A shiver ran down my spine. *Keep it together, Danny Boy.*

"So you're leaving tomorrow. If—when—you get the money."

I caught my fingers drumming the rudiment to "The Sash" on my thigh. "Aye."

Fiona picked at the colorful bands round her wrist. Her eyebrows knit. "I'll miss you."

My heart grew ten sizes bigger. "I'll miss you too." I traced my finger along her chin and tilted her face toward me. Those beautiful hazel eyes locked onto mine. I cradled the back of her head and kissed her hard, my nose pressing into her warm, soft cheek.

A horn blared from a passing water taxi as it slid under the Lagan Weir footbridge.

She pulled away giggling, cheeks pink. "What?"

Grinning, I shook my head. Words didn't exist for how I felt. I ran my fingers through her soft hair.

Fiona slipped a band from her wrist and slid it onto mine. Her fingertips traced the back of my hand. "So you don't forget my favorite color."

It was purple, but I didn't even care what wankers like Anto might say. I felt giddy, drunk, but this was a thousand times better than actually being drunk. "I wish I had something for you to remember me by."

Her fingers wove around mine. "I won't forget you."

"Even when you're back in America with all those American footballers?"

"Not really into jocks." Fiona squeezed my hand. "You'll still have access to the internet when you're in the army, right?"

I was utterly gobsmacked.

Her face went the most brilliant shade of red. "I mean, unless you'll be too busy saving lives to talk to a boring high schooler."

I threw up a hand. "No, no, I'll be waiting for every message with bated breath."

Fiona looked up at me through a veil of gold-tipped eyelashes.

Our faces were so close I could almost feel the heat from her skin. She pressed her lips against mine. Her heavy breath warmed my upper lip as her tongue gently opened my mouth and caressed mine. She tasted like mint.

My arms slid around her narrow waist. After our lips parted, I said, "You've no idea how much I fancy you. When I'm with you, I can forget everything. I never felt this way round anyone else."

"Really?" Her head nuzzled into my shoulder and the world was her warmth and apple shampoo and soft brown curls tickling my arm.

"Fiona," a man growled from a distance.

Fiona's gaze snapped to the footbridge. Some short lad with a chain on his jeans glowered in our direction. The color drained from her face. She broke free of my arms and jogged over to him. It had to be her brother—they looked almost identical—but I'd never seen a tourist in an O'Neills top.

Red-faced, he gestured at me as he spoke to her.

Back to me, Fiona clenched her fists. "You could have just trusted me to be an actual adult!"

I sprung to my feet. "You wee prick. Leave her alone."

That short twat's eyes shot bullets at me. "She's my sister!"

Her brother had a Belfast accent, and that top meant he was a Catholic. What the hell was going on? Her *brother*?

"What, did she tell you she's American, then? She was born here." He smirked. "She's from up the Falls, and our da's Peter Kelly."

The dirty, lying prick.

"Danny." Fiona ran to me.

"Tell me he's lying." I was shaking.

Her face crushed as her head drooped.

"Tell me he's full of shit," my voice quaked.

"I was going to tell you."

Ma's blond hair soaked in blood, blue eyes dead, pieces of her body scattered across the street. A closed casket, Da said. They'd never charged anyone with the bomb that killed Ma, but everyone knew. My heart hammered into my rib cage so hard it almost snapped my bruised ribs.

"So it's true, then."

Fiona's heel jumped to a steady beat, her shoe laces bouncing off the footpath.

"So it's Peter frigging Kelly who took you to Giant's Causeway."

"I'm sorry I lied. I only found out about his past the day I met you. And I *hate* what he did." Fiona's American accent cut through to me." But he... he was a volunteer, and he's been trying to make things better." She reached out for me, but I stepped back.

"Those fellas that bombed the Twin Towers, were they volunteers too?"

Fiona's chin trembled.

My body shivered with adrenaline. "My ma's six feet under. Your da did a few years and now he's walking round with his wee daughter like nothing happened. He stole everything from me. He doesn't deserve to breathe!"

Fiona paled as her eyebrows arched.

And that Taigy wanker was sneering at me like he'd won the World Cup. I wanted to smash his skull into a bloody pulp.

I had to go. I had to go right now.

"Danny..." Tears filled her honey-flecked eyes.

"I told you the things I hid from *everyone else*." My fists were ready to fly. "And you lied. Over and over."

I started walking. Electric pain snaked up my sides. I dug the whiskey out of my rucksack and let it rip down my throat and fill my chest with burning.

"Danny, wait. I know I lied, but I did it because I was afraid..."

I stopped and looked back. "Of what?"

Her eyes fell to my bottle, then she cuffed her tears away with her tiny freckled wrist. "That you'd lose your shit."

"I don't need you or your murderer father. I'm getting out."

"But . . . like five seconds ago, you totally just shrugged when I asked about jobs."

"Maybe there's no legal ones."

Her lip curled like I was a pile of rubbish. "What, like drugs?"

"I'm doing whatever I have to do."

"Oh, my God, you are! Are you in one of those racist bands that pee in people's yards too?"

"Aye, fuck away off to your 'RA scumbag daddy." As I walked away, I took another long drink of whiskey.

"Screw you!" she yelled at my back. "They were right!"

"Feck up, you dirty wee Taig!" I punched a lamppost.

# chapter seventeen
## *Fiona*

That red-faced, hate-filled drug dealer couldn't be Danny. It *couldn't*. But it was.

I stood there frozen by Big Fish like I'd been jettisoned into the vacuum of space. Tears poured down my cheeks as I watched Danny's tall, lanky form disappear behind a sandstone brick building. And I'd thought Mom was the doppelgänger.

"Fiona." Patrick jogged up to me. His voice had lost its mocking tone.

"What's a Taig?"

Patrick's wallet chain jingled against his skinny jeans. "You don't need to worry yourself with that."

I clenched my fists. "God, everyone stop *saying* that!"

"It's a bad word for us."

"I'm, like, barely one of you."

Patrick's eyes wandered to the direction Danny had gone. "Doesn't matter to the likes of him."

"I want to go home."

"Da's or Madison?"

I needed to be real Fiona again, not Belfast Fiona. I needed Nevaeh and Zion. I needed to mow a crap-ton of lawns. I scrubbed my eyes to force the tears back into my tear ducts. "Madison. I'm deleting all this bullshit from my brain."

"Fiona..."

I stormed over to the waiting taxi. Patrick messed on his phone the whole ride. When we got back to Dad's, I braced myself for his anger from yesterday times ten. For Seamus to cuss me out.

But instead, I walked into the usual scene. Men's underwear drying all over the place. Seamus drinking Guinness. Chipped teacups and coloring books covering the coffee table. I craned my neck to see into the kitchen; no sign of Dad.

Finn launched into Patrick's arms.

"Did you run in your jeans?" Finn asked.

Patrick must have covered for me and Seamus just glowered at the TV. My face flushed as relief cooled my veins. I ran up the stairs two at a time.

Maybe Finn could come visit in Madison.

I started throwing clothes into my suitcase.

My phone vibrated.

And I hated—hated—how my heart swooped, hoping it was Danny. A sensation of Danny's lips lightly brushing mine invaded my brain.

I snatched my phone off Seamus's bed.

`NevaehAngel: Zion asked me out!!!! Squeeeeeeeeeeeeee`

My heart plunged to the floor.

Whatever. Screw Danny. I rammed the memory back into the abyss.

Zion's dad had a criminal history, but Zion worked his butt off legally to help his family pay bills. He was still probably going to beat me out for valedictorian. Granted, Zion's dad actually loved him and pushed him to be everything he hadn't been. And Zion wasn't surrounded by a bunch of bigoted adults reinforcing his dad's formerly unwholesome views. But still, Danny had no excuses for selling drugs. For the way he'd treated me.

A gentle rap came on Seamus's door. "Fiona," Dad said softly, "can we talk?" It wasn't anger that laced his voice; it was desperation.

"There is literally nothing you can say to get me to stay." I zipped my suitcase.

A heavy sigh leaked under the door, but his feet didn't move.

I tossed *To Kill a Mockingbird* into my messenger bag. Under it was the old picture of all of us on the beach. I picked it up. Dad's proud smile before the scar, Patrick's arms protecting me.

Dad had been scared for my safety yesterday. He'd risked my anger, our relationship, to protect me from this.

I set the picture on the bedside table. "Fine."

Dad limped in wearing his Translink fleece. As he sat on the end of Seamus's bed, his eyes fell to my suitcase. His whole being wilted.

"What, here to do your touchdown dance?"

Dad's eyebrows rose, but his gaze didn't move. "Not quite sure what that means."

"It means rub it in already." Tears blurred the swimsuit model posters. I scraped them away. "Danny blamed me for everything you did."

Dad's head slowly pulled up. Red rimmed his tired eyes. "I never want you to be in pain."

"Well, here's another strike against that."

Dad was a statue as he frowned at his leathery hands folded between his knees, probably mulling over his precious words. God, why couldn't he be angry at me?

He cleared thick-sounding phlegm from his throat. "This boy, he can't help how he was brought up. In a few parts of Belfast, we've passed the legacy of the Troubles on to the next generation."

"Wait, are you *defending* Danny now?"

A sigh slowly leaked through his nose. "It's com—"

"Don't. Even."

Dad's head bowed.

If it was like this nowadays, I couldn't even imagine how bad things were back in the day. Dad had been Finn's age when he was burned out of his house by a mob of his neighbors. And that was just one of the horrible things he had to endure. I thought back to the black-and-white mural. "Oppression breeds resistance; resistance brings freedom."

I couldn't even imagine what all that would have done to me. *Fact*: Dad hadn't wanted to kill people. That I did believe.

Dad pressed his folded hands to his forehead like he was praying. "Please stay."

He looked at me. Sunlight highlighted bits of green in his tear-filled eyes that matched mine.

The hair on my arms stood on end.

God, he loved me so much. *Fact*: I wasn't sure I wanted to delete him from my life.

"Fine."

Dad's chin trembled. He squeezed his eyes closed and nodded.

My phone vibrated. Again, that disgusting hope swelled in my chest.

Dad cleared his throat and stood with a flinch. "Well, it looks like you've a call. I'll see to tea."

ZionMcD: I kinda asked out Nevaeh. Hope that doesn't make things weird...

It was selfish, but their happiness made Danny sting even more. A tiny, desperate part of me wanted to message Danny. I remembered what he'd screamed at me as he left. I responded to Zion.

FionaRuns: It's about freaking time. She's been crushing on for you for like five years.
ZionMcD: Whuuuuu???? Why didn't you tell me?
FionaRuns: Can't break a Best Friends for Freaking Ever promise. Sorry, bro.
ZionMcD: How are things with Belfast Boy?
FionaRuns: Don't ask
ZionMcD: Boarding a plane.

I almost laughed.

ZionMcD: What happened?

I couldn't go there with Zion. On so many levels.

Mom would know what to say. She always did. My eyes fell to the picture of us on the beach. Dad grinning as he hugged Mom. Seamus attached to Mom's hip.

*Fact*: Mom's family had been in the IRA forever; they raised her supporting it. She'd grown up walking the streets fearing drive-bys and UVF bombs, the people who lived twenty feet away, and the police and army—people who normally protected you. Mom's brother had been murdered by the UVF. If I'd lived through all that, maybe I'd believe the ends justified the means too. That Dad was a hero. *But, also fact*: Mom sacrificed her home, her husband, and Seamus and Patrick to save lives, to save the peace process. She could have just kept looking the other way, but she didn't.

I Skyped Mom.

The phone rang for less than ten seconds, then the screen filled with a face as familiar as my own. Light filtered through the maple leaves outside the bay window, shadows of leaves dancing on the living room wall behind her. Mom's face split into a tremulous grin. "Hi, sweetheart."

I set the phone on my stomach and draped my arm over my burning eyes. "Hi."

"Are you okay?"

My knee bounced off the pink comforter. "Not really."

I told her what had happened—all of it, more or less. Her eyes widened, and more than once she almost spoke but didn't.

"I wish I could be there for you."

"Me too."

"Sweetheart, maybe you should come home tomorrow."

"Dad and I talked it out."

The specter of a smile tugged on her lips. "As terribly as I've missed you, sweetheart, I'm glad." Mom gently cleared her throat. "And I can understand why it seems like I'm a different person, but I'm still the same boring mom who spends her Saturday nights doing paint-by-numbers. It's near killed me all these years, letting you hurt." Moisture rimmed her eyes; all I could think about was shattering plates.

You can't cry—you're the one holding my universe together. My chin quivered as my throat tightened.

"Your dad and I, we made the choices we thought were best, and the pieces fell where they did. And the thing I regret most is how much you, Patrick, and Seamus have suffered because of us." Her eyes squeezed closed. Tears rolled down her cheeks.

Aftershocks rattled me from across the world as her armor shattered. Warm tears streaked down my cheeks too.

Mom pushed up her glasses and rubbed her eyes. "You have a right to be angry. Perhaps I should have trusted your beautiful brain with the truth. But I'm glad you know now."

I could almost smell her apple shampoo. I sniffled and cuffed my tears away.

Mom looked exactly the same as she did when I left almost two weeks ago, but now I knew the ghosts that made her tough and vulnerable at the same time. I'd walked the streets that forged her. Now I felt like I actually knew her.

Mom drew in a shaky breath. Her lips pressed into a small smile that quickly faded. "So this boy."

"Yeah, so that was a mistake."

"We all make mistakes. It's dangerous to open your heart to someone, but life's too short to keep it locked away."

After we hung up, I blocked Danny so I never had to worry about hearing from him again.

# chapter eighteen
## *Danny*

Wearing that frigging baseball cap, I sat against the wall in between the double doors connecting the bus station to the Great Northern Mall. I hugged my rucksack to my chest in case any wee shit got any ideas about nicking it. The brightness from the station tried to fight back the heavy dimness from the shops.

As the hours passed, a bus or train would come, bring a wave of people, and then the station would empty. My head was swimming in whiskey as I waited for a peeler to grab me and ruin everything. But at least I felt nothing about Fiona—or the texts I got from Sinclair asking after my plane ticket.

The lad behind the Café Bar counter shot me dirty looks like he thought I might set the place alight. I hugged my rucksack tighter. How long could I blatantly loiter in the same place and not raise suspicion?

Then all I could think of was Fiona and her lies and her soft strawberry lips on mine and her fecking papist brother and the way her freckled nose wrinkled when she laughed and that she kept asking if I was okay, which nobody ever did. And the gold specks in her eyes.

Her da was Peter Kelly.

“Oi, mate.”

I dragged my head up. Liquor blurred the world. I squinted to focus my eyes on a shower of twats in polos from somewhere posh like Marks & Spencer. The fat one with an acne problem looked me over. Here it was, Danny’s first deal. A Kodak moment for Da. I dragged myself up, but my head was not properly attached to my body.

That fat twat sneered like it was me who was disgusting. “You’re new. Where’s the wee scumbag with the fake gold chain?”

His three mates sniggered. Anyone round the Shankill talked rubbish about Anto and I’d join in, but coming from that lot of bastards with their boat shoes, I almost lost my rag.

I gritted my teeth. “How many?”

“Ten.”

“Hundred.”

“What? Your dirty wee friend with the pencil arms, he sells them for seven.”

*Liar*. I stood up to my full height. *Keep your calm; don’t prove Billy right*. “A tenner each.”

Fat Twat’s friend with spiky hair leant over and whispered, “Just pay him. We’ve a bus to catch.”

Fat Twat scowled as he dug out the cash from his pocket.

Loads of people were coming and going, but nobody cared about us. My fingers were a bit numb, but I got the baggie open and found ten pills. We did this fruity handshake and I pressed the pills into his soft, sweaty palm. He slid me the cash.

They walked through the sliding glass doors, laughing like Foster’s shower of gobshites, and loaded a bus bound for

Donegal—where all the Taigs and middle-class Protestants went for the Twelfth. I hoped they got caught, but I knew the peelers never randomly searched tossers like them.

I'd made thirty pounds profit, but now I'd officially become a drug dealer for the UVF. The notes were dirty, oily in my pocket. What Fiona's da had done was a million times worse than selling a couple blues, but she'd stood there defending *him*.

As I staggered home, I chucked my stomach off the bridge over the Westlink.

Thoughts of Fiona and her 'RA daddy who killed people like my ma splattered on the road below with my sick. My hand was smarting. I'd punched that lamppost. I could keep all the profits from today if I steered clear of Marty. Then I'd need to make only twenty quid tomorrow.

But Peter Kelly was walking free, taking his wee daughter to Giant's Causeway while Ma got no justice. And I was about to join the British army—for the government that let the man who murdered Ma go free.

Maybe Billy was right. Me off in other countries? I'd never left Northern Ireland. I couldn't go off to some other place where people didn't even speak English and they might not have fish-and-chips. Plus I hadn't a clue which fork to use when, so I was screwed when it came time for the formal dinner at my Main Board.

And I didn't want to be surrounded by poncy twats in boat shoes.

Da was at work, so I nipped home and hid my rucksack and the drugs in the attic. Da was too fat to be arsed to look up there. When I came out, Mr. Sinclair's Volkswagen sat parked out front. Ah, bollocks, I couldn't deal with him too.

"Danny, wait."

A car door opened behind me.

Sinclair jumped in front of me. For the first time ever, he was wearing jeans.

"What happened to your face?"

I shouldered past him. Pain stabbed my ribs at impact.

"Are you drunk?" He followed me. "Your Main Board is in thirty-six hours. Have you got your ticket?"

"Piss off."

Mr. Sinclair pushed up his glasses. "Let me help you."

"Why don't you feck off and buck your wife for once so you can have your own kids to stalk!"

Sinclair's jaw tightened as red spread across his face.

Clarity cut through the fog. All he'd done for me. I couldn't see his face for one more second. "Leave me alone, or I'll call child protection and say you touched me up, you dirty knob jockey!"

Mr. Sinclair seethed, his breath coming out in shaky bursts. "Call me when you're sober, you wee shit." He went back to his car.

On the way to the boney, I finished off my whiskey.

"Remember, Danny, keep her lit, keep her safe," Community Organizer Rob, all official in his *Shankill Options* jacket, said as he scribbled something on his clipboard.

Four tricolors and a Celtic flag fluttered on top. Near the base was a massive sign that said "No surrender 1690," the year King Billy won the Battle of the Boyne. The boney dwarfed the houses behind—our biggest yet. They'd have to board up their windows this year.

I spotted Jon and some of the other band lads near the guard hut. They'd have beer. I headed past the shrinking piles of tires and pallets.

"Alright, mate, how's it going?" Davey tipped his baseball cap at me.

"Ooh, the professor's blessing us with his presence." Anto's eyes twitched. He was off his face again.

"The feck you looking at?" I grabbed a Dutch Gold from the twelve pack. I drained it straightaway and chucked the tin in a puddle.

"Danny, where were you last night? Me and Davey had ourselves some good craic," wee Jamie said. A shiny, new gold medallion hung round his scrawny neck.

"Same place as during the riot and the Whiterock parade." Anto sniggered. "Hiding at home like the posh wanker he wishes he was."

I shoved him, and he staggered back a few steps. "You shut up or I'll knock your bollocks in, right!"

Then Jon was in my face. "What's eating you?"

I pushed past him and grabbed a pallet from one of the rows. A splinter cut through my skin. I braced it on my shoulder and cut across the wasteland, my shoes sinking into the mud. I hoisted it up to two lads. They passed it up to the next pair of lads.

Jon came back with tins bursting out of his trackie bottom pockets. "Beat it down you."

We worked for hours. The drink kept me from getting sore. And then I was almost crying. I sat in the mud and buried my face in my muddy hands as all the alcohol made my head spin round and slam to a stop over and over again.

"Feck sake, Danny, what's your problem?" Jon nudged me with his toe.

"Her da," I said through my hands.

"Who's da, the wee American bird? What are you on about?"

"He's Peter Kelly."

A snigger. Frigging Anto. "I told you she was a Taig."

I sprang to my feet and threw an uppercut right into his jaw.

"Say one more thing and I'll beat your head in!" I screamed at Anto's back as he scarpered, Buckie spilling with each step. My knuckles smarted again. It felt good.

"Have you a death wish?" Jon asked.

"Shut up." I took his beer off him and finished it.

Shaking his head at me, Jon pulled out his mobile. "Peelers takin' down our flags in East Belfast."

It was the Taigs that hit a wee boy in the face with a rock on the mini-Twelfth. *Belfast Telegraph* never talked about that.

I chucked my empty tin in the mud. "Right, let's go, then." I knew as well as Jon did that this meant a riot would be starting.

Jon squinted at me. "But what about getting lifted?"

"That's political policing, taking down our country's flag. They never touch them tricolors hanging in all the Taig estates."

Jon looked me over like I'd sprouted a third head. "Are you certain? Aren't you away tomorrow for your wee test?"

"Shut your teeth."

"Right." Jon threw his hands up. "Davey'll give us a lift."

I tried to follow Jon across the wasteland, but it was tricky because the world was spinning. The sound in my ears wobbled as I focused on putting one foot in front of the other.

"Here, Danny Boy's back." Davey handed me a bottle of Smirnoff. "Happy birthday, mucker."

Right, I was eighteen now. I twisted off the cap and gulped it down so fast my eyes watered.

"Yeooooo!" All the lads cheered except Jon with his sour-looking gob.

We loaded up in Davey's naff Vauxhall Astra. I got squished in the back between Jon and Jamie, who reeked. Had his ma never told him about deodorant? He was thirteen, for Christ's sake.

Laughing like a buck eejit, Davey swerved round a bus and near took out a lady getting out of her car. Everything outside was moving slower than it should've been. I took another drink, vodka stinging my throat. Dubstep rattled from his desperate speakers.

Jamie, that wee knob, bounced in his seat. "Lemme take a petrol bomb to one of them'uns' houses this time. Unwashed Taigs—we'll show 'em."

I'd called Fiona a Taig, and she'd cried her wee lamps out.

I pressed the mobile to my forehead but couldn't feel it.

"What?" Jon lit up a cigarette.

Coals burnt in my chest. I gulped down more vodka. A quarter was gone. Had I drunk all that?

Jon watched me, face all scrunched up. He tried to take away my birthday present, but I wrestled it back.

The throbbing bass was making my head bang.

Davey sped across the bridge over the River Lagan. I could almost see Big Fish past the Lagan Weir. We passed terraces with Union Jacks and UVF flags; behind them, there was another peace wall between us and the Short Strand. He slammed to a stop by the UDA mural demanding the release of East Belfast Loyalist prisoners. We all climbed out. The H&W cranes glowed in the distance.

Hello and welcome? What a shit joke.

Jon was looking at me sideways again. "You all right, mate?"

I tossed back more vodka.

"Yeooooo!" everyone cheered. Alcohol pressed out against my veins.

"Look at Danny, he's a friggin' rocket!" Anto laughed.

The sun sunk below the horizon as we ran for Albertbridge Road. A wave of hot, messy drunkenness clean knocked me over. Streetlights buzzed on. Jon pulled a red scarf from his back pocket and tied it over his nose. Shaking his head, he handed me one too. My fingers weren't cooperating as I tied mine round my face. I tried to take another wee drink, but I'd lost my vodka.

"Look who's finally here." Marty slapped me on the back. Where'd he come from? He wore his *Shankill Options* jacket, which he usually had on when he decided to stop us fighting by our interfaces.

I flipped my hood up and charged through the throbbing mass. A rush spread through my blood. The buzz. The craic. I closed in on the police cordon. Barren lampposts. They'd already stolen our flags; proof that if you're law abiding, they'll still take it away. Those Taigs rioted, the Parades Commission rerouted our parades. Ulster was British. We should be able to fly our flags wherever we wanted.

Rocks clattered. Bottles shattered. A line of armored Land Rovers sat across the six lanes. Their pulsing lights flashed against the failing daylight. Taigs rioted on the other side; I could hear them lobbing shite and shouting. A bottle rocket shrieked and popped. Marty pulled on a balaclava. We burst through to the front line.

Dozens of us faced off against the PSNI. They were dressed in full riot kits, backlit by the blazing headlights. The police's clear plastic shields formed a wall. The water cannon stood ready, its floodlights on us.

Jon launched an empty beer bottle at the peelers.

A lad climbed up on top of a Land Rover and tried to cover the camera with a crisp packet.

"Bobby Sands is dead!" Jamie shrieked, voice cracking, as he, Davey, and Anto forced their way through the line and started kicking a Land Rover.

"Feck the PSN-IRA!" yelled Davey as he went buck mental on one's window with a brick.

A fist-sized bit of masonry ricocheted off a peeler's shield and rolled back a few meters to my feet. I grabbed it and pitched it at the line of police. "No surrender," I screamed so loud it hurt my vocal cords.

Something blazed. A wave of heat warmed my face. The crowd moved back. Smoke and flames curled out of a Corsa with busted windows.

"Disperse or we'll use the water cannon," a peeler said over a crackling loudspeaker.

"Yeoooo!" a hooded, masked boy shouted as he gave the peelers the finger with both fists. "Hullo, Hullo. We are the Billy Boys..."

Everyone followed. I sang it too.

"Hullo, Hullo. You'll know us by our noise..."

"Here, mate." Marty handed me a petrol bomb and a lighter. My hands were numb. It took three tries to light the flannel at the end. The fumes made my head spin. The brightness hurt my eyes as heat radiated through the glass.

I swung my arm back and lobbed it. My petrol bomb left a trail of flame as it streaked toward the police line. It struck a shield and exploded into a ball of fire that faded to nothing in a second.

I'd just thrown a bottle of flaming petrol at another person.

"Yeoooo!" a bunch of the lads yelled.

A sharp burst of cold water threw me. My back slammed into the pavement. Water filled my mouth and nose. I coughed it out as I scrambled to my feet.

Then an ear-shattering pop echoed off the terraces. I dropped to my knees. A gunshot—automatic rifle by the sound of it. When I was twelve, Da let me shoot a Sten gun up at Uncle Jim's.

The first time I'd fired, I thought I'd burst my eardrums, and I'd almost got knocked over by the kickback.

Another and another explosive clack ricocheted off the building. It came from their side. A scream from our side.

The line of PSNI facing us thinned as some of them cut between the Land Rovers to the Catholic side.

A hand grabbed my arm and pulled me back. "Let's go, ya wee melter. Dissos are shooting at us." Jon dragged me through the crowd. "And you've lost your scarf."

I touched my face with my numb fingers. Had I lost it before the petrol bomb? Peelers were always taking pictures and prosecuting later.

Water squished out of my Adidas, and my soaking trackie bottoms stuck to my skin. My hair was plastered to my forehead. I shivered. The shouts and shattering glass and rushing water faded as the crowd thinned to lads and girls drinking and smoking. I felt drunk again. Had I finished that bottle of vodka? What happened to that thing, anyway?

Then Da materialized. "Least you're finally ready to do your bit."

I coughed water out of my lungs and spit it at curb.

Marty's shiny new blue BMW 3 series pulled up, the streetlamp reflecting off the windscreen. Where'd he get himself that fancy car? My head got five times bigger all the sudden, and my vision went fuzzy. Then all the vodka caught up to me and I was drowning. In a car. Marty's swanky new car. With Da and Gusty. Had I taken too much drink? Where was Jon?

"The state of wee Danny. Sure he's about to boak."

They were laughing. At me. I was going to be sick. Groaning, I pressed my forehead against the cool glass. I couldn't get to my pocket to check my mobile. I wanted Fiona. I put a finger on the wee purple bracelet she'd given me.

Now they were singing, "Oh bouncy, bouncy, bouncy, la la la la la!"

That was my favorite Rangers song apart from "The Sash." I tried to sing along. They laughed. My head sank against my chest.

Lights spilt through a window. "Campbell Tattoo" was a shadow on the footpath. We were at Marty's tattoo shop. A door dinged. They pulled me inside. To a chair.

"Let's give Danny a wee birthday present, now that he's ready to be a man."

Da remembered it was my birthday?

I was going to be sick all over Marty's shop.

More laughing. It was too bright. It hurt my eyes. Music blared out, some kind of rock music.

Da pulled my wet hoodie over my head. My arms were lead. My birthday present. A tattoo.

"Do a Rangers flag," I said. Even in my state I knew it better not be something sectarian. The army would never let me in with something like what Da and Marty had on their arms.

A high, whining buzz. Cat's claws scratching my upper arm. I flinched. Marty grinned at me like a half-toothed Cheshire cat as he pressed the tattoo gun into my skin again.

Da held my arm down. "Get my boy a wee drink."

❧

I woke up with my cheek stuck to the toilet seat by coagulated drool. My cold, damp trackie bottoms chafed me.

My mouth had that sticky, sour taste, and my head pounded. The world spun; I was either still drunk or majorly hung over. Or could you be both at the same time?

I tried to sift through the black haze of last night. Had I drunk a bottle of Smirnoff?

My fingers smelt of petrol.

Shite, I'd gone down to the riot. I'd thrown petrol bombs at the peelers—mums and das and brothers and sisters just trying to do their jobs. And I claimed to want to help people on the front lines.

The room started to spin again. My stomach pitched, and I filled the stained toilet bowl. I pressed my face to the cool seat.

I wanted to die.

Christ, I was never drinking again.

What else had happened?

Fiona's da was Peter Kelly, and I'd called her a Taig and made her cry. I'd told Sinclair to sod off. I'd a hundred quid in my pocket, but seventy was meant to go to Marty.

Another wave of nausea rumbled in my gut. I groaned and pressed the heels of my hands into my sweat-covered forehead. As my hoodie sleeve grazed my bicep, my skin screamed like I'd burnt it. What the hell was wrong with my arm?

Marty's tattoo shop. I'd been there last night too.

My birthday present from Da. I pulled myself up and faced my reflection. Was that my face? That sick-looking patchwork of yellows and greens?

I yanked my hoodie over my head. There it was, covering my whole bicep—the red hand of Ulster in a six-pointed star with the Union flag and the Queen's crown, "No Surrender" and UVF underneath. Plastic was stuck to it by Vaseline.

A paramilitary tattoo. Not a Rangers flag.

It started as this cold tingling in my stomach that swelled with each heartbeat, bigger and bigger until it pressed against the inside of my skin and threatened to tear me apart.

Even if I made it to my Main Board, the army might take one look at that and say I couldn't join.

"Fuck!" I punched the mirror so hard it spidered and I had to look at dozens of me.

My knees caved. Blood dripped from my split knuckles.

Ma had wanted me to be a hero, not some hood with a UVF tattoo getting off my head and throwing petrol bombs.

My rucksack. What had I done with it? I dug through the bits left in the blackness of yesterday. I crawled to my room. And thank Christ, there it was on my bed with the baggie of ten deals.

Using my phone, I checked the flights. The only flight left at half six, and the website said you had to check in an hour early.

If I sold two pills—four to cover a taxi to Belfast International Airport—and avoided Marty, I could still pull it off. I went to grab a change of clothes, only to discover I'd nothing clean apart from one pair of boxers. I threw my boxers, a Rangers top, and my cleanest pair of trackie bottoms into the rucksack and left without brushing the alcohol from my breath.

As I nipped out the front door for the last time, I felt nothing, even though I'd lived there my whole life.

The clouds were so heavy with rain they grated on the peace wall. Christ, Fiona was just on the other side. I walked along it past a stretch of wasteland where rotting terraces used to be, heading for the bus station. The bag of ten deals weighed down my pocket as my body trembled from dehydration.

On the Shankill Road, the UVF mural across from my primary school caught my eye. It was of three men in a graveyard, one dressed in a World War I uniform from the Thirty-Sixth Ulster Division, two UVF lads wearing balaclavas and holding guns. Then the mural on the gable of the barbershop taunted me: a masked man with a gun, a badge at the center with the hand and UVF, "For God and Ulster" round it like the frigging ink on my arm. "The Peoples Army 1912–2002 90 years of resistance." The

UVF C Company mural with the faces of murdered volunteers and four masked men holding Sten submachine guns like the ones on my kitchen table a few days back. Heat pulsed from my tattoo.

Clutching the straps of my rucksack, I ran past the snapping Union Jack bunting zigzagging across the road. The wind whipped the little flags so fast they were red, white, and blue blurs.

I wouldn't be going to the bonfire tonight. I wouldn't be marching in the Twelfth parade. I'd never feel the drumsticks vibrating against my palms as I played a crushed five roll. Or the thunderous beat of the Lambeg drum reverberating in my chest. Or the pride I felt when playing "The Sash My Father Wore" marching down the Shankill Road next to Jon while everyone cheered. The army band wouldn't be the same.

I was abandoning my culture.

But in a few years, after I got my training and finished my term of service, I'd come back driving that nice car, see what everyone said then. And I'd be saving lives instead of taking them.

When I got to the bus station, I pulled on that frigging baseball cap and sat in the same spot as yesterday, wearing the same mud-caked clothes. A posh woman walked by clutching her purse to her chest. She wouldn't have looked utterly disgusted if I'd on my Ballysillan Boys' uniform or if I dressed like Foster or those tossers I'd dealt to yesterday. She definitely wouldn't have that dirty look if I'd on an army uniform.

My blue, blood-clotted knuckles smarted as I played with Fiona's purple bracelet.

I opened Fiona's picture with the ice cream and the massive smile and tried to remember the feel of her heart-shaped lips on mine.

I didn't care that Fiona was a Catholic, and she wasn't really from the Falls. Her da, I wanted him to suffer a fate worse than death and eternal damnation, but Fiona couldn't help who he was any more than I could help that during the Troubles, Da was a Shankill Executioner who had killed Catholics who weren't even in the 'RA. And the way I'd lost my rag, I'd proved her right about needing to lie.

I wanted Fiona in my arms again. I wanted to listen to her American accent when she asked if I was okay. I wanted to trace my finger along her collarbone, share my earbuds with her. I'd never felt that way about anyone else.

I dug out my mobile. No new messages.

DannyBoy: Im sorry for yesterday. I don't care where you're from or who your da is.

MESSAGE FAILED TO SEND

I tried four more times with the same result. She'd blocked me.

The thought of never looking into those green-and-gold eyes again, that she'd think I hated her forever, left me gutted. I hated myself. I sat there for hours, until it ticked past three. I must have looked so utterly dodgy and pathetic, people wouldn't even buy drugs off me.

Then I felt someone looming. A spindly woman with dead eyes and sunken cheeks stared down at me. Her bleached hair was growing out an ugly brown. She clenched the arm of a small boy with food on his face. My heart sped up to the beat of a single stroke roll. There were loads of people everywhere. Easier to get lost in the crowd.

Then a pair of peelers sauntered by. Today they wore their normal flak jackets over white shirts and police flat peaked caps, not riot gear. Holstered guns hung from their duty belts. One peeler's eyes locked onto me like he could smell the petrol still on my fingers—or the blues in my pockets. I hugged my rucksack against my chest.

But that bird was unfazed.

I'd to be to the airport in two hours. *No surrender.*

The peelers walked on.

We needed to do this somewhere private. I forced myself up and made for the men's toilet round the corner. No one was pissing, and the stall doors were all open. I drummed the cadence to "Minstrel Boy" on my thigh as I leant against the sink.

The door swung open and the woman jerked her wee boy inside, but not fast enough. The door slammed on his hand. I dove for the door and yanked it open. The boy screamed, huge tears pouring down his cheeks as he held his red hand up for her to see. She popped him across the face. "Shut your gob, wee skitter. You're fine, so you are."

I almost clobbered her, but that'd be bad for business probably. The stench of her oily hair almost made me puke yet again.

She opened her palm just enough for me to see a fifty note. Scabs and track marks covered her rail-thin arms. The boy stared up at me like he knew I was giving his mum the very thing that was stealing her away. He could have been Jon twelve years ago.

Christ, my future . . . but if I did this again, I was no better than Da. An officer would never hurt a wee kid for personal gain.

I grinned at her. "Sorry, I don't have drugs. I was hoping for a blow job."

The woman scowled at me with her greasy face. "Fuck up." She dragged the kid out.

I locked myself in the nearest stall and pulled out the bag of blues.

Mr. Sinclair was my only option. He might give me the cash if I pleaded. If he wouldn't, I'd go to Palace Barracks and beg to change my Main Board to January, get a proper job and a bank account and all that. I'd sleep in a frigging bus shelter until I had the cash for my own place. No more rioting. Maybe I'd stop drinking too.

The smartest thing for my survival would be to return the drugs and money to Marty, but I unzipped the bag, dumped the ten deals in the loo, and flushed. I'd done Marty out of a grand, but he'd never find me when I was in the army.

Feeling a thousand kilograms lighter, I binned the baseball cap and walked out of the bathroom.

And into the two peelers. The one with the pedophile moustache grabbed my arm and threw me against the wall face-first. Shocks shot from my ribs.

"Mate, did you bathe in vodka?" One frisked up my legs. "No doubt you were at the riot last night."

*Don't. Speak.* They couldn't arrest me because my fingers smelt like petrol. People going to the busses gawked at me like it was an episode of *Prime Suspect*.

"What were you getting on to in the toilet?" asked Pedophile Moustache as he crushed my face into the wall. My cheekbone screamed, but I forced my body to stay still. *Officer, Danny.*

"Selling drugs to a strung-out mum while her wee boy watched? Dirty wee scumbag." Dirty Old Prick's hand jammed into my pocket. I bit my tongue hard enough to taste warm, tangy metal. His hand slid into my other pocket. My cash fluttered to the floor.

Pedo Moustache's rough hand left my face.

I grinned over my shoulder at them. "She wanted to suck my knob, but I told her I have a girlfriend."

Shaking his head, the first one shoved the money back into my pocket.

Pedo Moustache dumped the contents out of my rucksack.

My taped-up enlistment papers, baby book, Rangers top, trackies, and boxers were all on display for the wee granny hobbling by with her cane. And…

Nothing else.

My passport was gone. The heat drained from my entire body. It'd been in there yesterday. And I'd not even unzipped my rucksack, apart from the one time I took the whiskey out.

As the peelers fondled up my sides, I felt nothing.

Then it hit me like a liver punch. Yesterday when I'd stumbled home and dropped off my rucksack, I hadn't left it sitting out. I wouldn't have done that. I'd hidden it, and Da had found it. Stole my passport, knowing I didn't have a driving license and couldn't fly without proper ID. He'd left the rucksack sitting out to taunt me.

"No son of mine is going to turn his back on his culture," that's what Da had said. And for once he'd kept his word.

Wasn't the tattoo enough? I wanted to scream. *Keep your calm. Keep your calm.*

Pedo Mustache gave me a shove. They left me standing there as people stepped on my enlistment papers. One wanker's boat shoe inched down on my baby book.

"No!" I scrambled for it.

The man in pastel shorts froze.

I grabbed my baby book and hugged it to my chest, then fumbled for my papers. The man handed me two pages with a quick smile.

My knees gave out. I pressed my back against the wall and buried my head in my hands. My clammy forehead was crusty with dried sweat and dirt.

*Soldiers don't give up. They solve problems under pressure.* Twenty quid and my passport. I'd to get to the airport by 17:30, and it was thirty minutes from here. It was 15:30.

I rang Billy.

"What now, you wee melter?"

"Da stole my passport. And I still need twenty quid."

"Sell some blues, then."

Shite, couldn't tell him what I'd done with those. "But I can't fly without ID."

Billy sighed. "I'm in Londonderry. I can be home in two hours."

"But I need to check in for my flight by half five."

"Christ, Danny. What do you want me to do? Fly? How do you always manage to make a bollocks out of everything?"

I hung up. Proved Billy right again. I'd to deal with Da myself. That's probably what he was hoping for, like a high noon shoot-out in some Western film.

But I still needed that money. I called Sinclair.

"Please don't be done with me," I begged as my mobile rang. And rang. And rang. My heart pounded.

"Hello?"

"I'm sorry. It's Danny. I've mucked it all up!" It all came pouring out. Da's beatings and stealing all my money and that frigging posh arse at the bank and dealing and rioting and the tattoo. And the passport.

"Jaysus, Danny! Do you *ever* stop and think? And all this for just a hundred twenty quid. Why did you not tell me sooner? I'll just buy the ticket for you."

That stirred something blazing hot like the sun in my chest. I tried to shove it back down deep inside, but bits kept bursting up into my heart.

"The only flight to Bristol is at half six."

"Get your passport. I'll pick you up at your house at five."

"No!" I couldn't risk him coming round my house. For his sake. "Can you meet me at the KFC on the Shankill Road?"

"Aye, sure."

A lump swelled up in my throat. I tried to clear it away, but my voice came out thick. "Thanks."

I dragged myself to my feet. My bruised ribs smarted.

Time to face Da.

He was probably waiting at home for me. If not, at the bonfire with the rest of the Upper Shankill getting ready for Bonfire Night. *No surrender*. I slung my rucksack on my back and ran out of the bus station.

That hyena cackle rang out behind me. "Oi, Professor."

I glanced back. Anto sauntered up to me, holding up his jeans that were three sizes too big.

"What do you want?"

"I'm here for Marty." He held out a slimy hand. "Give me the money you made. I'll give you your cut, so I will."

Ah Christ.

I dug out a fifty note and handed it to him. Mr. Sinclair would cover the rest.

"Marty gave you the best spot for the past two days and you sold five pills?" Anto squinted at me with his beady little rat eyes.

"I can't make people buy drugs off me."

"Well, since you're fecking off to England, give me the blues you didn't sell."

Fuck. Fuck. I folded my arms across my chest. "Lost them at the riot."

A sneer spread across his pimple-infested face. "You got rid of 'em, didn't you? You yellow bastard. You're well fucked now."

I broke into a sprint.

"Oh, and Danny Boy. Your Taigy wee slag...we're about to call round her house."

I slammed to a stop so fast my brain rammed into the front of my skull. "What?"

Anto sniggered. "We know she's a Kelly."

"How?"

"You buck eejit, I was standing right there when you were crying your wee lamps out telling Jon."

Coldness leaked through my veins.

"Her 'RA brother shot one of us last night. Your da saw that twitchy wee bastard running away with a gun. Recognized him from the Antrim Boxing Club. Got killed by your man Billy a few times" Anto's thin upper lip curled. "Tit for tat."

Fiona.

Her brother was in the 'RA? A son of Peter Kelly—I shouldn't be surprised.

But what were they going to do to him? And who was Anto going with, exactly? And what if Fiona got mixed up in it?

I couldn't even message her. I could just ring the peelers, but they wouldn't do anything. Hands shaking, I dug out my mobile and went to the Royal Mail address finder, then searched Peter Kelly Falls. And sure, he lived just on the other side of the wall from me. He didn't hide his whereabouts; people were scared enough of him that he didn't need to. It was taking their lives in their hands, for Anto and them to be going round Peter Kelly's house in the Falls. What were they thinking, even?

It was 15:45.

I steeled myself against the pain in my side and ran to the Shankill Road, then headed for the gate on Northumberland Street. Thank Christ, they hadn't closed it yet. I passed the mural that said "Welcome to the Shankill" with images of a bonfire, the bands, and the Thirty-Sixth Ulster Division. Two CCTV cameras watched from a tall pole as I walked through the gate for the first time. My throbbing heart near cracked my rib cage again as I waited for a Taig to jump me.

I wasn't wearing a Rangers or Northern Ireland top or my

school uniform, no sign of being a Protestant. *Act like you belong.*

Just on the other side, a brick wall was tagged with Kill All Huns, from their lot, and Kill All Taigs, from ours—our lads liked to sneak over and prove their bravery. I didn't want to kill anyone, and I hadn't a clue why we even called them Taigs. We just did it because that's what our das did.

It was a bit over a half mile to Fiona's house. The longest fourteen minutes of my life. I sucked in a breath to steady my nerves, shoved my hands into my pockets, and forced my feet to move along a wall topped with barbed wire, covered with murals. The first one had Martin Luther King Jr. and "I Have a Dream."

But then I saw the orange-and-green phoenix, the faces of murdering 'RA members like Fiona's da, like they were frigging heroes. I felt sick to my stomach.

*Fiona's innocent. Keep going.*

I put on blinders and stared straight ahead until I got to the crossroads with the Falls Road, the black heart of West Belfast. Terraces newer and nicer than ours, just like Da and Billy always said, stretched in both directions, and past that was red-and-silver Divis Tower. The British army had once put an observation post to monitor the IRA in there during the Troubles, and they'd been able to get to it only by helicopter.

Three wee lads in Celtic tops eyeballed me from the newsagent across the street.

I gritted my teeth and tried to act casual as I turned on the Falls Road. Cars drove past. My fingers twitched in my pockets as I walked past more Catholics, these ones wearing regular clothes, going about their days like I wasn't a foreign invader. The Falls Road looked the same as the Shankill Road really, apart from the green "*vótáil Sinn Féin*" signs on the lampposts instead of the red-and-blue Democratic Unionist Party ones. I'd been expecting tricolors to be draping everything, but there wasn't a single flag in sight. The delicious smell of sausage rolls drifted out of a bakery, but my stomach was too knotted to grumble.

Then I spotted, on the gable of a shop, a crown with an X through it and the words "Brits Out." Ulster *was* British. They had no problem taking money with the Queen's head on it for their nicer housing and social services.

I turned on Clonard Street and headed past their massive cathedral. Then I finally got to Fiona's street. On the gable of a house was a billboard with burning terraces that said "Bombay Street Never Again." Bombay Street happened only because they'd been shooting police, though.

That was Fiona's house.

I froze. DJ Mikey's thumping music from our bonfire echoed over the wall through their area.

My heart pounded in my ears, each beat spreading ice through my chest cavity, as my fingers drummed against my thigh.

I checked the time on my mobile. It was 16:00.

Why was I risking this? And what if *he* answered?

# chapter nineteen
## *Fiona*

The doorbell rang in the middle of some *Spider-Man* movie. Finn started. His arms tightened around my waist. As Patrick opened the door, Peter Parker confessed to his aunt that he had caused his uncle's death. Cool air fought back the smell of frying meat.

"You little Orange bastard!"

I peeled back the curtains behind me. Danny stood at the door wearing the same Nike T-shirt and track pants as yesterday, now smeared with dirt.

My heart tried to soar. I rammed it back down. But my blazing anger still hadn't managed to immolate the memories of his adorable cockeyed smile, his terrible John Wayne impression, or the picture of his mom cuddling him in the hospital—or the fact that all that felt just as real as the bigoted drug dealer he'd revealed himself to be.

I kissed the top of Finn's head and scooched him off my lap. I pushed past Patrick.

Danny's pale-blue eyes met mine. His black eye had faded to green and opened all the way again. Sweat beaded on his forehead and above his upper lip. His face twitched into a small smile. I hated how it weakened my knees.

"Em, hiya." His voice was soft and gentle like a wounded dog backed into a corner. A single butterfly tried to flutter its wings in my stomach.

Patrick smirked as he chewed on an unlit cigarette. "What do you want?"

Danny clenched his teeth so tight tendons popped out of his neck. Like yesterday, I felt every inch that he was taller than me.

"Go inside." I shoved Patrick back in and closed the door. I folded my arms over my trembling chest. "So what's with the recon mission into Taig Territory? Aren't you supposed to be leaving?"

Danny's jaw relaxed; his gaze dropped to my Chucks. "I'm sorry I called you that, and I don't care where you're from."

"I'm from America." I hated how much I craved his arms around me.

"Well, you did lie." Danny ran a huge hand through his flop of sandy-blond hair. He still wore my bracelet. "Your father and people like him took everything from me."

His words stole my righteousness. I picked at an orange bracelet that had slipped below my flannel sleeve.

"I was going to come clean when I came over, but you, you were so hurt," my voice cracked, "and then my family figured out where you lived. They said that I couldn't see you again because you weren't safe to be around."

Danny's eye flashed up to me. "I *never* hated you, no matter what."

"Yeah, well now I don't even know who you are anymore."

"You think I wanted to sell drugs? And I made only one sale, then I flushed them down the loo. *I* didn't kill anyone."

My cheeks flamed.

"This isn't going as I planned." Danny's fingers drummed on his thigh. "Look. I will *always* hate your da. But I shouldn't have lost my rag at you for something you can't help." His voice quaked. "I need to warn you. The UVF is coming. You know who that is?"

"The bad guys from your hood. Coming where?"

"Here. For retribution. Your brother shot a Protestant last night at the riots. He's a disso. Dissident Republican opposed to the peace process."

"Seamus?" I gasped.

Danny's eyes darted to Patrick, who was still shooting psychic daggers at him through the front window.

The ground plummeted from under my feet. "No. Just no. Patrick sits around reading books when he's not working at the gas station. He's a dad, a mentor." Goose bumps prickled my skin. "You're wrong."

"My da saw him with a gun after one of ours got shot. It's not like America, where everyone can own AK-47s."

I glanced back. Patrick watched me, ready to spring to my rescue at a millisecond's notice.

"Patrick would never risk getting arrested and leaving Finn without a father," I spat through my teeth. "And he'd *never* put Finn in danger. Besides, how would your dad even know what Patrick looks like?"

"Remembered him from cross-community boxing." Danny's eyes locked onto mine, and I felt the spark of synaptic connection again.

Seamus—the rioting punk—wouldn't have really surprised me. But *Patrick*?

Then again... Patrick was gone a lot at night. He'd said so much crap that I just let him play off to his "mentoring" role. Then all his socialist stuff.

I felt stupid for the second time in twenty-four hours.

If it was true, we were all in danger.

*Fact*: Danny was risking his flight, his whole future, to let me know because he was scared for me. That fizz filled every part of my body.

"Danny, go. Please go. Your army test."

"Fiona." Danny's voice trembled as he reached for me.

I couldn't let him screw this up. "Get the hell out of here, or I'll send Patrick after you." I planted my hands on him and shoved.

Danny sucked in a sharp breath as he stumbled backwards. Crap, his ribs. I'd hurt him. His face tightened and then he limp-jogged down Bombay Street toward Finn's school. The sun cast a long shadow behind him. I'd never feel his long fingers wrap around the back of my hand or breathe his smell—fresh-cut grass with a little bit of sweat.

The door cracked open. "Glad you gave him a proper seeing to," Patrick said. He had the same freckles and hazel-green eyes as always; he still dressed like an early 2000s skater punk lit major, not a terrorist.

"Are you all right? Did he say something to you? I swear to Christ, if—"

"What was that about?" Dad stuck his head into the stairwell. He gripped a tray of teacups in his hands.

I slipped past Dad. "Finn, go in the kitchen."

Finn's eyes flitted up to me from the TV. Green Goblin dropped both Mary Jane and a tramcar filled with people from the Brooklyn Bridge. Spider-Man swooped after the tram.

"Why?" Patrick folded his arms across his Rage Against the Machine T-shirt.

"Trust me, he doesn't need to hear this," I said.

Dad set the tray on the coffee table, cups rattling.

Gripping Bucky, Finn darted for the kitchen. The door slapped closed behind him.

"Did you shoot someone last night?" I tried to sound indignant, but my voice was a whimper. *Say he's wrong, please, Patrick.*

Patrick's eyes protruded from their sockets. "That dirty wee scumbag."

I said, "Just tell me—"

"Oh, for feck sake, Paddy!" Dad yelled, veins bulging from his forehead.

Patrick rammed a finger in Dad's face. "We were aiming for the PSNI."

It. Was. True. "You're in the ONH."

Patrick shot me a scathing look. "It's a war of liberation against an exploitative government rejected by most of the island."

"The UVF's coming for retribution right now," I said. "That's why Danny came."

Dad and Patrick's eyes both jumped to me.

"That pack of used-up thugs is more interested in drug dealing and selling counterfeit rubbish than in me," Patrick scoffed.

"Don't worry yourself about it, Fiona." Dad's hands flew up like I was a feral cat. "We haven't seen tit-for-tat revenge in ages."

"Oh, my God. Stop telling me not to worry about things!"

Of course he was taking Patrick's side; they both had terrorist on their résumé.

Finn peeked through the kitchen door with eyes that filled his whole face. When he saw I'd caught him, he bolted back into the kitchen.

Danny wouldn't have risked his future if we weren't in danger.

I followed to find Finn huddled against the oven, crying as he covered his ears. Bucky lay abandoned by the door. I pulled him into my arms. He pressed his hot, tear-soaked face into my shoulder.

Dad and Patrick's muffled argument leaked under the door.

More than anything I just wanted Mom to stroke the back of my neck and tell me everything would be just peachy. But she was thousands of miles away, and now it was me who had to protect someone—because Dad and Patrick were doing absolutely nothing.

Hands trembling, I dug out my phone and made an emergency call. As the ringtone pulsed, all I could see was the picture of Patrick holding me right after I was born. He'd looked almost exactly like Finn, who was now quaking in my arms. I was about to get Patrick arrested.

What if they arrested Dad too? Who would take care of Finn? Seamus wasn't really a functional adult.

Patrick left me with no choice.

"What's your name, caller?" a woman asked.

I kissed the top of Finn's curly head and whispered, "Cover your ears."

Blubbering, he pressed his hands to his ears.

"Hello?" a tinny voice called.

"Hi, um, I'm calling to report something," I choked out.

"Okay, would you like to remain anonymous?"

"Um, yes."

"Okay, caller, how can we help you?"

I squeezed my eyes shut as tears dripped from my chin into Finn's hair, "Someone"—my voice caught, but I forced the words out—"just confessed to shooting that guy at the riot last night. His name is Patrick Kelly, and he's in that ONH."

"Where does he live?"

I gave her Dad's address, then hung up.

Finn's whole body shuddered with staccato sobs. I wanted to grab him and run, but out the back door was the cage protecting us from Shankill projectiles and the front door was blocked by Dad and Patrick. The minutes ticked away like hours. Patrick and Dad's indecipherable shouting continued.

Mom must have felt five hundred times worse. I could almost see her throwing a few things in a bag, including the tiny purple *Star Wars* T-shirt I still had. Breaking into sobs as we drove away in a cab, leaving Seamus and Patrick to an uncertain fate.

With my free hand, I messaged Mom.

FionaRuns: Patrick's in the ONH. He shot someone yesterday. I called the police. I'm scared.

Just as my phone vibrated, the front door rattled. "Armed police! Open the door!"

Finn cried out.

I had to make sure the police took the right terrorist. "Stay here, Finny." I stroked his sweaty, tear-stained face. His eyes pleaded as he grabbed handfuls of my flannel shirt.

My eyes burned. "I'm just going to the kitchen door. I'm not leaving. Please, Finn, just stay here." I loosened his tight fingers and gave him Bucky. He collapsed into a puddle of sobs.

My heart hammered into my sternum as I opened the kitchen door.

Flashing blue-and-red lights cast through the window onto the ceiling.

"It was you, wasn't it? You tout!" Now a red-faced wompa, Patrick screamed so close his tobacco-laden spittle spattered on my nose. He was only an inch or two taller, but, in that moment, he towered over me. "You betrayed your own flesh and blood, just like *she* did!"

Dad grabbed Patrick and slammed him into the wall. "You stay away from her!"

Patrick shook his head, in a daze.

Fresh tears streaked down my cheeks. How could that be *Patrick*?

Dad pulled open the front door. "Evening, Constable. How can I help you?"

"Peter, have a seat on the sofa there," the officer said. "You, too, Patrick."

Dad sat down, hands up. Three cops entered wearing bulletproof vests and black baseball caps that said *Police*. Seething, Patrick stared them down from by the TV. One of the *Die Hard* movies was on now.

"Jesus, Mary, and Joseph, Paddy, just do it, you hellion," Dad said.

Patrick glared at the cops for a few more seconds and then sat on the other end of the couch. His wallet chain danced as his leg jerked.

"What's all this, then, Sergeant Webb?" Dad balanced his forearms on his thighs and stared at his leathery hands.

"We've received word some individuals here may have been involved in a bit of trouble we're keen to resolve," said Sergeant Webb.

"No trouble here. I can assure you of that," Dad said.

Why was Dad covering for him? I bit the inside of my lip so hard I tasted copper.

A tiny hand rested on my back. Finn. Shit. I hugged his head to my stomach. His tears soaked through my shirt.

"As you know, under the Terrorism Act, a constable may enter and search any premises if he reasonably suspects that a terrorist is to be found there." The policewoman's eyes moved between Dad and Patrick.

The stairs creaked as two cops ran up. Sergeant Webb rested a hand on the butt of her gun.

Finn broke free of me and bolted to Patrick. Patrick kissed his head and whispered something in his ear. I stared at the cop's black boots, inches from Patrick's copy of *To Kill a Mockingbird*. The crash of furniture overturning echoed downstairs. We waited. And waited. I'd done something stupid, I realized; I didn't have proof of anything. The cops wouldn't find anything up there. They'd dismiss my call or maybe just give Patrick a warning, and I'd have burned my bridges with my family forever.

"Gun up in the wee boy's room," a cop shouted from upstairs.

In *Finn's* room? Lead sank through my stomach.

Dad lifted his head and glanced around Patrick at me, a tightness around his eyes that crinkled his scar.

"Is it yours, then, Peter?" another cop asked.

Dad let out a slow, heavy sigh and covered his face with a hand.

I waited for him to tell them, to deny the gun was his.

"Right then, Peter; let's go." The cop sauntered around the coffee table.

Dad stood up and turned around.

"Peter Kelly, you're under arrest for possession of firearms and suspected membership in a proscribed organization." The cop handcuffed him. Each click punctured the air.

I cried, "It's not—"

Dad shot me a look that could cut diamonds. I shrank against the wall. Finn buried his face in Patrick's chest.

More police officers slipped past Dad and his arresting officer. They walked right by me into the kitchen. Cupboard slammed. Dishes shattered on the floor. Seamus's lemon cupcakes lay scattered across the linoleum.

"Keep moving, Peter." The cop rested a hand on his back.

Dad stepped through the front door. Before he was out of view, he looked at me. I thought I saw tears in his eyes, but he was too far away to tell.

The officer shoved him out the door. Camera clicks followed by the high whine of the flash drifted from upstairs.

Another officer came into the living room, eyes on Patrick. Finn's body shook with sobs. Patrick hugged him tighter.

I found the courage to beg, "Can I take my nephew to our neighbor's?"

Sergeant Webb squinted at me sideways. Right, accent.

"Please?" I asked. "He doesn't need to see this."

She glanced at Finn. "All right, then."

I tried to pull Finn off Patrick. Patrick gripped his arm. I peeled his calloused fingers off.

"Daddy!" Finn bawled as I tugged him away.

"On your feet," a cop said to Patrick.

"Fuck you!" Patrick shouted.

Two cops slammed him face-first against the wall, floor quaking at the force of impact. Finn's choked scream cut over a car explosion on *Die Hard*. The painting of the Virgin Mary stared down on the scene with a serene smile, one hand outstretched toward Patrick, the other holding a stem of white Easter lilies like the ones on our mailbox back home.

As I carried Finn through the door, Patrick yelled over them reading his rights, "I'm coming for you, Finny. I promise. Ah! You bastards! Police brutality!"

Three armored police cars sat out front. Dad sat in the back of one, head down. Two guys came out of the house next door. Police ushered them to the other side of the white tape. Some of the police wore helmets with face shields.

"What'd you take him for?" a woman yelled.

"Frigging bastards!" a guy decked out with ridiculous gold chains from Jonty's pack shouted.

The air thickened, buzzed.

Sobbing, Finn clung to me. I ducked under the police tape and did my best to jog with him braced on my hip.

I kissed Finn's cheek, covered with hot, salty tears. "Show me which one's Mrs. McMahon's."

He limply pointed to one with a little flowerpot hanging next to a white door. I pounded.

A girl wearing a pink Abercrombie sweatshirt opened the door. She looked at me like I was an alien, but then she noticed Finn. "You all right, wee Finny?"

Mrs. McMahon poked her head in from the kitchen. "Mary, put the kettle on."

"It's okay, Finny. It's okay. You're safe." I set Finn on the couch and hugged his tiny, trembling body.

Finn wiggled free of me and nestled into Mrs. McMahon. And I felt utterly alone.

"You needn't worry, love, it's just a show of strength." She was talking about the police arrests. Holding Finn, Mrs. McMahon picked up the ancient cordless phone from the doily on the coffee table. "Seamus, it's Mrs. McMahon. Did you hear the police are at your house?"

I grabbed the phone, earning me a shocked look from Mrs. McMahon. "Patrick shot someone at a riot. Danny came to warn me."

Seamus's voice rattled the earpiece. "That wee Orange wanker!"

"Wait, you're blaming—"

The phone disconnected.

"Call him back!"

Mrs. McMahon frowned as she dialed. Seamus didn't answer.

Seamus's douchebag friend had followed me to Danny's house. He knew where he lived. If Danny was home...I unblocked Danny from WhatsApp. An apology I ignored. I sent him a message, but he might not get it in time.

"I'll be back." I kissed Finn's head and bolted for the door.

"Fiona!" Mrs. McMahon called, but I sprinted away.

# chapter twenty

## *Danny*

Fifteen minutes.

Sweat ran down my back as I sprinted for the Lanark Way gate, not even caring how many Catholics saw me, not quite crying but it hurt like hell to swallow.

Christ, when Fiona first laid eyes on me, she had this look like I'd ripped her heart out and sliced it up into five million pieces. It'd been physically painful not to touch her. Then she'd shoved me and threatened to send her 'RA brother after me. It ripped a hole in me that kept getting bigger until I near broke in two.

I'd had my shit kicked in so many times, but I'd never hurt like this.

I reached the gate. Their side had an image of peeling skies and faded hills, just like ours. I crossed back into our area. The bonfire towered over the already packed wasteland. The smell of barbecue wafted over. Mrs. Donnelly was probably making one of her famous tray bakes that very minute, but for the first time ever, it didn't make my mouth water.

Each foot impact was a knife to the side, but I kept running down Cupar Way. The peace wall separating me and Fiona towered over me. Da's car was gone; he was out. Adrenaline surged through my veins. I flew through the house, turning over everything for my passport. And finally, there it was, in the drawer of his bedside table on top of some porn and a bottle of Bushmills.

Now to the KFC, then I'd be free. I slipped it into my rucksack with everything else that mattered in the world and charged out of the house.

Into some red-headed, broad-shouldered, ape-looking lad.

"You!" His fist caught me in the side. My bruised ribs howled. "You called the peelers!"

"Seamus, stop!"

Fiona.

Both me and that ape dropped our fists. There she stood by the peace wall. Our eyes met.

"Feck sake, Fiona! Are you mental?" Her brother jogged across the street to her.

Tires squealed. Marty's swank BMW turned down my street, sunlight gleaming off the windscreen.

"Get Fiona out of here," I said.

Fiona's brother squinted at me, then the car, then back at me. Seamus grabbed Fiona's arm.

"No!" she cried, curls flying as he dragged her away. Thank Christ, that brother was a bruiser.

Car doors slammed. Laughter echoed off the peace wall.

Marty and Gusty strolled toward me. I turned to face them.

Marty stopped inches from my face, wearing his Cheshire cat grin. "We know what you done."

"Come on then, you bastard, you!" I threw an uppercut into

Marty's chin. My side screamed. The teeth he had left clattered together.

He shook his head, eyes unfocused for a second, then grabbed me by the neck and wrestled me to the ground. I tried to fight to my feet, but Gusty's trainer drilled me in my already bruised ribs. A crack. My body gave out. Gusty ground his fingers into my scalp; my cheekbone bowed. The grainy pavement, still warm from the sun, cut into my skin. His meaty knee dug into my back. Pain tore through my ribs as the air was forced out of my lungs. Gusty's cheap digital watch said it was 17:05.

The click of a sliding mechanism. I squeezed my eyes shut. "Please."

"You binned a grand worth of ten deals," Marty said.

I'd been so close.

# chapter twenty-one

## *Fiona*

Seamus dragged me toward the gate. I tried to wrench my arm free of his iron grip.

Through the rails in the rusting fence, I watched them pin Danny to the ground. Seamus's fingers tightened around my bicep as his picked up the pace. My legs tangled, but Seamus caught me before I face-planted. Now decaying row houses blocked my view of Danny.

An ear-shattering pop like those boom fireworks on the Fourth of July—but sharper and more focused. The air shuddered. A scream.

"No!" My shoulder socket strained as I fought to pull my arm free. "We have to help him!"

"We can't!" He yanked me in the wrong direction.

Another explosive report echoed off the peace wall. A blood-curdling scream. *No*.

I punched Seamus in the side of the head. Pain shot through my knuckles. A drop of blood ran down his chin.

"Fuck, that hurt." He dropped my arm and smeared the blood away.

I scrambled, but Seamus got his arms around my waist. "He told me to get you out of here."

"No!" I drove my elbow into Seamus's muscular side, but he barely flinched.

Danny might be dead. The ground rushed toward me. Pebbled glass cut into my palms. My knees stung. Seamus slung me over his shoulder like a doll. I slammed my fists into his back, kicked his thighs, but he pushed forward.

"Here, will you listen to me? Two shots. They kneecapped him, Fiona, they didn't kill him."

"They what?" My arms and legs went limp.

His arm crushed around my waist as he pulled out his phone. "Wee lad got shot. Shankill, Lawnbrook." Seamus hung up. "One bullet in each knee."

"How do you even know that?"

"Frigging paramilitaries. Your man made a bollocks out of something."

He'd flushed the drugs, that's what this was about. "But, but he's supposed to have his army test tomorrow."

"He'll not be making that."

Fresh tears blurred the red brick around us. The street was empty. A graffiti-covered fence made of rusting, mismatched sheets of corrugated metal separated us from an unlit pyre towering higher even than the peace wall. "*It's all good*" filled several sheets in massive red-and-white letters. Thumping eighties rock reverberated off the wall, and I could hear people laughing.

"The UVF is coming for revenge. Danny wanted to protect me—us. And Patrick had a gun hidden in Finn's room."

Seamus finally set me down, but his beefy hand clenched my upper arm like a vice so I couldn't escape. "In *my* room?"

"So you weren't in on it?"

Veins bulged out of Seamus's freckled forehead. "I didn't know about *that*."

Back at Mrs. McMahon's, she tried to question us as she cradled sobbing Finn, but I made Seamus call hospitals until we found Danny.

"Probably took him to the Royal." Seamus looked up the number and put his phone on speaker. My heart throbbed so hard it squeezed the air from my lungs. *Danny.*

"Royal Victoria Hospital, how may I direct your call?" an elderly-sounding voice said.

My throat tightened.

"Hello?"

I fought for my voice. "Hi, um, I'm calling to see if someone was brought in tonight."

"Around thirty minutes ago," Seamus said.

"We can release information only to immediate family members."

"I'm his sister."

Smirking, Seamus raised an eyebrow at me.

The tapping of a keyboard came over the line. "What's his name?"

"Danny Stewart."

"Yes, he was admitted at 5:27. He's in surgery."

"So he's alive?"

"Yes. I'm sorry, but I haven't got any more information."

I squeezed my eyes closed as happy tears burned. *Thank God.*

Seamus ran a hand through his sweat-crusty red curls. "Well, you're not going anywhere tonight. Huns with their bonfires, wrecking the place."

All I could imagine was Danny's long body laid out on an operating table, surrounded by surgeons wearing masks and head covers as they cut him, not knowing that he'd spent months training for his army test.

I curled into a ball and dissolved into sobs until I was drained of tears.

# chapter twenty-two

## *Danny*

Ma's singing came to me—"Danny Boy." And it was beautiful.

Low, quiet beeps grew louder until they drowned her out. Then I remembered I couldn't recall Ma's voice.

I opened my eyes. Everything was cloudy, but I could make out dark strip lights over me. And whiteness. Dull light slipped through the vertical blinds. I felt too heavy to sit up, shattered even though I had just woken. Something cold hissed up my nostrils. I felt my face with my numb hands. Tape held a tube in my hand that snaked over to a machine. I had a tube under my nose too. A monitor was clamped to my finger.

An alarm went off on the IV machine next to me. Curtain rings rattled.

"You're awake." A woman in a blue uniform leant over me and grabbed a remote attached to the rail next to my head. A light blinked on. I squinted against the brightness. She adjusted the clear IV bag and pressed some buttons on the machine.

"Where am I?"

She smiled down at me with kind eyes like Mrs. Donnelly's. "Royal Victoria Hospital."

After the first ear-shredding explosion happened, my brain didn't register it. But the second, I felt the bullet, like all my nerves had been set alight. My blood on the ground, the fence, pumping into puddles with each heartbeat as the world faded away.

Fiona had screamed.

I tried to prop myself up. My head wobbled.

"Wait, love, use this." She pointed to the remote and then pressed a button.

The back of my bed rose up. My right knee was wrapped in gauze. My left knee had this cage round it. Metal rods went through it into my bandaged flesh. Into my bones.

"I'm Nancy, the surgical nurse. How are you feeling?"

Now everything was crystal clear, like the camera had focused.

"Daniel, is there anyone we can call? Your parents?"

Then the pain started, a dull throb, like somehow seeing my injuries made my brain feel it.

Billy, he wouldn't come round for me. They'd ask questions he wouldn't be too keen on answering. And Da . . . shook my head.

"Surely there's someone for us to call, love."

"David Sinclair."

"Of course. What relation is he to you?"

"My teacher."

"We'll find him." She dug in her blue hospital scrub pocket. She held out Fiona's purple bracelet. "We had to remove it while you were in the operating theater. I thought you might want it back."

I slid it on my wrist with my hospital bracelet. Some doctor with her hair in a bun came in. She looked at me like I was a piece of pure rubbish and started talking in a low, serious voice. A hand squeezed mine, skin soft like Fiona's. "Are you listening, Daniel?" Nurse Nancy asked. "This is important."

I forced myself to look at the doctor's thin lips as she read from the clipboard about compound unstable fractures and patellar fracture and vascular damage and fixators and more operations. It sounded like she was talking through a wall, and I had to focus on each word and string it together.

"But I'll be okay, right? I know I've missed this Main Board. See, I'm going to be in the army. I want to be an adult health nurse. But come January, I'll be ready, right? For the fitness tests?"

That wee bitch finally looked up from her clipboard. Her lips pressed into a brief frown. "Your right leg is a flesh wound, which will likely heal fine in a few weeks. But your left kneecap was pulverized. You'll be able to walk eventually, but likely with a limp."

"But I won't pass the army fitness standards if I've a limp."

The doctor's brows pursed as her eyes fell to her clipboard again. "I'm sorry."

She left me there watching the shattered bits of my future drift out of reach.

Nurse Nancy squeezed my hand. "I'm sorry, love."

A tidal wave of fire burned up my legs—the entire bottom of my body dipped in a lake of fire. I pressed fingers into my eyes and screamed.

"Oh, dear, you're in pain. Just press this when it gets to be too much." She pressed a button on a cylinder-shaped thing, and it all went away.

❧

When I woke, I was staring at the dark strip lights again, but this time I knew where I was. I fumbled for the remote and pushed the button. The back of my bed slowly rose until I was half sitting.

I couldn't bring myself to look at the mess that was my left leg.

It was the whiteboard by the door that caught my attention.

Date: 12 July
RN: McGuinness
RT: Irving
Family Contact: ___________

Everything I'd worked for. Two years of sixth form, studying and doing homework instead of running about, all the sit-ups and press-ups and people slagging me off for running like a poof, the list with Sinclair, practice for Main Board, facing Da for 730 frigging days when I could've just got a job and moved out.

All for nothing.

It felt like someone had fired a petrol bomb at my chest. My eyes tingled. I draped my arm over my face. The IV pressed into my cheek.

Shoes clicked on the tile. I peeked under my arm. Nurse Nancy led in a smartly dressed man and woman with badges who walked like they'd got something shoved up their holes.

"Danny, there's some detectives here to talk to you. Would you like me to stay?"

I shook my head.

The woman settled into a chair next to me. She flipped open a little black notepad that had "Police Service of Northern Ireland" embossed in silver. Her partner dragged a chair to the foot of my bed.

"Just press the call button if you're in need of anything." Nurse Nancy squeezed my big toe before she left.

I folded my arms across my chest. Rain beat on the window to the tempo of a multiple bounce roll, almost synchronized with my beeping heart monitor. It was the Twelfth still. The Shankill Young Conquerors would be returning from the field by now. I'd never march with them again. Or anyone probably.

"I'm Detective Dunlop, and this is Detective Maginnis," said the woman as she tapped her Biro on the notebook.

"Look, mate, we're not here to give you a hard time." Detective Maginnis's face softened as he looked at my knees. "That nurse mentioned you were supposed to be at an army test today."

My eyes dropped to the metal screwed into my leg, holding the pieces together. "Whatever happened to patient confidentiality?" I squeezed my eyes closed.

"This isn't what you wanted." And his voice was so friggin' gentle, like when Mrs. Donnelly used to read me bedtime stories. "This was done to you. Someone stole your dream."

I saw red through my eyelids. Fire sparked in my chest, swelled into my throat. Choked me. "Shut your teeth, you bastard!" I pressed my fists to my eyes.

"Tell them who did this to you, Danny Boy."

My fists dropped. Mr. Sinclair stood behind Detective Maginnis. For the first time ever, his shirt wasn't tucked in.

Sinclair's jaw set, but his eye twitched as he stared at my legs. "Tell them who did this to you." His voice shook.

The blaze holding my chest open died. I caved. Screw them. Screw them all. I wanted to make them pay. It meant I could never go back to the Shankill again—most likely that I'd be exiled from Northern Ireland—but I didn't have anything left here anyway.

"Marty Campbell. He's the CO of the West Belfast UVF. Gusty Johnston was there when I got shot too. And my da, Rab Stewart, he's got Sten guns and drugs hidden in the freezer, the toilet tank, the dirty laundry, the attic, and under the oil tank."

Dunlop's jaw dropped.

"Aren't you going to write that down?" I asked.

That got their Biros moving.

Somewhere in the Shankill—Jamie or Anto or someone—would spray-paint "Danny Stewart is a tout" on something, but I didn't care.

Dunlop snapped her notepad shut.

"If you think of anything else." Maginnis held out a card I couldn't reach. Sinclair took it as they left.

"You've to find Fiona for me," I said. "Make sure she's okay."

Sinclair shook his head like he was startled. "Calm down, you wee fiend." His voice came out soft, which just made me feel worse. Sinclair settled into Dunlop's chair. "You're in a right state at the moment, and I'm playing catch-up. Now, who's Fiona?"

The whole story poured out of me.

Sinclair gaped at me. "You've been seeing *whose* daughter?"

"Well, I didn't know, and sure it's not her fault who her da is."

He shook his head in disbelief. "No, you're right, of course. I'm just—"

The curtain tore back. "Ah, Christ!" Billy, dressed in his usual red-and-white Adidas tracksuit, pulled at hair he didn't have while he stared at the cage round my knee.

He'd missed the Twelfth parade to see me.

Sinclair eyed Billy up. Billy's gaze was locked on my ruined legs, hands laced behind his head like he was under arrest. "Why could you not apply to uni?"

"Feck up, you pikey bastard."

Billy sniffled and swiped his nose with a fist, same empty look on his face as when he was twelve and had to call 999 after Da beat up one of his ex-girlfriends. He pulled my rucksack off his shoulder and handed it to me. "Knew you'd be wanting this, ya wee melter."

I opened it. My taped-up enlistment papers, passport, and baby book. My skin tingled as my breath got stuck below my larynx. The world got fuzzy.

"I'll help get Danny sorted," Sinclair said.

Billy cleared his throat, then nodded. Finally he looked at my face. "Em, I'll stop round later when you're feeling better."

We both knew that was a lie. He would likely be the new UVF CO, and I got his predecessor arrested. I stopped myself from drumming on my thigh and nodded.

"Right, I'm away out." Billy's head dipped as he headed for the door.

"I'll go to uni," I said.

Billy stopped at the curtain divider. "Glad you'll be getting on with something useful with those qualifications." He shoved his hands in his trackie bottoms and walked out.

I'd probably never see him again.

# chapter twenty-three

## *Fiona*

I brushed the tear-glued hair from my cheeks to find sunlight streaming through lace curtains.

My whole body ached, and my head was filled with the same packing peanuts as the first morning I woke up in Belfast. My aching fingers were swollen. I was surrounded by pink walls adorned with One Direction and Justin Bieber posters—Mrs. McMahon's daughter's bedroom. I ran downstairs. The living room was filled with the smell of fried meat. Finn sat with his head pressed against Seamus's shoulder. My heart sank. What if they kept Patrick and Dad and put Finn in foster care? Because of me.

"Good morning, Fiona," Mrs. McMahon called from the kitchen.

I gripped the doorjamb. "What's happening to my dad?"

Mrs. McMahon set an old-school teakettle on a burner. "They're likely holding him in the PSNI Serious Crime Suite in Antrim." She sighed as she steeped her tea. "Fiona, your father can look after himself."

The front door opened. Sunlight spilled across their wood floor. Dad walked in, wearing the same Restorative Justice Ireland fleece as yesterday. The bags under his eyes were heavy enough to sink him to the bottom of the ocean, but there were no bruises on his face.

Finn darted to Dad. Dad kissed Finn's head and then lumbered into the kitchen, leaning heavily on his left leg. Mrs. McMahon set a stack of plates in the sink and slipped past Dad. My chest trembled as I braced myself for Dad's deep, rumbling yell. I hugged my arms to my chest.

Dad stopped a yard from me. His weary hazel eyes, spotted with green, looked me over.

As much as I tried to picture Dad's sordid past—fingers nestled in blue-and-red wires making bombs; wearing the ski mask, sunglasses, and the beret with the Easter lily; shooting at British soldiers—I couldn't. Right after I was born, he'd held my whole body in his hand.

My tears broke free. "I'm sorry."

"Sweetheart, you have nothing to be sorry for." Dad pulled me against him.

I pressed my face into his shoulder. The smell of his leathery aftershave mixed with cigarettes calmed me. "Are you okay? Did they hurt you?"

"I'm all right. They know I've been done a long time." He stroked the back of my head, fingers curling into my hair. "I'm sorry you had to go through all that."

A tiny choked sob came from the living room. Over Dad's shoulder, I saw Finn staring at the front door, Bucky dangling by an arm.

Dad gave me a quick squeeze and then hobbled to Finn. I felt cold. With a grunt, he kneeled down and hugged him. "You'll see him soon."

"How soon?" My heel jumped on the linoleum.

Dad sighed and rested his cheek against Finn's curly head. "Seamy, can you help wee Finny find something to watch?"

Seamus peeled Finn off Dad. Dad shut the door and settled into one of the white kitchen chairs. The lines in his forehead became chasms as he frowned at the lace tablecloth.

"Paddy confessed to the shooting, the grenade attack a few days back, even an assault on a prison guard a few years back."

"He confessed?"

"To ensure they'd let me go."

"But... what's going to happen to him?"

Dad rubbed his eyes and let out a guttural throat clearing. "He'll go to trial."

"But Finn—"

"I'll look after him."

"Finn needs Patrick." Tears distorted the cheesy print on the wall about being stronger and more brilliant than a star. I buried my face in my arms. "If I wouldn't have called..."

Dad's rough hand wrapped around mine.

I choked on a sob as tears soaked through my shirtsleeve. Chair feet scraped on linoleum, and Dad's arms encircled me.

"Why did Patrick go and do the same thing you did? After he saw what it did to us?"

Dad got up and stood in the open door to the backyard. He lit a cigarette. "He continues the fight so his suffering has meaning." The cigarette dropped from his lips into the McMahon's pebble-filled backyard. Dad buried his head in his hands. Gray-peppered curls poked through his fingers. "And that's *my* fault. Christ, who Patrick could have been."

Without his dad around, Finn would be burdened too. And he was already fragile.

And it was *Patrick*.

But Patrick had been involved in that grenade attack in the paper and that weird conversation between Dad and him about Jonty joyriding…Patrick probably kneecapped hooligans in the Falls or something, followed through on that spray-painted ONH threat against heroin dealers. He'd said himself that's the only way they'll listen. Patrick shot someone and almost brought UVF revenge to our doorstep.

And he'd hidden a gun in *Finn's room*.

Had what I'd done hurt Finn, or was it for the best—safer for him—this way? And I might have saved lives, kind of like Mom. I'd never know…and that would be my burden to bear.

❦

As I stepped into the Critical Care Building, the pea-sized pit in my stomach grew into a watermelon.

Reception told me he was on the third story. As I cut through the white halls with gleaming floors, choking down the smell of Band-Aids and antiseptics, I shivered. In the third-floor waiting room, a muted TV played choppy images of a burning Loyalist effigy. A crying woman held a boy about Finn's age.

Signs for Critical Care pointed to wide silver double doors. I'd never visited anyone in the hospital. Did I just stroll on in?

The doors swung open and a nurse walked past me reading a clipboard. I slipped through before they closed. A sign directed visitors to use hand gel from the dispenser. I squirted the cold slime on my hands and rubbed it in.

"May I help you with something?" a young doctor with a tight bun asked.

My heartbeat roared in my ears, drowning out the doctors

and nurses talking in quiet voices. I hugged Bucky to my chest. "Danny Stewart?"

She flipped through some pages on a clipboard. "Right, *that* one."

Like he was one of Seamus's punk-ass car-stealing friends. Like he didn't even matter as a person.

The doctor looked up at me. Her face unstiffened. "Last room on the right." She left me standing alone by the hand sanitizer.

The hall felt five kilometers long as the pit in my stomach swelled *Titanic*-sized. I pressed my hand against the door and pushed. The closest bed was empty. A cream-colored curtain divided the room. Some kind of medical equipment beeped on the other side. I gripped the curtain and pulled it back.

Danny grinned so wide it overtook his face.

An IV sprouted from his hand. One leg was bandaged; the other knee had a cage around it. Seamus had made it sound like kneecappings were just flesh wounds, like people just bounced back. But this was serious.

Danny struggled to sit up, but a man in his late thirties with hipster glasses pushed him back down.

"You must be Fiona," he said. "I'm David Sinclair, Danny's teacher." He held out his hand, but mine was too heavy to lift.

"Right, well, I'll leave yous alone." Mr. Sinclair left with a newspaper tucked under his arm.

"Are you in pain?"

"Nah. They give me drugs." He still wore my bracelet along with a hospital one. "*Legal* drugs."

The cage around his leg, it had to be screwed into his bones. "What about the army?"

Danny's perfect smile faltered. "I'll find something else to do."

He'd lost *everything*.

"I'm sorry. I'm so, so sorry. God. If you hadn't come to my house—" *You'd be at your test today*. Tears rolled down my cheeks.

"It looks worse than it is like. Come here, please come here."

A haze crept across my field of vision. I crouched down and put my head between my knees. All the blood in my head roared as my empty stomach churned like the day we'd met.

"Fiona, please."

His voice cleared the world. I pulled myself up and gently sat on the edge of his bed. Danny wrapped his arms around my waist and pulled me to him. Fizz rushed through my veins. Today he smelled like tangy antiseptics.

"What happened to me, it's not your fault." Danny tucked his finger under my chin and tilted my head toward him. He wiped my tears away with his calloused thumb.

His breath tickled my lips as I stared into his eyes, the color of the sky on a hot, cloudless July day.

I pulled Bucky out from between us. "Um, my nephew wanted me to lend this to you."

Danny took it. "He hasn't got rabies, has he?"

I grabbed Bucky back and bonked him on the head. He always knew the right thing to say. "I've had him since I was like five, so I can guarantee no."

Danny set him on his table. "Tell him thanks. I feel better already."

I traced my fingers along his strong jaw, rough with a hint of blond stubble. "I missed you."

A massive, lopsided grin split his face as he tucked a curl behind my ear. "It's been torture without you."

Thousands of butterflies fluttered from my heart to my fingertips. It was electric. I planted my lips on his. I felt his lips twist into a smile as he kissed me back.

"What?" I breathed against his mouth.

Danny's cheek slid against mine, stubble tickling my skin. "Christ, you're amazing." His warm breath in my ear sent shivers down my spine. He kissed my forehead.

I slid my fingers through his hair, pulled him closer, and parted his lips with my tongue. Danny sucked in a sharp breath; his tongue caressed mine. Then his face went even redder than Seamus's when I'd said boob. He snatched a pillow from behind him and smooshed it on his lap.

"Did I do something?"

"Em, I've a catheter shoved, em, up . . . there."

My cheeks blazed. "Oh, um . . ."

Danny's fingers drummed on the pillow. "So, em, are you still leaving in two days?"

I closed my eyes, imagined myself standing on the observation deck overlooking the one-thousand-foot-wide telescope built into a sinkhole surrounded by mountain rainforests. I pictured myself sitting in a tiny lab filled with computers, helping a real astronomer interpret radio frequency radiation emitted by quasars. Finding a spare minute to run into the warm, tropical ocean and feel the warm waves lap at my legs.

It stung to give up summer jobs and lawn mowing and therefore Arecibo, but not as much as leaving would. I wasn't ready to go, especially after so many people had gotten hurt. Even Mom understood. "I'm going to stay for the summer."

"But what happened with your brother?"

I picked at some threads hanging from the hole in my jeans. "I called the police. He's in jail for a long time, Dad said."

Danny's fingers froze midbeat. "Won't they be coming after you?"

I shook my head. Dad had asked Patrick, and he swore he'd told no one. I was safe.

"What about you? Will you be safe?" I asked.

Danny blinked rapidly at the ceiling. "I'll be fine, so I will."

I stroked the back of neck. His shoulders relaxed.

In that moment, there were literally no words to say. I lay my head on his chest and felt his heartbeat against my cheek through his thin hospital gown. It was the cadence to "Hero's Heart." He rested his chin on the top of my head. His shaky breath tickled my scalp. We melted together as minutes passed.

That pretentious doctor kicked me out at three thirty because they had to do x-rays. Our kiss was long and deep. We didn't say goodbye.

When I got out of the hospital, boiling blue-gray clouds drizzled on the red brick surrounding me. I tossed up my jacket hood and put on Fading Stars. As I walked home, I savored the lingering taste of Danny on my lips.

When I opened the front door, I found an empty living room but *New York Supermodel* on TV. The air was thick with the smell of warm chocolate.

"Simone, can you at least pretend to be turned on by Fabio?" Beau Braxton's New York accent cut in. "You look like you're going to puke on his six-pack."

In the kitchen, I discovered an explosion of flour and mixing bowls and baking contraptions. Seamus spooned batter onto a baking sheet while Finn colored at the table, chocolate smeared on his lips.

"That dirty wee slag Simone just made the black doll cry her wee lamps out because she said she had a 'nappy-ass weave,'" Seamus said, like everything was totally cool. After what I'd done. To his brother, his nephew. What I'd brought on our family.

I took one of the cookies stacked on a frilly flower plate and bit into it. Through the gooey chocolate, I tasted peanut butter. They were like Mom's, but better. "Well, bro, in my professional, mostly American opinion, you've mastered the art of baking with PB."

Seamus looked up from the baking sheet. "Well with that ringing endorsement, I reckon I'm ready to open shop across the pond." He shoved a cookie into his mouth.

"God, I cringe to say this, but your accent might attract some business."

Seamus shot me a grin bursting with cookie before cramming another one in there.

"Okay, so how do you not weigh five hundred pounds?"

Seamus guffawed, bits of half-chewed cookie flying out of his mouth. He flexed his huge biceps, then kissed each one. "All goes to these."

We were cool.. Laughing, I sat down next to Finn. His tongue poked out through his missing front teeth as he colored Obi-Wan's lightsaber blue. I grabbed a brown crayon and started in on his robe.

Finn launched into my lap. My chair rocked onto its back feet. That filled me up past the brim. I wrapped my arms around him.

I heard the front door open over the muffled *New York Supermodel*'s dubstep catwalk music. Dad pushed open the kitchen door. His gray-peppered curls were plastered against his forehead, phone pressed to his ear. His eyes darted to me, expression unreadable. Finn tensed. My heart throbbed faster than a millisecond pulsar.

Frowning, Dad motioned for me to follow him into the living room.

I kissed the top of Finn's head, then slid him back to his seat. My ears started ringing, drowning out Beau Braxton's adulation of Mia's shots, as I dragged myself to the living room. I grabbed the remote off the newspaper and muted the TV.

Dad set the phone on top of a coloring book. "Patrick would like to have a wee chat with you."

All I could see in my mind was the rabid look on Patrick's face as he screamed that I was a tout. But he confessed everything so Dad could go free. I sat on the edge of the couch. Dad stood next to the arm.

Dad's callouses caught on my flannel as he squeezed my shoulder. I leaned my head against his stomach. He brushed my curls over my shoulder.

I could picture Patrick leaning against a pay phone in whatever color prison uniform criminals wore in Northern Ireland, his heel bouncing just like mine was that very second.

I forced my foot to be still. "What?"

A heavy, rattling sigh came through the line. "Fiona..." A liquid ton of desperation dripped from that one word.

The picture of Patrick carrying baby me on the beach haunted me. A few months after that photo, he'd had our parents and me ripped away.

He continues the fight so his suffering has meaning.

"Did you finish *To Kill a Mockingbird*?" I asked.

"Nearly."

"Maybe we could do a book club someday."

Patrick sniffled and cleared his throat. "I'll find a way."

# chapter twenty-four

## *Danny*

Fiona slipped past the curtain divider the second visitors' hours began; thank Christ I'd got Nurse Nancy to bring me a toothbrush three minutes prior. I still couldn't believe we'd six more weeks together.

She wrapped her fingers round the nape of my neck, leaned in, and parted my lips with her tongue. My whole body was set alight. She tasted like mint mixed with peanut butter, and it left me starving for more. Cupping her chin, I kissed her forehead, her eyes, and then brushed her lips with mine.

Fiona pulled away. The pink in her cheeks drained. She bit her lip as she stood at the side of my bed. "Okay, look, can we talk?"

That was always a bad sign in films. I pressed my fingers into my eyes so I couldn't see her freckled face.

"Say it, then."

She stroked my chin. "We need to talk about my dad."

A burning pain sparked in my mangled knee. My nails cut into my skin as fire radiated out from my shattered bones and shredded muscles.

Fiona peeled my hands from my face and squeezed them in her clammy grasp. "I hate what my dad did. And"—her eyes closed—"none of this is fair to you. I'm, I'm so, so sorry. But he's my dad, and he's trying so hard. It's like you said the second time we met, I can hate what he did but still love who he is today."

I had said that. But I hadn't been talking about *him*.

"I don't know if I love him yet. Maybe Dad doesn't deserve that chance, but I want to try."

I twisted my hands free of hers. How could she care about me and love that man, who set the stage for everything bad that ever happened in my life? The blaze spread through my chest, my arms, out to my toes. Sure I'd mucked up plenty, but there were far worse people out there in the world. Like Anto and my da and Peter Kelly. And I'd been trying so frigging hard. Couldn't I have *anything*? The burning pain consumed me.

I mashed my fists into my temples. "Why are you telling me this now?"

"Because," her voice quaked, "I want you in my life. Which means I can either lie again and hurt you even more or just get it out there now so we can hopefully move forward together."

I could hear her tears and I hated them, but I couldn't look at her.

"I'm not asking you to talk to him or even see his face. I just needed you to know that I'm trying to build a relationship with him."

I'd have been fine ignoring her da, but her honesty meant she did care about me. She'd spent her whole life wishing she had a da and now she did, and by all accounts he treated her like a wee princess. How could someone not love Fiona?

I wasn't sure I knew what love felt like. Maybe Billy loved me. Ma had loved me, but I couldn't remember it. I imagined it felt like you were two perfectly matched puzzle pieces and when you were apart that piece of you still existed, but you felt half empty. And each day those feelings grew stronger.

The fire cooled and shrank.

"Danny, say something."

My hands dropped to my lap. Fiona looked at me, pale and wide-eyed as tears streaked down her freckled cheeks.

I fought back the clog in my throat. "As long as I don't have to see his face."

Fiona sniffled and nodded.

"Can you promise me one thing?"

"Of course." Fiona carefully climbed onto the bed next to me, on the side with the flesh wound. She rested her cheek on my chest but gave my leg six inches of space.

I wrapped my arms around her. "When you look at me, can you try to see who I want to be? Not who I was."

Her voice reverberated through my chest as she spoke.

"I want to help you build something new."

# chapter twenty-five

## *Danny*

*Six Weeks Later*

Skyscrapers glittered in the sun as the plane descended over Lake Michigan.

Fiona pointed out Willis Tower and the Hancock Building. Seamus almost pissed himself laughing at the name, but the death glare Fiona shot him stopped me. He wasn't so bad yet, but it'd been only a few hours and I'd be staying at their mum's for a whole week. Seamus was staying a fortnight.

Sinclair had found me a cultural exchange program that taught boxing to troubled lads living in gang-infested areas in that city thousands of feet below. You didn't need good knees to teach it; my coach at the Shankill Boxing Club had been over seventy. Before I was accepted, I'd to survive three pure terrifying Skype interviews. The program director, DeVontae, told me all the mental things the kids did and asked what I'd do. Since I'd done most of them myself, I thought of what Sinclair would do and said that. DeVontae agreed to take me on. The program was run by the University of Chicago, so in a week I'd be living in a dorm room and eating their food. I'd take the "L" every day and tutor at the lads' school, then teach boxing.

Fiona had been helping me revise for my ACTs, which I was to take on sixth September, so I could apply to universities for spring term—semester, they called it in America. Her mum was going to help me get asylum, like she'd got.

We flew over a patchwork city grid that stretched to the hazy horizon. Cars and American things like baseball diamonds and swimming pools in people's massive back gardens grew bigger and bigger. Their traffic drove on the right, which I knew, but it still did my head in.

Sinclair was always on about how moving to Chicago would be nothing compared to what I'd already gone through, but I'd never been more than a hundred miles from Belfast. Surrounded by all these American accents, as the runway rushed toward us, I didn't feel so brave.

I gripped the armrests as I braced for impact—what if the wheels didn't come out? The plane juddered and jumped as we touched down.

As terminals whizzed by, I said, "I'm in America."

Fiona's tiny hand squeezed mine. "You're adorable."

"Welcome to O'Hare International Airport. Local time is 4:47 p.m. central time. The temperature is a steamy ninety-one degrees Fahrenheit."

"How hot is that?" Seamus asked.

"Em, about thirty-three," I said.

"Bloody hell."

"Dude, at least we have sun here." Fiona flicked his thigh.

"Are we in your state?" Seamus asked.

"No, she lives in *Wiscahnson*." I tried to say it like Fiona.

Her freckled nose wrinkled as she giggled. I couldn't stop

myself from kissing her cheek, even with her bruiser of a brother right there.

I loved Fiona. I'd known for certain since I learnt she'd chosen to stay in Belfast for her wee nephew, even though it cost her the telescope thing. Then it was impossible not to love her. But I was such a yellow bastard I hadn't told her, because if she didn't love me back, it would make a bollocks out of everything.

Fiona dug out her phone and called her mum.

Then I remembered, I'd promised Sinclair I'd open his letter after we touched down. Saying goodbye to Sinclair had been harder than with Mrs. Donnelly when she dropped off the wee tray bake and Jon with his last KFC delivery.

I opened the envelope. Inside was a single piece of A4 lined paper. As I unfolded it, two American twenty-dollar bills—bucks—fell out.

*Take Fiona on a proper date. And remember, now you have infinite possibilities.*

*Sinclair*

I'd thought about still being a nurse, but I'd watched Nurse Nancy and the others wait on me hand and foot for the past six weeks. I wasn't sure I'd be able move like that anymore. Which left my entire future a blank sheet of nothingness.

"Love you to Neptune and beyond." Fiona rolled her eyes with a grin as she hung up. Then her eyes danced across my face as she stroked my arm. "You okay, Danny?"

I rubbed my nose with the back of my hand. "Em, aye." I rammed the envelope into my pocket. I could take her somewhere posh for dinner; she wouldn't care if I used the wrong fork.

The clicks of seat belts unfastening filled the cabin. Sticky heat leaked onto the airplane.

Fiona wrangled Seamus and me in by our necks. "I super-dooper-pinky-promised Finn I'd send him a landing selfie."

I gave a thumbs-up and Seamus plastered an evil clown smile on his face as Fiona snapped the picture.

Fiona pulled her satchel from under the seat in front of her and shoved in her copy of *Brave New World*.

I grabbed my rucksack with my baby book and then my cane from by the fuselage. Dr. McIlroy finally let me start using it instead of crutches two days ago, so at least now I had a free hand. As I stood, a stab of shooting pain radiated from my bad knee, the one with the new kneecap. I drew in a sharp breath. I'd popped as many paracetamols as I reasonably could, but after sitting for seven hours, nothing could improve the situation. Fiona's eyebrows knitted. I'd all but begged her not to feel guilty, but she couldn't stop herself.

Fiona stroked the back of my neck, the magic spot she'd discovered the first day she visited me. The pain faded to a dull throb.

"Your hair feels so cool." Her fingertips ran up and down my freshly trimmed hair. "And with those fancy clothes, you kind of look like a different person."

Sinclair had bought me new clothes from Marks & Spencer for my fresh start. "Do I look American, then?"

Seamus snorted. "You look like a posh twat."

"Feck up, I have to make a good first impression." I did look a bit like Foster, even without the boat shoes. Jon might even call me a poof with these clothes.

"Stop being a douche." Fiona's eyes raked Seamus's Kappa trackie bottoms.

I leaned heavily on my cane as I limped off the plane. Fiona gripped my hand. My knee started loosening. Since we'd done immigration in Dublin, we headed straight for baggage claim.

We stepped on a moving walk. Rainbow neon lights ran the length of the entire walkway, reflecting off the marble ceiling behind them.

"Hello, gorgeous," Seamus said.

Then I realized a group of girls rode by wearing tops that said Purdue. A bunch of them were eyeballing me.

Fiona's arm slipped around my waist. Her hand squeezed on my hip bone. "Mom's waiting by baggage claim."

Seamus's eyebrows furrowed. Fiona had said yesterday that I'd talked to their mum more than him.

"The first time I met Dad, I was scared too, bro." Fiona pushed her shoulder into Seamus's hulking mass.

"I'm not scared. Jaysus, I need a cigarette."

My cane caught me from stumbling off the moving walk when it ended.

Once I moved into my dorm room, Fiona and I would be three hours apart, which wasn't too far in America. Fiona said she'd come pick me up whenever she could, but that would be twelve hours of driving a weekend. I could take a bus to Madison sometimes, but I got only a small stipend and I'd to pay for my mobile, the launderette, and university application fees.

And she'd be back to her life as an American high schooler with all her hard classes and running clubs. When Fiona Skyped her friends, the way she talked, the words she used, even the way she sat all changed. They talked about things I hadn't a clue about. She became American Fiona. I acted different round Jon and even Sinclair, but it made me wonder if I knew the real Fiona. And we had no idea where she'd end up going to university or if I'd get accepted anywhere, even though I'd promised Billy I'd go.

I clutched the strap of my rucksack.

I'd never have another sausage roll from Arlene's Bakery. Eat one of Mrs. Donnelly's tray bakes. Go to another bonfire. I'd never get pissed up with Jon again. And I'd never be in the army. Mr. Sinclair had sworn he was going to stalk me over Skype and Facebook, but he'd other students, and sure he and Mrs. Sinclair would have miniatures running about eventually. I'd no plan come December when the exchange program ended, and all the spelling differences did my head in. And my knee was aching again after that short walk from the gate.

Of course, I'd had all these thoughts before, but now, standing in Chicago, they were real. All I wanted was a hug from the ma I never knew. My eyes burned as my throat thickened. I pressed my fingers into my eyes.

Fiona grabbed my wrist and pulled my hand down. And I was pure scundered to be almost crying. As her gold-flecked eyes searched mine, that connection locked between us. Fiona wrapped her arms around my waist and pressed her body against mine; her heart pounded through my yuppie checked shirt.

"I love you, Danny."

Oozing warmth flooded my veins. My heart swelled so huge, it forced the air from my lungs. The tears broke free. "I love you too."

Fiona wound her fingers around the back of my neck, got on her tiptoes, and pulled me down for a soft kiss. "Mom's got only like thirty-minute parking. We better keep moving. You ready?"

My arm hair stood on end.

I gripped my rucksack strap. Sure, my future was a blank page—and I was pure terrified. But there were other ways to save lives. Perhaps I could be a teacher, like Mr. Sinclair. That would make Ma proud, and Principal Doyle would shit himself if he found out.

Ahead of us, a blue sign over the escalators said "Attention, you are leaving the secured area."

I blew out a slow breath. "No surrender."

# acknowledgements

*All the Walls of Belfast* took over five years to research and write. And re-write and re-write. This book wouldn't have been possible without a tremendous amount of help from many tremendous people. It really took a village... that spanned three continents.

First off, I want to thank my agent, Claire Anderson-Wheeler at Regal Hoffman & Associates, for liking my tweet in a Twitter pitching contest. Thank you for not only believing in my potential as an author, but also believing in the novel now known as *All the Walls of Belfast*. It took three years of your expert guidance, and several complete re-writes, to help me find the heart of Fiona and Danny's stories. Not only is this story better because of you, I'm also a better writer. I'd also like to thank Heather Howell, Lindsey Johnson, Stephanie Beard, Madeline Cothren, and everyone else at Turner Publishing Company for, first off, appreciating not only *All the Walls of Belfast* as a story, but also seeing the potential it has to expand readers' worldviews and challenge their thinking. Thank you for bringing my dream to life so beautifully. When it comes to all your hard work, I only saw the tip of the iceberg.

Now we'll get into the whole three continents thing. *All the Walls of Belfast* was inspired by a trip I took to Belfast in 2011, but I actually wrote the first few (of many) drafts while living in Singapore. It was the Singapore Writers Group, an extremely talented mix of Singaporeans and expats, who heard the very first version of the very first chapter. Members of that group challenged me to strive for authentic representation of culture and characters, as I was writing outside my lane. Specifically, I want to thank my some of my earliest readers: Xiuhui Lee and Caitlyn Sarkar, my Fellowship of the Writers, and also Helena Ryan and Rachael Lille Moore.

After a few years in Singapore, I returned to the US and, although my adventures across Southeast Asia were over, my journey of writing All the Walls of Belfast was really just beginning. Which brings me to my next lovely group of critique partners. First and foremost, my sister Melissa Bergum. Even though I'm the big sister, you've always give me the feedback I need to push my craft and my novels to the next level. I love you, Seeeester. And I cannot NOT acknowledge my favorite critique group of all time, my Far-flung Crit buddies Dina Von Lowenkraft, Katya Dove, and Rose Deniz (my brain twin). Finding Skype times to accommodate three or four time zones was always a bit of a challenge, but you all helped me tremendously in improving both *All the Walls of Belfast* and my writing craft as a whole. We've all lost count of how many Fiona chapter ones you've looked at.

Now to that third continent. This book could not have happened without help from some absolutely amazing writers and editors from Belfast, who were open to a crazy American's out-of-the-blue email with a strange request, to help me capture dialect, culture, and history from both sides of the Peace Wall. I'd like to thank Averill Buchanan and Janine Cobain. And Emma Warnock, hands down, this wouldn't have happened without your dialectical and cultural guidance and your willingness to go so far as to venture around the Falls and the Shankill with me while we were both pregnant. I will forever treasure the lovely "Suggested Swearwords" word doc you so meticulously prepared for me.

I'd also like to give a shout out to a fabulous group of debut authors, the Novel Nineteens. We've shared so much talent, wisdom, and debut angst. It's been a wild, amazing roller coaster as our dreams are coming true.

This book would not be possible without the support of my wonderful husband, Mark, who shouldered a heavier burden with housework, among other things, to afford me the time to write even when there were no prospects for publication. Thank you for your patience and support. Thank you for believing in both me and my dream.

And lastly, I want to thank my parents for always, always supporting me in my many quests. You always pushed me to develop my talents and interests, and challenged me to think deeper. My mom says that once I put my mind to something, whether it's moving back to Milwaukee or taking a group of students on an all-expense-paid service trip to Pine Ridge or getting a book published, I make it happen. The reason I have the confidence and drive to do so is because of you, Mom and Dad. Your belief in me and my potential has given me the strength and courage to persevere and follow my heart.

# about the author

Sarah Carlson, born in Scranton, Pennsylvania, is the eldest of five children. She spent the first few years of her life in dying coal mining towns in the Pocono Mountains. Her father's career as a Methodist minister took their family to Wisconsin, where Sarah spent the rest of her childhood growing up in places ranging from unincorporated towns of four hundred to the suburbs of Milwaukee. Sarah received a Bachelor of Science in Psychology, a Master's of Science in Education, and an Education Specialist Degree in School Psychology.

Currently, Sarah lives outside Madison, Wisconsin with her husband and young daughter. She works as a school psychologist in an elementary school with a diverse, mostly low income population. Sarah's professional areas of focus include supporting the success of children with behavioral and mental health needs and helping to promote resilience in children who have been exposed to trauma or toxic stress.

Sarah has had the opportunity to live in Singapore for a year and a half; there, she had the unique chance to be enmeshed in cultures different from her own. As a lover of adventures; she has been lucky enough to travel to seventeen countries on four continents and counting, including multiple trips to Belfast and broader Northern Ireland, staying at places such as Queens University Belfast and a local hostel in the Falls run by an organization that works to foster cross community development. All the Walls of Belfast is Sarah's debut novel.